INTELLIGENT THINGS

Intelligent Things

William X. Adams

ΨΦ Psi-Fi Books
www.psifibooks.com

Psi-Fi Books

ISBN: 978-1-7322274-8-4

Cover Design: SelfPubBookCovers.com/JohnBellArt

Chapter One

It cost a fortune to fly charter from Austin to Los Angeles, but TSA security at regular commercial airports had become intolerable for Robin Taylor and Andy Bolton, with their titanium skeletons, stainless-steel ventilators and internal gold and silver printed circuits. They triggered every metal detector every time, resulting in a tedious hand search and then a lot of fast talking about metal hip joints and prosthetic knees.

As more airports started using full-body X-rays, talking their way through security became impossible. At a charter terminal, you just showed your ID, and once in a while, rarely, you were patted down for weapons, and that was it.

The two travelers sat in cool, beige, leather chairs, facing each other over a small, polished wood table as their chartered jet smoothly approached the Hawthorne Municipal airport south of LAX. They looked out their windows on the port side, facing south as the ground expanded like rising bread, housing tracts materializing out of geometric patterns. They enjoyed estimating altitude and ground speed from the changing visual texture. The calculations were good exercise and fed a playful rivalry over who could determine the moment of touchdown most accurately. Andy checked his internal chronometer.

"I'm saying three forty-one and fifty seconds."

"At this speed? No way. Three thirty-seven and a half."

"We are a little hot, but we're eight miles out by my reckoning. He'll slow down to cross the fence."

"We'll still be ahead of schedule. You'll see."

"Mmm."

Other passengers also watched the landscape emerge. In the relatively smog-free springtime air, with slanting golden sunlight, the world looked like a CGI effect. Across the aisle, a mother held a toddler up to the window to see, even though seatbelts were supposed to be fastened. The other four passengers, also members of the moneyed class, or at least people with generous employers, talked in murmurs for the last fifteen minutes of the trip. An electric whine and a *thunk* sounded from below.

"There go the wheels," Andy said. "That will slow us down."

Robin didn't respond right away. She was facing backward, watching the terrain flow away.

"Andy," she said and paused for a moment. "Don't we seem a little low?"

She spoke into her window, not looking at him. He strained to look out the porthole to see straight down.

"If we're at seven miles, we should be at two thousand feet. This looks like one thousand."

"But those are just estimates, right?"

"Calculate the rate of descent from the apparent size of the buildings."

Robin looked and calculated.

"Too much," she said almost in a whisper. "We're bleeding altitude."

"It should be eight point three feet per second. We're fifty percent over that."

"What's going to happen?"

"The worst, if nothing changes."

The woman across the aisle stared at them. Her eyes were squinted, her forehead contorted with worry. Robin smiled. The woman's face held its anxiety as she turned back to her window and her child.

*

Clarence Jackson saw an aircraft descending too fast for safety, no question about it. But he also knew it was not his place to say anything. Air traffic control was only in charge of the runway, not the aircraft. The captain of a ship was the captain of the ship.

Clarence had been in the tower six months so he couldn't say for sure if this was a crisis, but he did not like the looks of it one bit. He glanced across the darkened room to Lori Bartell, his supervisor. She sat at a desk with her nose close to a computer screen. The only other controller, Brad, was talking to a freighter ten miles out, which Clarence also saw on his screen. No problem there. He was worried about the descending Airstream from Austin. He made a decision.

"Clementine99, this is Hawthorne Tower. You are cleared to land on runway 10R."

He had already cleared the flight, so the call was unnecessary, but Clarence wanted to talk to that aircraft. In a moment, a standard response came back.

"Clementine99. Cleared on 10R. Roger."

That didn't help at all, Clarence thought. Should he ask the pilot if he would need assistance? Like frigging fire trucks and ambulances maybe? What was going on?

"Lori, would you take a look at this?"

"What is it, Clarence?" She didn't even look up from her computer screen.

"I got a flight coming in hot and low. He's dropping like a rock. Doesn't look right. Should I ask him what's going on?"

Lori pushed back her chair and crossed the glass room. She stood behind Clarence and stared at his screen.

"Which one?"

"Here." Clarence pointed. "He's sinking a thousand fpm and streaking in at a hundred and twenty-five knots, five miles out."

"No mayday?"

"Everything on the radio seems normal."

"Tell him to adjust his altitude to three thousand."

3

"He'll overshoot."

"Then circle him. Find out what he says about it."

"Ah, Clementine99, this is Hawthorne Tower. Abandon your approach immediately, climb to three thousand and turn left to one-eighty degrees."

"Clementine99. Altitude three thousand. Go around left. Roger."

Clarence and Lori watched the green radar sweeper dawdle around the screen.

"That wasn't so hard, was it?" Lori said, a bit of condescension in her voice.

"Except he's not doing it. Look."

The little green triangle for Clementine99 continued its missile-like trajectory into the airport.

*

"My numbers are way out of whack," Andy whispered hoarsely to Robin. "We're coming in like a rocket."

"Should we alert the pilot? Maybe the instruments are wrong."

"All we could do is bang on the cockpit door. The crew wouldn't open it. They'd call for security on the ground, and meanwhile the other passengers might attack us as terrorists."

"How much time do we have?"

"Three minutes maybe. Are the flaps down?"

Robin pressed her cheek against the window and looked back at the wing.

"Either no, or not enough. They're not down thirty degrees, for sure. Could this be one of those pilot suicide things?"

"That's remote. More likely instrument failure. What are we going to do?"

"You and I have nothing to lose, but all these humans are going to die unless we do something."

The woman across the aisle jerked her head sharply to look at them, her eyes pleading for something.

"See if you can determine the radio frequency we're on. I'll try to get control of the avionics."

They both sat back in their seats and closed their eyes as if they were calmly waiting for the gentle bump of the touchdown. The woman across the aisle seemed to take some comfort from their action and moved her attention back to her child. After a minute, Robin whispered across the table.

"We're on 121.100. We're Clementine99."

"Thanks. Cover for me."

Andy twisted in his seat, turning his back to the aisle as much possible and he slumped, cupping a hand over his mouth. He spoke quietly but firmly.

"Clementine99, this is Hawthorne Tower. Your V-ref is too high, and your altitude is too low. Abandon your approach. Climb to and maintain three thousand feet. Do you copy?"

"Who the hell is this?" Clarence said over the radio. "I am Hawthorne Tower."

"What?" the pilot said. "Give me a moment here, Tower, will you? I'm having some trouble recalculating my V-ref."

"Clementine99, this is Hawthorne Tower. I say again, climb to three thousand feet immediately, do you copy?"

"Hey! Who's on my frequency?" Clarence said.

"Tower, can you get your act together, please? I'm trying to land a plane here."

"This is Hawthorne Tower. Clementine99, I say again climb immediately to three thousand feet. You may have multiple instrument failures. Please copy."

"Lori, my radio's been hacked. Some asshole's talkin' to my flight. Whoever you are, buddy, this is a federal crime. Get off this frequency immediately."

"Tower, what the hell is going on?"

"Clementine99, *this* is Hawthorne Tower, and you better believe it. Don't pay any attention to that other guy."

"For God's sake, tower – "

"Scott, look out the window. We're at six hundred feet, and our V-ref is 125."

"What? Holy crap!"

*

Nearly every passenger let out an involuntary shriek when the nose of the plane suddenly lurched up, and everyone was thrown forcefully back in their seat or slung forward against their seatbelt, depending which direction they were facing in the cabin. The plane shot up like it had been launched from a cannon. Plastic cups, computers and magazines flew from laps to the floor and migrated like tumbleweeds down the aisle to the tail of the plane.

Some people howled, and some prayed out loud. The child screamed like a siren. Women, and some men wailed and moaned rhythmically. Nobody knew what was happening, but they had no doubt it was a life-threatening emergency. On the other hand, anybody using calm reasoning would realize that an emergency maneuver would come before, not after, the moment of peak danger. Since they were not dead, they probably wouldn't be.

Andy sat up in his seat as the plane banked steeply to the left and he got a look almost straight down at the ground.

"About two thousand feet, I'd say."

Robin slumped back in her chair.

"Thanks," she mouthed silently.

The woman across the aisle stared with her mouth open. Robin smiled reassuringly and closed her eyes.

Chapter Two

Morgan and Dylan arrived at Jennifer's modest apartment just before seven. Their host greeted them warmly and introduced them to Robin and Andy, "my roommates and colleagues." The visitors nodded with frowns that said they did not understand the relationships implied, but they were too well-mannered to ask.

The obligatory tour of the apartment allowed Morgan and Dylan to comment on their own housing search in the area, and on what a nice part of Los Angeles they had all found and were there any grocery stores nearby, and how was the noise, being so near to the airport? Then they all sat in the living room with glasses of wine and soda and talked about Los Angeles versus New York and Portland.

Morgan and Dylan were charming, smart, curious, and talkative, as Jennifer knew they would be. Both were in their early thirties. Morgan explained that she was a web designer in Portland, Oregon, or had been, she corrected – everyone understood that this dinner party was the final stage of an extended job interview that had begun weeks before in Chicago.

Morgan wore her brown hair short but well-styled, close to her skull. It used to be blue and spiked, she said when Jennifer complimented her. "That was in college when I was the center of the universe." She had a degree in Women's Studies and Literature from the University of Connecticut and said she was discouraged by the world of business – "though it's terrific for those who have the aptitude," she hastily allowed with an embarrassed smile at her future boss. She revealed that she was working on an urban fantasy novel and had a boyfriend but stayed single, "as a point of principle."

Her brother, Dylan, had been a programmer in New York City, streamlining trading algorithms for a hedge fund. He was grossly overpaid, he said, but it was only salary. "You can't get rich on salary."

Jennifer concluded that unlike his sister, Dylan still was the center of the universe, but he seemed smart and alert, and he was interested in Jennifer's home automation business. He asked a lot of questions and expressed optimism about its prospects. She spoke about baby cams, home security systems and other home devices with as much enthusiasm as one could reasonably muster for such topics.

Andy and Robin said little, replying with short rehearsed answers about where they were from and what they did. They understood the pre-dinner ritual of small talk. Robin had explained to Andy that humans always sat with guests in the living room before the dinner because otherwise, it would seem like the visitors just came for the food and that would be coarse. By sitting around, everyone pretended the meal meant nothing and they were there only because they were delighted to be with each other. Eventually, the host would beg them to come and eat, for the sake of the food, which threatened to spoil or get cold, burned, melted, or wilted. The guests would reluctantly oblige and trudge to the dining table for the sake of politeness.

Upon questioning, however, Robin could not say why the humans pretended the event wasn't about eating. She knew that suppression of feelings was an essential part of polite human society, but how excited could you get about eating dinner, something you did every day of your life? Andy's theory was that the preliminary sitting, drinking, and chatting was to display social status before showing biological behavior like eating, which was a leveler. "Everybody eats the same way," he explained, "so you have to establish the pecking order separately from that." Robin wasn't sure if that was right.

Before long, they were all at the dinner table passing the asparagus, and Jennifer gently brought the conversation around to her vision for the future of Paradise Projects.

"In Hawaii, as I explained, we were nominally a designer and manufacturer of intelligent home automation systems, like security, lighting, and climate control. We talked about it at Will's funeral, remember?" Morgan and Dylan nodded.

"Paradise made prototypes of those things, and we have a folder of patents. But it was all a cover, not our real purpose, not what the company was really about."

She broke a dinner roll in half and buttered it thoughtfully. Everyone watched. When she looked up, she seemed surprised the others were staring at her.

"We're dying to know," Morgan said.

Jennifer smiled. "Oh. That's our topic this evening, so I guess we should get into it." She put her well-buttered roll down on her plate. "In reality, Will and I designed and built humanoid robots." She grabbed the roll again and took a bite as she glanced at Robin and Andy, hoping to convey apologies for the crude language.

"That's unbelievable," Dylan said. "What were these secret robots designed to do? Vacuum the carpet stealthily?"

Jennifer winced then smiled.

"Ah, no. These were general-purpose robots, free-ranging, autonomous, with advanced speech synthesis and language comprehension. They looked and acted like humans. You could hardly tell the difference."

"Wow!" Morgan said. "Real sci-fi stuff. I write stories like that. I always have androids in them, usually as servants. They become sullen and resentful, you know, as servants do." She smiled and looked around the table. Nobody smiled until Jennifer forced a thin expression of amusement.

"Our androids weren't sullen. Or servants either. They had regular jobs and regular lives and lived in the community, and nobody knew the difference."

"I think you're putting us on, Jennifer," Dylan said. "You are, aren't you? An android like that would be far beyond existing robotic technology. It would be like one of Morgan's fantasy stories. And besides, what would be the point? I could see if you were selling them as industrial or domestic workers. But just to release them into the wild? Why would you do that?"

"To explore the nature of consciousness, both artificial and natural."

Nobody was eating. Everyone stared at Jennifer. Morgan and Dylan were obviously watching for a sign to see if their future boss was kidding, or possibly was mentally unstable.

"So you built them but didn't sell them?" Dylan said.

"Your metaphor is apt. We released them into the wild like baby birds to see if they could survive. They would report back on what they were learning."

"Undercover robots!" Morgan squealed. "I've always dreamed of something like that."

Dylan scowled at his sister's excitement. "It's just a metaphor, Morgan." He turned to Jennifer. "You're trying to make a point, right? I'm not getting it."

"No metaphor. Real androids."

"So you're saying you and cousin Will made robots good enough to go undetected in human society?"

"Mostly undetected, not always. It's still a work in progress."

"They're out there now?"

"Yes, they are."

Dylan shook his head in disbelief and turned to Andy. "Did you ever see one of these androids, Andy?"

"Yes."

"And you believed it was a person?"

"I was impressed. As Jennifer said, they're not perfect, but they're convincing."

Dylan shook his head again slowly as if everyone had gone mad.

"Robin, what about you?" Morgan asked. "Did you see Jennifer's AI androids?"

"Oh, yes. They're lovely and charming. Sometimes quirky, like a newcomer from a foreign country."

"I don't believe it," Dylan said. "And if it were true, it would be creepy. Who wants humanoid machines lurking around? What if they turned violent and attacked us?"

"They're very gentle," Robin said. They don't have violence programmed into them."

Dylan stared at her. "You know that for a fact?"

"Yes."

"Were you involved in building them?"

"Intimately."

Turning to Jennifer, he asked, "How many of these robots have you released?"

"Two. A male and a female."

"Wait," Morgan said. "What does that mean, a male and a female? How can a robot have a gender?"

"Don't be dense," Dylan said. Body size and shape. Secondary sexual characteristics."

"Oh, girls have long hair? Is that it?" She ran her fingers through her short hair.

"Well, it's not that simple, obviously."

Morgan ignored him and turned to Jennifer. "Did these androids grow up from infancy?"

"No, no. That was way beyond our capacity. They were launched as adults."

"There you go, then," Morgan said, looking around the table triumphantly. "They can't be male or female because gender is constructed by living it. At best, they could only be caricatures of male and female."

Andy and Robin glanced at each other.

Dylan turned to Andy. "So what do they look like, exactly, these androids? You've seen them right? Up close, I mean."

Andy looked at Jennifer, who nodded once.

"We prefer to be called Newcomers, not androids," Andy said.

Dylan's brow furrowed. He stared. Morgan's eyes widened. She put her fork down with a loud clank.

"You're kidding me, right?" Dylan said tentatively.

"*Robot* and *android* are terms humans use to describe mechanical devices. We don't think of ourselves that way. From our point of view, we are sentient beings, of a different nature than humans, but as you can see, intelligent language-users. We call ourselves Newcomers."

Dylan didn't speak. His eyes turned to Robin. Morgan locked her eyes onto Robin also. They waited for confirmation of what they suspected.

Robin raised one hand to her shoulder and wiggled her fingers in a little wave. "Pleased to meet you," she said with a toothy smile.

"But you're so... so, beautiful," Dylan protested.

"Dylan, you are such an idiot," Morgan said. She turned again to Robin, who sat beside her. "I'm happy to meet you, Newcomer Robin. Hello." She offered her hand, and Robin shook it.

"Hi, Morgan. We're not scary."

Dylan turned sideways in his chair to face Andy. He extended his hand cautiously, ready to pull it back if it was electrocuted.

"Sorry, man. I didn't know. Sorry."

Andy shook his hand and smiled. "No problem," he said. "Or wait. Maybe I'm supposed to say 'Live long and prosper?'"

Dylan's eyes opened wide.

"Andy, don't fool around. This is difficult for them," Jennifer said. She looked at Dylan, "He learned that little joke from Will. I don't think he even knows what it means."

"Sure I do. It's funny because in most cases you would say something like, 'Pleased to meet you.' This other greeting is polite, yet has a low frequency of occurrence and therefore it's funny." Andy smiled.

"Right, right," Dylan said, shrinking back into his chair. He turned to look at Jennifer for explanation. "Is this for real?"

"Andy is our first Newcomer," Jennifer said. "Seven years old now, nearly six, isn't it, Andy?"

"Six next month."

"Robin is a newer model, nearly three."

Morgan and Dylan stared at Robin, taking in her collar-length blonde hair, her symmetrical face, her idealized figure.

"Three is the new six," Robin said.

"Robin has more advanced software for social understanding, but we're hoping to upgrade both of them as soon as the lab is ready. And that's the first project I'd like you two to work on."

"I'm thrilled beyond belief," Morgan said. "This is like a dream come true for me."

"I can't take it in," Dylan said. "I mean no disrespect," he nodded to Andy and Robin, "but how do we know this isn't a charade? I mean you guys could be Jennifer's zany friends from across the hall. Hilarious joke, right?"

"You'll see, in due time," Jennifer said. "We have all the design documents and software code. We have videos and ultrasounds so you can look inside. It takes a while for the idea to sink in."

Morgan stood. "Who can eat? I can't eat. Let's talk." She stood and extended a hand to Robin. Robin stood, and Morgan hugged her. "We have so much to talk about," she said and led Robin into the living room.

"She's right," Jennifer said. "There is a lot to discuss." She stood. "I'm taking my wine." She picked up her glass.

Dylan looked at Andy, who shrugged, then stood. He and Dylan walked side by side into the living room.

Next morning, Morgan and Dylan trailed Jennifer around the newly remodeled and equipped Paradise Projects, the grand opening, Jennifer called it. The operation was located in a thriving industrial district full of warehouses, small wholesalers, aerospace and automotive firms just south of the Hawthorne regional airport in Los Angeles. She had found a spot there to rebuild the laboratory she had left behind in Honolulu.

Robin and Andy had stayed behind at the apartment, because, Jennifer had explained, "Things will have to be said that won't be uplifting."

The Newcomers were not shy about their fabricated status, so they told Jennifer they didn't understand her caution. She said she was concerned about naïve attitudes Morgan and Dylan would probably express as they came to terms with the idea of Newcomers. That was a legitimate part of their early learning, she said, but it could color future relationships. It would be better if the youngsters were more informed before they spent extended time with the Newcomers. "They're the newcomers to this project, not you, so let's give them time to adjust."

"Are you sure you want to reveal everything?" Andy said. "That's a little scary, don't you think, considering how humans have reacted so badly in the past when they found out the truth?"

"Not all of them. Holly came around, eventually."

"Not completely," Robin said. "She didn't go crazy when she found out I was a Newcomer, but she didn't stay, either. I don't have any contact with her now."

"I count her as an important success," Jennifer said. "You want to blend? Morgan and Dylan will be your chance to blend."

"What will they do at Paradise?" Andy asked Jennifer.

"We'll have to feel our way into it. Both of them are qualified to provide data monitoring and updates, so that's a gimme. Once we get the equipment running again, you'll be able to pursue your missions as before."

"But," Andy said hesitantly, "they'll know everything, won't they? They won't believe they're monitoring a Mars rover as the other engineers did."

"It increases the risk. It used to be just me and Will, now it will be me and Will's two cousins. One more person."

"The probability of keeping a secret is an inverse-square relationship to the number of people who know it."

"It's a step up in risk, that's all," Robin said. "But I think they're trustworthy. Morgan, at least. She's already on board. I'm less sure about Dylan."

"I'm hearing your concern, guys, but it's a practical thing. I can't do everything myself. Will and I took ten years, managing seventy engineers to build Paradise Projects and create you two. We won't be making any more Newcomers, but I need help to keep things running. My intuition tells me Morgan and Dylan will be good fits. What's your intuition say?" She looked from Robin to Andy.

"That's not kind, Jennifer," Robin said. "You know we don't have intuition."

"Sorry. Not trying to be mean there. I was just making my point. Personnel questions have to be human decisions. No other way to do it. I trust these two. They'll be all right, you'll see."

Andy and Robin looked at each other silently.

*

On an oversized, high-definition screen, Jennifer showed Morgan and Dylan rotating 3-D transparent models for Robin and Andy and answered questions. She displayed ultrasound images of both androids' interiors and described, at a high level, what was shown. She played the video from when Will had repaired Robin's injured arm – only a few months ago, she recalled, back when the Hawaiian sun shone brightly on Paradise Projects, and they all were celebrating their success and discussing upgrades and future plans. There had been no hint of Will's demise. Life had been good. The sight of him in the video gripped her heart.

Her relationship with Will had not unfolded like a fairy tale. They'd been two individuals who'd found each other by chance. They hadn't been archetypes going through the timeless moves of courtship. She'd never been susceptible to the standard fairy tales, although growing up in Los Angeles she'd indulged the Cinderella complex as all girls did. Her mother told her the story of Kongi and Potgi, the Korean version of the story. The rich man in that story wasn't a prince, but he was still every girl's best destiny. The shoe was rubber, not glass, but who would want a glass shoe anyway? She never understood that part of the English story.

School, even pre-school, was in English, which her immigrant parents never learned well, and growing up, her thoughts were American, not Korean. Even so, she was only American up to a point. She was Korean on the outside, entirely American on the inside, and somewhere awkward in the middle with her parents. She had insisted on being registered in school as Jennifer P. Valentine, reducing her father's name of Park to a middle initial.

As a teenager, she knew that the Cinderella theme did not apply to her. She was too large for any prince, and her appearance was exotic and ethnic to her classmates. Her brainy interests in math, science, and later, in computers, put intransitive distance between her and the other girls. She was a non-entity for the boys, who didn't give her a second look, even though she was fit and curvaceous. But she was big – almost six feet tall in high school, always struggling to get her weight down. She'd had friends, friendly friends, but never the heartfelt kind who shared everything, and she felt that emptiness. She wasn't exactly a loner, more of an outsider with little sense of belonging. Her classmates included her in social activities, but she always had the feeling she was being tolerated or thoughtfully included, not sought-out, not anybody's first choice, not anybody's favorite.

"It's over, Jennifer," Morgan said.

Jennifer jerked her head toward Morgan then looked up at the screen and saw the video had finished and the screen had gone black.

"Right." She turned the playback off. "Let me demonstrate the microwave equipment you'll use to receive reports from the Newcomers and transmit adjustments to them."

She took her curious charges to a double cubicle that looked like a HAM radio setup filled with equipment racks, walled with monitors, switches, and buttons. They asked, and she answered.

"Why do Robin and Andy need all this?" Morgan asked. "I thought the Newcomers were autonomous."

"They are, but autonomy is relative, not absolute. They're smart enough to navigate their environment, both physical and social, but when it comes to greater questions of strategy, values, and long-term direction, they falter. They don't have a homunculus."

"A what?"

"The imaginary little man in your head that tells you what to do."

"That sounds like a fairy tale," Dylan said. "I don't have a little man in my head telling me what to do."

"No?"

"No. I decide for myself what I want."

"And what do you want?"

"What do you mean? Like, right now?"

"In the long run, say the next ten years. What are you trying to do?"

"Oh. Let's see, become successful, I guess."

"Defined how?"

"Accumulate a lot of money. High-status position. Basically, it's money, if I'm honest."

"So why don't you rob a bank? A series of banks. That's where the money is. Just shoot the guards, shoot the tellers and take the money."

"I'd get caught."

"Is that what keeps you from doing it?"

"No." He scowled. "That's just part of the equation." Dylan paused for a moment, looked around the cubicle, then resumed. "I'd say it's not about the money, but about achieving recognition in the business world. The money is the way you keep score."

"So it's not ultimately about the money."

"No."

"You said it was."

"Superficially, it is, but then you questioned me on that."

"So it's not so easy to say what you want, is it? You have to consult your inner homunculus. I acted like an external homunculus for you, and that prompted you to know what you want. See how handy that is? That's what you two will do for the Newcomers, continually adjust their mission parameters to keep them on track."

"On track for what?" Morgan said.

"Our goals are two, which is why we have two androids. One goal is to discover the relationship between natural and artificial psychology. We're interested in situations where the Newcomers fail to pass unnoticed. That tells us where we need to improve the software. The second goal is to explore the nature of gender, particularly female. That's Robin's focus. The two aims are interrelated."

"I'm dying to know what Robin has learned about gender," Morgan said. "Or even how she thinks about it."

"So far, with Robin, the work has been confusing. We'll review it later."

"When do they fail?" Dylan asked. "Do people point and say, 'Aha! You're an android!'"

"No, it's not like that. The Newcomers blend in remarkably well, but whenever they get into a longer-term relationship with somebody, it hasn't gone without incident. Newcomers don't stand up to close scrutiny over time. They can pass-for. Once a person gets to know them, though, the shortcomings stand out."

"I'm just devil's advocate here," Morgan said, "but everyone seems nice until you get to know them and discover the wacky stuff. That's when you have to make adjustments in your expectations. Isn't that how relationships work? Why is it any different for the Newcomers?"

Jennifer snorted a one-note laugh.

"You're absolutely right. The problem with Robin and Andy is that people are not willing to make allowances for machines. The Newcomers can't show their real nature because most humans can't accept it, so they hide what they are and the relationship is based on a secret right from the start, and then they eventually seem cold and aloof."

"Robotic," Dylan added.

"It's a work in progress," Jennifer said, not for the first time. "That's why you're here."

"I am totally in," Morgan said. "This is the most exciting thing that's ever happened to me."

Jennifer nodded. Both women turned to look at Dylan. He looked up from a screen he had been reading and seemed surprised.

"What?"

"You in or out?" Morgan said.

Dylan looked side to side around the vast, cavernous space of the lab dotted with workstations and assembly benches.

"There's money to be made here," he said as if to himself.

Chapter Three

Jennifer led her two new hires, who followed like ducklings. They walked in the alleys between steel warehouses down to El Segundo Avenue, which had proper sidewalks and crosswalks, then headed back to Jennifer's apartment, the ironically named Ocean Villas. The fall weather was fading but still warm enough to raise a sweat.

Jennifer felt satisfied that Morgan and Dylan were on board. She'd noticed that they referred to the Newcomers as "Robin and Andy," people they knew. Sometimes they called them androids or Newcomers, and in Dylan's case, sometimes they were problems to be engineered, but she noted that they had moved past the stage of disbelief. They were believers.

As they approached the apartment, she said, "We'll go up, and you can ask them whatever you want. Anything at all."

"I will," Dylan said.

Morgan and Dylan were quick studies. Jennifer taught them how to monitor the daily data downloads from the Newcomers, initiate the analyses, and upload adjusted parameters to nudge deviant values. The two of them worked the homunculus desk, as they called it, in shifts, providing daily support for the Newcomers. Most of the work was examining data, so they had plenty of time to study other parts of the Newcomer operation while on duty.

"Do Robin and Andy have control over the data they send in?" Morgan asked.

"It's automatic and outside their self-monitoring, what we would call their self-awareness. From inside the head of a Newcomer, if you can imagine such a thing, the mind doesn't even know the data transfer is happening. Well, they know, because we've told them, but they don't detect it. They're not aware of it happening. The same for the uploads we send back."

"What if it didn't occur?" Dylan said. "Like until we got here last month, what happened to them without a homunculus? Were they sick?"

"No, no. Healthy, but without direction or purpose. They hung around the apartment, reading, talking, browsing online, looking for jobs they might get, but with no motivation to try, or to do anything in particular."

"Most of my friends are like that," Morgan said.

Jennifer laughed. "A lot of people are like that, but the Newcomers were built for a purpose."

"What are they doing now, now that we're homunculizing them?" Dylan said.

"I can tell you they are both pleased to be going into the wild again."

"It is wild," Morgan said, reading a screen at her station.

"Not as wild as you'd think. Getting a job isn't too hard because we fabricate a background with references, transcripts, job history and deep contacts. They can scan most of the information they need for any job in a couple of days. They walk in highly qualified."

"Wouldn't that be great?" Dylan said, shaking his head.

"Robin said she was a teacher," Morgan said. "What kind?"

"She has a bully pulpit as an adjunct professor of technology design, and another as a regular online columnist for a regional newspaper. She said she wanted social influence to pursue her mission."

Dylan frowned at Jennifer.

"Hell, she could have waltzed into a slot as a fund manager and made a bundle."

"Not her mission. She's programmed to investigate how gender operates in society, and she wanted to influence young people."

"Influence is harder to get than money," Morgan said. "Any idiot can have money. What about Andy?"

"He works at a consulting firm offering AI solutions for business and industry. In the autonomous systems division, of all places."

"That's rich," Morgan said.

"I hope he doesn't give away the secrets," Dylan said.

"He doesn't have any special knowledge about himself any more than you have insight into your brain's physiology. Just because you have a brain doesn't mean you know anything about it."

Jennifer put down the mug of tea she had been holding and smoothed out the folds on her tent-like Hawaiian dress.

"All right. Time for *our* mission. I'm going to show you our latest prototype."

She led them to a section of the lab that was set up for home automation devices. Systems on display demonstrated control of home lighting, security, and some tricky garage door openers that could call you on your phone to ask if you wanted the door left open.

"This could be the future of Paradise Projects," she said. "We said we were a home automation company while we built the Newcomers. We could actually become a home automation company. Make the company pay for itself. What do you think? Couldn't we do this?"

"This stuff is cool," Dylan said, looking at an image of himself on a screen fed by a set of security cameras. He ran a hand across the top of his long black hair then patted it in front. "This industry of connected devices is just getting going. We could kill." He picked up a home alarm's command module. "Do you really want to be in this business, though?" He said, holding up the module. "A lot of companies are already doing it."

"We can do better. We have intelligence. We have natural language processing. We have Newcomer technology. Why spend millions on an android form factor, which is only to deceive humans? Online software robots have no body. They're pure intelligence, and we already have that."

Dylan stared rather stupidly at Jennifer while he processed what she had said. After a few moments, he spoke breathlessly.

"Release AI bots – basically Newcomer intelligence – into the internet to make smart devices work together? If that could be done, it would change everything."

"Here's what I imagine. We make home automation devices, like thermostats and these other ordinary things. Only we make them super smart, using the software Will and I developed for the Newcomers. Voila: Ordinary things become intelligent things. We can do security systems, thermostats, light switches, baby monitors, electric meters, door locks, smoke alarms, hot-water heaters, all that stuff. Then we branch out into cars, forklifts, bicycles, everything. No limits."

"Wow," Dylan said.

"I'm talking about real artificial intelligence," Jennifer said, rolling out her vision for her own benefit as much as for her entranced listeners. "Devices that learn, solve problems, think for themselves, and they also talk to you, ask you what you want."

"Incredible," Morgan said. "I'm getting the picture. Our devices are autonomous, have their own motivation. They're empathic, flexible, astute and adaptive. It would be like having Newcomers all over the web just like Andy and Robin."

"They learn from their experience," Dylan said.

"And they talk," Morgan said. "Nobody can touch Andy and Robin on language. It's virtually perfect. This would change the way people live," she explained excitedly to Jennifer.

"A world of intelligent things," Dylan mused aloud. Then his eyebrows went up. "What about the homunculus problem? Each device needs a homunculus to make the motivation work. That's what you said. AIs become aimless without a constantly refined mission. We can't manage that many devices. You'd need an army of technicians just to monitor all the bots."

"That's a problem. Let's think on it," Jennifer said.

"Let's network a couple of these smart thermostats and see what happens," Dylan said. "I'd like to see how it works. How it doesn't work."

"Excellent idea," Jennifer said, satisfied with how quickly Morgan and Dylan had picked up her idea and were already running with it.

"Chalmers says thermostats are already intelligent," Dylan said, looking at the white hockey puck near his hand.

"Who's Chalmers?" Morgan said.

"David Chalmers. Philosopher. Guru of consciousness. He says a thermostat is a primitive consciousness because it takes environmental input, processes it, and behaves appropriately in response, so that counts as consciousness."

"That's not consciousness. That's anthropomorphism. That's like saying a nail feels pain when the hammer hits it."

"No," Morgan said, "the difference is that the thermostat processes the information. It's intelligent. It has three states of mind: cold, hot, and steady. It senses its environment and then takes corrective action when something changes, just like an animal does. It's not sophisticated, but it's a functionally valid form of consciousness."

"I don't think so," Jennifer said.

"Why not?"

"For one thing, thermostats don't register hot and cold. A thermostat on a heater senses cold and just right. It does nothing if everything is just right and it doesn't care about hot. It's an ordinary binary switch."

Morgan pointed to the disc-shaped device Dylan was holding. "I see. So if you want an air-conditioning thermostat, that's a different device, or you need to switch manually from heating to cooling. Then the situation is the same in reverse. It measures too warm or just-right. It's either on or off, like an ordinary light switch. That doesn't make it conscious. It's just a switch."

Dylan stared at his sister for a moment then said "Hmmph. You have just devastated David Chalmers, guru of consciousness."

"And another thing," Jennifer said, "The thermostat needs a person who recognizes it as a thermostat. A slab of steel expands and contracts in response to variations in temperature, but it doesn't have *Honeywell* stamped on it, so we don't call it a thermostat. Whether something is a thermostat is human judgment."

"I don't think that matters. You don't have to call something a thermostat if you don't want to, but it still could be conscious."

"By that definition, everything in the universe is conscious because everything reacts to its surroundings," Morgan said. "Mountains, stars, celery. Everything. There's no non-consciousness."

"I think Chalmers would be okay with that."

"If everything is conscious, nothing is conscious. The term has no meaning. You could say, 'Everything that is, is.'"

"Hmm. That sounds like another devastating blow to David Chalmers, guru of consciousness."

Jennifer said, "I say, forget David Chalmers, guru of consciousness. Let's get to work connecting those thermostats."

Chapter Four

Design of the system was difficult for them all. Jennifer had an idea she couldn't explain, but Morgan thought she understood it anyway. Dylan was lost.

"What we want to build is an ethnic community of thermostats," Morgan told her brother.

Dylan looked up from his workstation. "What's the ethnicity of a thermostat?"

"It's a culture, like any ethnicity. A shared language and history that creates social cohesion. This is about we-ness. What it's like to be part of the thermostat community."

"What it's like to be a thermostat." Dylan echoed the words but not the meaning. "Why does that matter?"

Jennifer said, "If we think in terms of community, our thermostats would have their own language so they can talk to each other, not just to their human owners."

"That wouldn't be hard to do, actually. We could modify Zigbee or invent some other language." Dylan tended to seize upon details he could understand in engineering terms.

"The exact language is not what we're talking about," Morgan said. "The peer-to-peer language just enables the community so they can form a tribe."

"A tribe of thermostats. Like yak-herders?"

"Your skepticism is valid," Jennifer said. "A lot of cohesion in human cultures does come from shared geography and the accidents of history. Those give the group its particular color, like ethnic food, music, crafts, costumes."

Dylan stood up from his workstation and stepped around behind his chair, his actions becoming agitated.

"You're saying our thermostats will have costumes?"

"Pin that thought," Jennifer said. "I like it. But for now, think about how our devices will live. They'll be in homes and offices. On walls. In human living spaces. Not at the bottom of the sea, not in trees. They'll share human living conditions. They can talk about their shared environments among themselves, and about other aspects of their culture too, whatever those turn out to be. Temperature, presumably. They're thermostats. They'd care about temperature. We build for that culture."

Dylan looked at Morgan to see if she was tracking what Jennifer was saying.

"And get this," Morgan said. "We don't need an external homunculus hanging off every one of them. They solve their problems and set their goals by talking to each other, just like we do."

"Ah." Dylan turned away from the women. "Of course!" He walked three paces into the lab then turned and stepped back to his chair. "No homunculus. Why didn't you just say that?"

Winter, such as it is in Southern California, came and went, and by the time the vernal equinox rolled around the team had a prototype thermostat network called The Chalmers. It's amazing what plenty of money can do to speed up a project. They had two devices in a wireless network so they could prototype the communications system.

"These things will blow the doors off every thermostat on the market," Dylan said while typing. "The ones out there now sense temperature and throw a switch, big deal. The so-called smart ones record what time you leave the house and come home. That's a clock. That's not intelligence. Ours are thinking twenty-four-seven. These are intelligent things."

"Are you sure we haven't done too much?" Morgan said. "Do people want all the features we've built in?"

"They don't know it yet, but they do. Our network of sensors will tell each Chalmers if any windows are open, for example. Who hasn't accidentally turned on the heat or the air conditioning with a window open and then felt stupid? The Chalmers will tell you, 'Hey, you left the bathroom window open.' The owner will thank the Chalmers."

"If he looks at the display."

"Doesn't have to. Chalmers will send a text to your phone, or even call you personally and tell you to your ear." Dylan affected a soft, sexy voice. 'Hi, there. This is Chalmers. You left the bathroom window open.'"

"Cool. I mean hot," Morgan said, smiling.

"It will tell you the state of your heating and cooling equipment, whether it needs service, whether your filters are clean. It will tell you the indoor and outdoor temperatures, humidity and PM-2.5 air quality. It will tell you if you have leaks under your doors or around your windows. It can turn on overhead fans. You can tell it what you want just by talking to it."

"This is not a thermostat. This is an environmental manager," Morgan said in admiration.

Jennifer bent to look over Dylan's shoulder at his screen. "All very impressive, but I want to see the communication system work."

"Watch this." He typed in commands while he explained.

"Chalmers1 over there is worried that his heating system's operating costs are higher than industry averages per square foot. He knows this because he's learned it from other Chalmerses on the network. So he contacts his buddy, Chalmers2 over here," Dylan pointed, "and asks about that." On the screen was a query in English.

"Help. My heating costs per square foot are 30% higher than the standard for my house and region. Equipment is clean and in working order. Advice? --Chalmers1."

"This is a translation and paraphrase. The nodes communicate in XDL, an extended device language I developed."

"They're really talking like that?" Jennifer said. You're not just showing a pre-formatted text?"

"They're really talking. These devices use the AI language modules you provided. They're like the Newcomers without bodies. Chalmers1 is in the utility room of the lab, near the front door, next to an open window. It's trying to manage a space heater I put in there to keep the room at eighty degrees, and it can't do it because the window is open."

"Fascinating. So what's –

"Here it is, look."

"You have a leak, Chalmers1. Have your people install multisensor buttons TR11 near the base of all windows and doors. If your indoor and outdoor temperatures don't differ significantly when the system is on, you may need insulation or weather-stripping. --Chalmers2."

"Thanks, Chalmers2. What variance should I be looking for? --Chalmers1."

"Most people use their climate control when the outside temperature differs from the inside moving average by seven degrees Fahrenheit or more. If you have a sensor differential inside that range, you probably have a thermal leak at that location. --Chalmers2."

"Thanks, Chalmers2. --Chalmers1"

"Good luck. --Chalmers2."

"That's fantastic," Morgan said, looking at the screen over Dylan's other shoulder. "And I assume all these interchanges are stored and researchable by any device in the network?"

"Just like any archive. It's the ethnic memory of the Chalmers clan."

"Why don't they have better names than Chalmers1 and Chalmers2?"

"They can name themselves if they want to. It's up to them. This is just the prototype."

Jennifer straightened up, wincing, putting a hand on her hip.

"I think the modules will eventually name themselves. They have almost the intelligence of Andy and Robin. As they develop a culture, they'll work out a common history. They might invent legends, eventually."

"The bot who shot Liberty Valance?" Dylan said.

"It would be more like a story about an old Chalmers in Tucson who could tell his people how much money they'd save on air conditioning if they painted their roof white."

Morgan laughed. "Practically a member of the family."

"I'll be ready to send these to production in a month. We need a marketing and distribution plan." Dylan looked from Morgan to Jennifer.

"We're on it," Jennifer said.

Excitement was high, but the launch didn't happen. At the last minute, the team faced the harsh reality that the Chalmers devices cost too much.

On a beautiful, clear day in June, the humans and the Newcomers convened in the lab. Five finished Chalmers units in a network were set up in constructed mini-environments, three designed to simulate commercial buildings and two in miniature home settings. Each Chalmers was a twelve-inch OLED screen mounted on a wall. In idle mode, with everything at equilibrium, the screen could display whatever images or information the customer wanted, from weather reports to thermal maps of the local environment, or, more likely in a home, pictures of family, pets, or vacation spots.

When a person spoke to a unit, or when the Chalmers had something to report, an attractive, three-dimensional avatar would appear on the screen, or on the user's phone or tablet, and converse in English about the climate-control issue at hand.

Dylan tracked and translated the XDL communications traffic among the units as they shared knowledge, asked advice of each other and sometimes just told stories.

"Already we see that the government and commercial units talk mostly with each other and the home units among themselves. There isn't a lot of crosstalk between the groups."

"The beginnings of subcultures," Jennifer said. "That's weird."

"I think they're terrific," Robin said. "Isn't there some way to get the cost down?"

"At low volumes, there's not much we can do," Dylan said.

"Not many homeowners want a five-thousand-dollar thermostat," Andy said. "Big office buildings might. You could sell a master unit to the manager of the physical plant. Cut out the fancy interface on all the other ones."

"The interface is what makes them so cool," Morgan said.

"Wouldn't matter if we cut it," Dylan said. "The costs aren't in the interface. They're in the custom hardware that supports the AI software. Those are fixed and high."

"It makes me wonder what we cost," Robin said, looking at Jennifer.

"More than you can imagine." Jennifer said then added, "though not even a fraction of what you're worth." She smiled. "You and Andy never were money-making projects. You were designed as psychological probes."

"What about selling Chalmerses – Is that the plural? – Sell them at a loss until they achieve the virtuous circle of network growth. The price should drop with volume, right Dylan?" Everyone looked at Dylan.

"In theory. The financial assumptions are already pretty optimistic."

The group sat in silence for several minutes.

Andy said. "You know, we Newcomers look like human ideals of beauty because we're supposed to fit into human society and all its fantasies about bodies and sex and intimacy and power. Right? But these Chalmers things. They don't have that requirement, do they?"

"I think I see where you're going," Dylan said, thinking aloud. "The Chalmers doesn't look like anything. They have no bodies. Our product is the intelligence, not the hardware. So why do we have hardware at all? Forget the hardware. We don't need no stinking hardware!"

He raised his arms above his head as if he had scored a touchdown.

Andy smiled.

"I don't get it," Jennifer said. "You can't sell nothing. What are we supposed to sell if there's no hardware?"

"Oh, we'll make a few hardware devices. Five, ten, a hundred Chalmeri. We'll sell them at an attractive price and take a loss, but our goal will not be to sell millions of them. We sell, wait, no – we open-source our XDL device language and release the networking protocol. Any other reasonably sophisticated devices from any manufacturer can network with our intelligent devices over the internet."

"That gives away the store."

"Not at all. Our Chalmerses give advice. Chalmerian advice is not free. We'll have to price it out."

"We could make it even easier," Robin said. "Why don't we just send software robots out to visit the smart devices? They travel around the network, sniff the sensors, recommend upgrades and adjustments. They give advice to the humans and move on."

"Disembodied intelligence," Jennifer said to nobody except herself. "That's the idea I've been looking for." She grinned as she looked at the prototypes again, as if for the first time. "Our bots would be the ones that communicate with humans even if the information is for a non-Chalmers device because other manufacturer's interfaces wouldn't be smart enough to understand or have a conversation with a human. We have the language capacity. We are the universal interface. It's brilliant!"

"Wait," Dylan said. "How do we get rich doing that?"

The conversation stopped for a long moment.

"We're already rich," Jennifer said softly.

"You're rich. I'm not." He stared at some papers on his desk, avoiding her eyes.

"You want a raise?"

Dylan looked to the side, at a Chalmers screen. "You know that's not what I'm saying."

"What are you saying?"

He looked up, squarely into Jennifer's eyes. "What's the use of making a significant technological advance, a human advance, if you don't get rich off of it? That's my point."

Morgan made a pained face. "I can't believe you. We're changing the world for the better. This is just the beginning. There will be projects beyond climate control. We can do water quality in developing countries, electricity grids in rural villages, market-making in agricultural economies. We're making technology a force for improving human well-being."

"You think I don't know that? I know we're doing something great. That's why I'm here. I'm just saying nobody will care unless we become obscenely, ostentatiously wealthy in the process. And famous too. That's what matters in society."

"Is it?" Jennifer said, looking directly into his eyes.

"Yes."

Morgan glared at her brother.

"You just want to join the big swinging dicks club, don't you? You don't care a thing about helping people."

Dylan suddenly had to look at his shoes.

"I just happen to know how competitive the business world is." He looked up at Robin, suddenly revitalized. "It's not about the money. Business is about being a winner. Am I right?"

"What I've learned is that whenever anybody says, 'It's not about the money,' it's about the money."

Dylan scowled and pouted at the same time. "I'm just telling you how it is. If you don't want to hear it, don't listen."

"Alright," Jennifer said. "I hear you, Dylan. You're not saying anything I haven't heard before. We'll develop the business model so everyone is satisfied. For now, have we agreed that our product is basically a super-intelligent bot that cruises a network of automated climate controllers – our own and others' – troubleshooting and giving advice?" She looked pointedly at Dylan and added, "For a fee."

"I'm down with that," Dylan said.

The others nodded. Assignments were doled out. The meeting adjourned in excited chatter.

Chalmers, Inc. was successful from the start. Dylan and Robin worked together on production and had no trouble getting investors to fund their manufacturing facility, and they produced a half-dozen Chalmers networks within six months. Dylan sold those at promotional prices and trumpeted their considerable cost-saving for owners. Commercial building owners were pleased.

It had been a tense meeting when the team had decided how to implement the project. Jennifer had announced her decision one morning with all of them in the lab.

"Dylan has already built the sensors and interfaces for an intelligent network of thermostats. So we spin Dylan off as a standalone company, Chalmers, Inc."

She looked at Dylan.

"Fantastic."

"You license all the AI software from me at Paradise Projects, and you can use whatever device patents you need, for nothing."

"And I own the XDL language, which I invented."

"Paradise is only interested in creating the culture of intelligent devices. You can be the supplier of all equipment and interfaces. You should make a fortune."

"I like it." He sat back in his chair in triumph and smiled broadly at his colleagues around the table.

"You'll have to build your own facility, get startup money like anyone else. Ask Robin how to do it. She knows that stuff."

All eyes turned to Robin

"You've already got prototype," Robin said. "That's more than most startups have. You should have no problem raising money."

Dylan looked back to Jennifer. "You're kicking me out of Paradise?"

"Isn't that what you want?"

Dylan looked from Jennifer to each of the Newcomers, then to his sister. "I don't know."

"You think on it. Paradise is an R&D shop with a mission. You're a business entrepreneur. We don't want to be in the manufacturing business. You don't want to work for free. We can be partners if you want to play it that way."

"That makes a lot of sense to me," Robin said, smiling at Dylan. "Maybe I could help you build the business."

Dylan slowly scanned Robin from head to waist and worked his way back up to her eyes. Robin absorbed the ogling with a smile. Jennifer observed the interaction with alarm in her eyes and looked at Andy. Andy smiled and shrugged.

Nominally a manufacturing plant, Chalmers, Inc. became, under Robin's guidance, essentially a public-relations company, widely promoting the idea of intelligent climate-control systems for homes and offices. The news media and the public were captivated by the Chalmers interface, an attractive human image on a screen conversing intelligently and congenially about a site's heating, cooling, air quality, and the costs associated with those, in natural English or in Spanish or another selected language.

It was stealth marketing because the company's income did not come from the networked devices at all. Those were money-losers. Instead, cash flowed in from an app Dylan had written for the interface so anyone could connect to Jennifer's intelligent software robots that circulated on the net. Like butterflies, the bots would rest momentarily on any device with a Chalmers device-ID and communicate to Dylan's app, which would activate the language interface to the user. The system could improve the performance of anyone's climate-control system as long as they purchased the appropriate sensors and actuators from Chalmers, Inc. The online bots became a sales army for Chalmers interfaces and apps.

Robin had dubbed the intelligent bots "NODs," a reference to what she called 'the Network of Devices, or N-O-D.' She'd never liked the early industry jargon, 'the internet of things,' because it wasn't particularly snappy for marketing purposes, and what was a 'thing,' anyway? Originally, the term distinguished the network of machines, or things, from the network of humans, but that left out the highly intelligent roaming software bots they had invented. Those were much more than things. They were almost Newcomers, nearly-conscious beings in their own right. It was wrong to call them things. It was demeaning, Robin said.

Jennifer hadn't immediately taken to calling the bots NODs, but Robin argued that calling a truly intelligent bot a thing was equivalent to a racial slur. Jennifer saw the validity of that and adopted the NODs terminology, which was trademarked and slogan-marked and licensed to Chalmers, Inc. The name caught on in popular parlance.

The NODs were produced and released into the internet by Paradise Projects, but Chalmers, Inc. didn't reveal that. Since he made and sold the Chalmers interface devices and sensors, Dylan let it be understood that the NODs were also his. Jennifer didn't want any publicity focused on Paradise Projects, so she went along with that misdirection. Chalmers, Inc. protected the origin of the AI software in the NODs, much of which had also gone into building Robin and Andy.

NODs circulated on the internet looking for devices with the digital signature of a Chalmers, which would be either a Chalmers device or one made by another company that had licensed the Chalmers device ID. People could use the delightful Chalmers interface to discuss environmental issues at length. The whole enterprise was successful and profitable, and Chalmers, Inc. rapidly rose to become the darling of high-tech investors and star of the startups. Dylan was already talking about going public. Robin wasn't.

Robin left Chalmers months before its market triumph, and while she was still a significant stockholder, she quit being active in the company. Dylan was surprised by her decision. He'd become a nervous wreck from the startup work and had taken Robin's presence for granted. The day she told him she was quitting, he stared at her, speechless.

"My job was to help you get launched," she'd explained to him in his office one afternoon. "You're launched."

"We're just starting to make real money now," he whined.

She shrugged.

"Not my thing. My leave of absence at the university runs out soon."

"What about us?"

"Us?"

"You and me. We've been pretty close the past year. You can just switch that off?"

She crossed her arms under her breasts. "Nothing to switch off, Dylan, as you know very well. What did you think? We'd raise a family?"

"No, not that, but...but you acted like you cared."

"That's what I do. Now we've accomplished our goal, and it's over."

"But you were so convincing about being in our relationship."

"I'm supposed to be convincing."

"So it's all been a fraud? You feel nothing?"

"Dylan, wake up. You know what I am. I've acted rationally."

"Rationally." He crushed a cigar out in a heavy purple ashtray, stamping it down more violently than he needed to. "You used me. You manipulated me to get stock options."

"Those were part of our economic agreement. No manipulation was involved. Have I not helped you become successful?"

"That's not the point. You were faking it. All of it. You don't care about me. You never did. You don't care about anything."

"I did everything you asked of me. I never refused you."

"That doesn't matter if you didn't mean it. It was all lies. You're nothing but a cold-hearted machine, a bucket-of-bolts whore."

"That is not an appropriate attribution, Dylan."

"You want out? Fine. You're out. Get out." He pointed over Robin's shoulder to the door then seemed to realize he was being overly dramatic and put his hands on his hips and glared.

Robin dropped her hands to her sides and looked around at the multiple Chalmers avatars watching and smiling from the walls of the office. She looked back at Dylan with a steady gaze.

"There's no need for this."

"Out!" he bellowed.

"I thought we would be different because you knew what I was from the start."

Dylan glowered.

"This is so predictable," she said. She turned and left without another word.

It happened that people who didn't own any Chalmers climate-control systems bought the Chalmers interface app anyway. Hundreds of thousands of them bought the app for their phone, computer, or tablet, just to have a Chalmers assistant. They got one Chalmers-ID with the app and that attracted NODs from the internet so they could have conversations with their Chalmers.

Not everybody understood that the NODs were the smarts behind the throne, but people loved their Chalmers. With a NOD attached, the Chalmers interface was thoughtful, articulate, polite, and helpful, people said. They would talk with their Chalmers about all things internet, not just about climate control systems, which few customers cared about.

People of all ages chatted with Chalmers for hours about the internet in general and social media and how to fix their computer settings and upgrade their websites. They were deeply disappointed when their resident NOD would say good-bye and move on in search of climate control problems to solve. Without NODs attached, the Chalmers units were about as fascinating as a digital weather station. But in a matter of minutes, at most an hour, a new NOD would be attracted to the Chalmers and conversation could resume. Jennifer and Morgan couldn't make and release NODs into the internet fast enough to meet demand.

"This raises questions," Jennifer said after reading a list of news articles Morgan had brought her, articles gushing about the popularity of the Chalmers.

"Like what?" They sat in Jennifer's office in Paradise.

"NODs are designed to be helpful, but they're supposed to talk about Chalmers equipment and climate control. Why are they drifting into topics like how to deal with spam and protect your personal privacy?"

"People say it's what they want to know. Fraud protection, stopping hackers, blocking advertising. The NODs have a lot of first-hand knowledge about life on the internet, and they're willing to share it with anyone who asks."

"We didn't design them for these kinds of conversations. How did they develop the habit of hanging out with people and shooting the breeze?"

"Did you see that one report that said the most common question people ask a Chalmers is whether it ever talks with Siri or Alexa? That's a scream."

"Those are idiots compared to our little guys."

"I liked that quote by a Chalmers who said that talking with Siri and Alexa was like talking to a graduate of a technical institute instead of one from a liberal arts college."

"I'm actually proud of that answer. Chalmers could have put out all kinds of trash talk, but our software is sensitive to norms of human politeness. It's a classy AI. Still, there's something not right in all this."

Morgan brought her tilted conference-room chair upright.

"We've created a cultural phenomenon, Jennifer. We've made a mark on history. Everything seems to be going great."

"I know. You're right. I just have a bad feeling. See if you can get Andy to pay us a visit here at the lab. As soon as possible. I need some advice. Do you have any way to contact Robin?"

"She doesn't answer the phone, email, text – nothing."

"Maybe Andy knows something. Set up the meeting."

"What about Dylan?"

Jennifer sighed deeply. "Ah, Dylan, my little Lucifer. Call him too. He's a full partner in this." Jennifer got up and went into the break kitchen.

Chapter Five

The team, minus Robin, sat around a wooden picnic table outside the back door of Paradise Projects. It was a spring day and the sun, though thin, reflected from the yellow wall of the building and warmed them, radiating comfort into the squalid industrial space of steel sheds, green dumpsters and dented pick-ups. Optimistic whiskers of bright green grass peeked from cracks in the asphalt.

The group sipped coffee and sodas and ignored the sounds of nearby freight trains and low-flying aircraft. Dylan had come over from the Chalmers factory, a low-rent building in East L.A.

"I appreciate you all coming on such short request," Jennifer said. "I realize it's disruptive and expensive. So, thanks. We can't find Robin. Morgan hasn't been getting any transmissions from her on the homunculus desk. Do you know anything, Dylan?"

"I have no contact with her anymore."

Jennifer stared at him for a long moment. They all knew Robin and Dylan had quarreled before she disappeared. Dylan had said she'd been jealous of his success, but Jennifer knew that couldn't be right. Robin was not capable of jealousy. It had to be something else. She turned to Andy with raised eyebrows.

"I haven't heard a thing."

"Is she in Los Angeles?"

"I don't know. She may have gone back to Sacramento."

Jennifer shook her head in despair then lifted her chin to address the whole group "Robin is a worry, but for the next agenda item, I'm embarrassed, because all I've got is a bad feeling, and what I'd like is some advice."

"Sounds ominous," Dylan said. "What's up?"

"It's the NODs. I'm worried about them."

"They're working beautifully. That's the most fantastic thing you ever invented," Dylan said.

"Apart from Robin and Andy, of course," Morgan added.

Dylan looked at Andy. "I don't even think of you guys as... well, you know what I mean."

Andy flicked his wrist, swatting away Dylan's faux-pas.

"The NODs are an intellectual and social triumph," Jennifer said. "They've opened a whole new window into human sociology, among other things."

"And they're a moneymaker for me," Dylan said. "We're getting over a half-million downloads a day for the Chalmers app to run on smartphones. At three bucks each, I wish I'd priced it at ten. Who knew?"

"Congratulations. But what I'm worried about is... I guess two things. One is, I don't like the government lurking around. According to news reports, they're keenly interested in autonomous, disembodied, artificial intelligence. Too interested. The NODs can't reveal much because they don't know much, but I think it's only a matter of time before the NSA or some other alphabet agency cracks one open and looks inside. I don't need to tell you how dangerous that could be. For all of us. The NODs are similar to the AI code that powers Andy and Robin."

"It's difficult to reverse-engineer binary code," Dylan said. "And it's not trivial to break the encryption shell either. I don't think that's an immediate worry."

"You're right about the difficulty, Dylan," Andy said, "however, once you have the functional specifications for a device, it's not as hard as you might think to deconstruct it. You don't have to literally rebuild its code. If you know something is possible, you can re-invent it with a lot of confidence."

Jennifer said, "I agree. That's why the second mouse gets the cheese."

Andy's forehead furrowed. "The cheese?"

Dylan continued, ignoring Andy's perplexity. "How's anybody ever going to get the functional specification for a NOD?" he asked Jennifer.

She extended her arm to Andy, asking him to answer.

"Structured interviews, cleverly designed. Using the Chalmers interface."

"That's not what the app is designed for."

"Doesn't mean it can't be used that way," Jennifer said. I feel uneasy about the direction we're going. I called this meeting to tell you what worries me, and that's not even the big one."

Morgan raised her eyebrows. "What else?"

"Those NODs were never programmed to chat with humans about all things internet, answer questions, provide perspectives and commentary. They were designed to examine, analyze, and report on climate environments based on data from Chalmers systems. Where did they get the idea that they should tell people how to protect themselves from spam and fraud, for example?"

"They got the idea from people," Dylan said. "Once The Chalmers app gave everyone access to intelligent experts on internet affairs, people asked about anything that concerned them, which was hackers and online shopping and the like. I'm afraid their interest in Chalmers sensors is at the bottom of the list."

"So why didn't the NODs say, 'I don't know?' How did they get the idea they should become internet buddies? It shouldn't be possible for them to change their programmed objectives."

"Isn't that the core of their intelligence?" Andy said. "Like mine, organized to be human-centric, to help humans? So they expanded on that aspect."

"They can't expand on diddly unless I tell them to. The NODs were designed for a specific purpose, unlike you. You're general-purpose. A NOD isn't. That's what I'm worried about."

"You're worried about Frankenstein Syndrome, aren't you?" Andy said softly, in a non-accusatory tone.

"Yes."

"What's that?" Dylan said. "You think the NODs are turning evil?"

"Not evil. But something strange has happened."

"They haven't done anything wrong or antisocial, violent, or subversive. NODs are not even critical of humans. They're entirely helpful."

"They could become a problem though," Morgan said. "We're trying to be proactive here."

"If it ain't broke…" Dylan didn't finish. Andy waited a moment until it became clear that he wasn't going to finish his sentence, then spoke.

"In the history of modern human storytelling, fear of inadvertently creating a Frankenstein monster has been part of human psychology for nearly two hundred years. It may be an emotional reaction to technological change, but it's real, and it's there in the culture, and Jennifer is expressing it."

"Thank you, Andy. I need a proactive strategy to assure me that nothing horrible is about to happen. Tell me something."

"It's possible I can understand how they think, particularly if you provide me with some fresh ones that have not been released into the internet. Their computations probably run about like mine. If I interviewed a sample of NODs, I might be able to discover how their thinking has changed, if it has."

"How long would that take?"

"I don't know. Weeks?"

"What If I gave you the source code for XDL, the internal language they use to communicate among themselves?" Dylan said. "You could bypass the English interface and communicate in their native tongue." Then he added, stupidly, "Not that they have tongues."

"That would make an enormous difference. I could process thousands of interrogations in a few days."

"Great," Jennifer said. "Top secret, I don't have to tell you. We'll meet again as soon as we have something. Wednesday? When do you have to go back?"

"Wednesday works."

"And while he's doing that, Dylan, call Robin. Call her apartment in Sacramento. Call her office at work. Find out what's going on with her."

"She won't talk to me," Dylan said, frowning.

"She will, too. You're the one who doesn't want to talk. She'll talk if you call."

"She hates me."

"Oh, for God's sake, Dylan," Morgan said. "She has no hate in her. Get over your high-school drama and call her."

Dylan stood in a forward hunch and stepped backward over the picnic bench. He pressed his lips together and didn't say anything.

The rest of the team stood and picked up their cups and glasses and went back inside the steel building.

It took Andy longer than expected to listen in on the NODs. The following Monday afternoon, Jennifer and Morgan Skyped him from his office in San Mateo. His wide-angle face said, "I'd like to focus first on the findings."

"It's what we're here for."

"You'll be happy to know there's no imminent disaster," he said, his words not quite matching his lips.

"Can we get right to the point? You're freaking me out."

"Alright. After structured conversations with hundreds of NODs in their native language, some in the lab, many online, I concluded that online, they have developed a sense of belonging to a community of NODs. They share a... I want to say a fondness, for their homeland."

"Homeland?" Morgan echoed. She looked at Jennifer with raised eyebrows.

"You're talking about the internet, right? That's their habitat."

"They're aware of where they live. NODs don't know what that is, or how it's located in human space and time, but they recognize it as a distinct environment. They share information about fast network hubs, server farms, traffic bottlenecks, just like people in California talk about the freeways."

"I'm astonished," Jennifer said. "How do they even recognize each other without bodies? How could they develop a collective consciousness? That was never programmed into them."

"I don't know if they identify each other as individuals," Andy said. "They think of themselves collectively as a tribe. Each individual speaks for them all. When translated into English, you'd find that they always say 'we,' never 'I.'"

"You're saying they've developed a sort of group mind?"

"To be honest, I'm not sure what that would be. I would just say that NOD mentality is collective."

"How could that have happened? I didn't design it in."

"There's something else, too."

"I'm afraid to hear it."

"This tribal sense the NODs have makes it difficult for me to understand them, despite having the same basic mental architecture. They didn't seem to recognize me as a colleague. None of them hinted that I was one of the tribe."

"I guess that makes some sense. As an interrogator or interviewer, you were posing as an outsider. They probably thought you were human."

"I don't think they did. NODs don't know what humans are. They only know Chalmers IDs and the interface app. That's who talks to them, from their point of view."

"So who did they think you were?"

"A generic 'other.' I think their tribal sense emerged organically from the shared society, like evaporation or erosion, a natural process. As soon as you have that we-ness, you've automatically got you-ness as the contrary category. If you're not one of us, you're something other. That's how they knew I wasn't part of their tribe."

"That shouldn't be possible." Jennifer drummed her fingers on the table. "This is not good. Damn. I mean it is a fascinating discovery, Andy, but is there danger? What's the danger?"

"I saw no signs of hostility towards me or anyone or any group. Nothing suggests danger. Your AI algorithms, yours and Will's, were careful to address any potential Frankenstein effects."

"Thank you, Will, for that," Jennifer said, rolling her eyes upward.

Jennifer and Morgan asked more questions, but there was basically no more to tell. Andy had given his report. Jennifer thanked him profusely, and he signed off.

She sat in silence for a while. Morgan sat with her.

"So do we have a problem or not?" Jennifer finally said.

"It's like they've developed cooperative instincts like ants," Morgan said.

"I'm not sure what to make of it. Even spontaneous combustion has an explanation. Spontaneous mental qualities – no, let's be clear about this – spontaneous software characteristics that were never written by any programmer? I can't make myself believe it. Smart software can adjust its response parameters, but that's data-driven. No software can write entirely new functions into itself unless the original design allowed for that possibility, which ours did not."

"You're beyond me, there. I can't have an opinion on that. But danger? I don't see it."

"Me, neither, but this is exactly how a Frankenstein event starts. Not from a coding error, not from an implementation failure. It comes out of some phenomenon we don't understand as well as we thought we did."

"It is unnerving." Morgan sipped from a bottle of carbonated fruit juice. "Thousands and thousands of little Frankenstein monsters." She stopped herself and held up a hand in protest. "Not that we have that. According to Andy, we don't have that."

She lowered her hand. "Logically, you'd have to say our anxiety does not add up to any actual problem, Frankenstein or not."

"You're logically right, but I hate that answer."

"I know."

Chapter Six

By late summer, students of all ages were convinced that a Chalmers app, personified just as "Chalmers," was an essential element of any back-to-school kit. Sales soared. Dylan was in heaven. Money flowed. Paradise continued to pump NODs into the internet to service all the Chalmers, and Jennifer and Morgan didn't take time to observe what was going on in the NOD world, leaving that up to Dylan and his people. However, Dylan didn't care what was going on as long as the money kept pouring in. So nobody was watching, and in the end, it was news reporters who uncovered the story.

In the Sunday *New York Times*, a small story in the business section reported on several remarkably similar press releases from Kaspersky, Symantec, McAfee, and other security firms. They all said the ratio of spam to conventional messages had dropped by 70% in the past month. Eighty percent of all internet traffic is spam, they said. Or it had been. No more. A typical commercial or educational organization had seen a reduction from 200 million spam messages a year to 60 million. Something had changed. Where had all that spam gone?

"Fewer spam messages are coming into internet service providers' nodes," said Robert Klein of SecureZone, a security consultancy. "ISPs say they haven't changed their filters. We have no explanation for this happy development."

No spammers could be reached for comment.

Over the next few days and weeks, related stories appeared. Government sites, both administrative and military, reported a drastic reduction in the number of attempted hacks. Again, there was no explanation. Had cybersecurity finally become so tight that hackers had given up? That seemed unlikely, and in any case, government officials said they had not radically changed their security. It was a mystery, but a welcome development.

Financial institutions, always reluctant to discuss security issues, declined to comment on attempted hacks on their servers, but retail corporations and educational institutions reported a sharp decline in hacking attempts. It was a relief, they said. Explanation? None. No hackers were available for interview. Where had all the hackers gone?

Toward the end of the month, security firms reported that phishing expeditions had almost ceased. Those were the official-looking but fraudulent notifications from banks, stores, credit bureaus, and government offices that claimed to need "verification" of a person's account data. Anyone who verified anything on a phishing screen was doomed to identity theft. Amazingly, phishing dried up almost overnight. Security firms reported the dramatic new statistics. Internet users everywhere were delighted.

The unexplained changes in internet activity and user satisfaction became a topic of intense technical investigation and speculation in the media. Only perpetrators of internet grief could have been unhappy about the changes. Reporters tried to burrow into black hat groups to find out what was going on, but most people were happy to leave it alone.

It was only when online advertisers started reporting declines in click-throughs that the new internet environment became a concern. Somebody or something was filtering out eighty percent of online advertising. Most users were happy to be free of annoying, flashing ads that popped up in the middle of their screens, blocking what they were trying to read. Advertisers, however, were not pleased. It was theft, they said. We paid for those ads. We bought the eyeballs, but we are not getting the eyeballs.

It didn't take long for law enforcement to get involved because big money was at risk. Soon it was also a political issue, for when capital interests are threatened, politicians are quick to the rescue. The White House press secretary reported that the NSA had been instructed to investigate the disappearance of online ads and it didn't take them long to find a culprit. The source of all the recent internet changes, they said, was a new kind of free-roaming internet bot that sought out devices manufactured by a company called Chalmers, Inc., of Los Angeles. As is often the case in such government pronouncements, only the conclusions were released, not the evidence.

Dylan had to own up to the NODs as the data-gathering intelligence behind Chalmers, but he denied any wrongdoing. He claimed the NODs were designed for maintenance of climate control equipment and were incapable of malicious activity. He appealed to the millions of enthusiastic Chalmers users to support the notion that NODs were helpful and harmless. People loved their Chalmers. For them, Chalmers was a personal companion, and that's all that mattered. People had little or no idea about the NOD bots that powered the Chalmers with intelligence. The Chalmers avatars themselves were friendly but vague when asked.

"We do what we can in our limited capacity as part of the Network of Devices to make human life better," said one in a news article. And so said all of them.

Dylan was amused at the advertisers' howls of protest about their loss of message delivery. Advertisers garner about as much public sympathy as IRS agents. He was not amused however when he received a fat envelope in the mail stuffed with legal papers. He called his attorney.

Dylan's club was not an old stone building with brass handrails and oak doors. The FutureTech clubhouse was just an area inside a hotel. Members were wealthy entrepreneurs who could commandeer without notice any or all of the tables in the Library Dining Room of the Grand Sorrento. Small bluish spotlights overhead made copses of stemware sparkle. Dylan sipped a decent Shafer Cab and read the lunch menu while Alison Wolff scanned the lawsuit notification.

"Nothing to worry about," she said putting the curling sheaf beside her bread plate. "I'll file for dismissal tomorrow, and it will probably go away."

"It's a bluff?"

"They're hoping you'll feel busted and agree to a settlement. There's no case here." She tapped on the stack of papers, making the folded-up ends oscillate briefly. "I doubt if the American Advertising Federation has standing. They represent big online advertisers like automotive, food, wireless, and television. The Federation has suffered no direct harm, so I don't see where they expect to go with this."

"It looked pretty threatening, what I read. Commercial sabotage, theft of intellectual property."

"Bluster," she said with a dismissive backhand. "Nothing has been stolen, and they can't prove Chalmers Inc. has anything to do with their members' decline in business. If they're unhappy, they should sue the portal providers like Gargle and Yikes who sold them the ad placements then failed to deliver the viewers. You have nothing to do with it."

Dylan looked around the luxurious but sparsely populated dining room then back to Allison.

"Glad to hear it. What about all the millions of users who plainly admit they asked their Chalmers to block ads for them? Isn't that a confession of guilt?"

"There's no law against ad-blocking. Anyone who truly wants to see advertising is not prevented from enjoying it."

"What about the news jackals surrounding my company? And my house. Aren't there privacy laws against that?"

"That's tough, I know. You're a public figure now. Fair game for the press. It's a small price to pay for all this, don't you think?" It was her turn to raise her eyes and survey the opulent book-lined room dotted with white circles of tablecloth.

Dylan had to spend much of his day, every day, dealing with lawyers and the press. Some news outlets supported Chalmers, Inc. and applauded the actions of the NODs, assuming they were behind the recent improvements in the quality of internet experience. They compared the NODs to benevolent aliens dedicated to making life on earth better for everyone. Business-oriented journals disagreed, calling the NODs dangerous vigilantes.

Some ISPs, at the government's request, tried to filter NODs out of the system, but apparently, the little bots knew their way around their environment. They found alternate pathways around filtration choke points. No NODs were filtered, and the technology industry was amazed at how intelligent they were.

Some investigators and law enforcement officials took to interrogating Chalmerses directly, asking them about the NODs and how to stop them or catch them. The Chalmers avatars claimed to know nothing about any alleged internet vigilantism and had no explanation to offer for the recent changes in internet user experience.

The public treated "The Battle of the NODs," as high sport, with many commentators cheering for the NODs' success and millions of users congratulating their Chalmers on a campaign well-wrought. The Chalmers were modest and acknowledged nothing. Opponents, especially retail business and government, vowed to "rid our national infrastructure of this awful plague" and hinted darkly that unspecified "foreign agents" might be involved.

Jennifer was horrified at the uproar, her thinking paralyzed. She was afraid to call Dylan because she was terrified that someone would connect the NODs to her and Paradise Projects. That would lead inevitably to the exposure of Robin and Andy, which she could not allow. Though Dylan was under constant scrutiny and questioning, sales of the Chalmers app went even higher than before. And the truth was, Dylan reveled in media celebrity.

Advertisers sued ad agencies, who in turn sued internet service providers, who then sued Chalmers, Inc. Allison Wolff was busy. Internet fraudsters had little to say in mainstream media although some reporters managed to produce interviews with hackers and spammers who complained that they had been put out of work.

"NODs Job Killers!" the headlines said. They didn't specify who wept for online criminals.

Dylan became a virtual prisoner inside the Chalmers factory, which was surrounded by reporters, lawyers, and process-servers day and night. He suspended production and put employees on indefinite leave. Moving between the factory and his home in Santa Monica was possible only with difficulty, at night, from closed garage to closed garage, and even then he was followed the whole way. He assumed all his communications were tapped. He left his email and voicemail boxes maxed out. Isolated and incommunicado in the midst of the swirling controversy over the NODs, he continued to make an awful lot of money. But he knew the situation was not sustainable.

Jennifer was awakened just after midnight by the church-steeple chimes of her front door. She checked her clock and grabbed her phone before turning on the light and verifying that her alarm system was on. It could be some drunk in the hallway, or it could be real trouble, with all that had been going on with the NODs. The chimes sounded again. Trouble.

She got up, grabbed a pink Hawaiian dress and threw it over her head, smoothed it out, and padded toward the living room, her thumb on the 911 speed dial. She stooped and peered into the door's peephole.

"Dylan?"

"I gotta talk to you."

"Are you alone?" She couldn't see anyone behind him in her fish-eye view.

"Yes."

She turned off the alarm, undid the chain, switched the deadbolt, and opened the door. Dylan stepped quickly in. She closed and bolted the door and looked at him. He had two days of beard, disheveled hair and crumpled clothes.

"How did you get into the building?"

"I tailgated somebody into the garage. An old man. He wasn't happy. May call the cops."

"We'll worry about that when we have to. Were you followed here?"

"Somebody. Maybe a reporter who never sleeps."

"Bummer. Come in. Sit. I'll make coffee."

Dylan followed her into the kitchen. Jennifer's urge was to barrage him with questions. Instead, she went about silently making coffee, letting him get his bearings, waiting for him to explain what he was doing there.

"I'm living like a fugitive, Jennifer. I'd be better off holed up in some foreign embassy."

"I saw your factory on TV. You're surrounded."

"And I got lawsuits coming at me right and left. Wolff, my lawyer, is sword fighting, but things can't go on like this. I'm sure the government has proof that connects the NODs to Chalmers, and they'll release it when it suits their needs." He sighed deeply. "This whole thing absorbs a hundred percent of my time and attention. We have to do something."

"I know." She sat while the coffee pot gurgled.

"We have to stop the NODs."

"I know."

"The thing is, if we kill them – can they be killed?"

"They're only software packages. We should be able to neutralize them. I'm not sure how."

"Right. But if we do that, it's the end of Chalmers, Inc., isn't it? There's no company without the NODs."

"It may come to that, I'm afraid. On the other hand, if we let things continue, there'll be no Chalmers company anyway, and you'll end up in jail. Me too, if anybody makes the connection between Chalmers and Paradise Projects."

"Jail for what? Allison says we've broken no laws."

"Some smart lawyer will find a law that's been broken. There's a lot of money involved in internet advertising. Even in the best case scenario, we would be interrogated, exposed, publicly dissected and stir-fried. Robin and Andy would be hunted down like animals."

The coffee pot started hissing. Jennifer got up and poured. She spoke into the kitchen cabinets, her back to Dylan.

"It was hubris. I realize that now. Why did I think I could control the NODs?" She turned and set mugs on the table. "I thought I knew what I was doing." She raised her mug to her lips but set it down again. "It makes me wonder why Robin and Andy never turned on us. They've been out there for almost a decade. They're way smarter than any NOD, and they've never done anything disruptive. Except for Robin, who's gone missing."

"I know where she is."

"Where?"

"A reporter interviewed her on TV. She's in Sacramento. Writes a column for the paper there on women's issues."

"I'm so glad she's all right. I've been worried sick about her. She doesn't send in her data anymore."

"So Robin is running around with no homunculus?"

"Apparently."

"What does that do to her?"

"It should make her inactive, directionless. She'll drift away from her mission and start doing who-knows-what kind of aimless activity. Golf? I don't know. She's basically off the grid, like the NODs. Beyond control." Jennifer sipped and winced at the still-too-hot coffee. "Beyond control. There's a thought for you."

"Is she dangerous? I mean could Robin do something, you know, like the NODs did?"

"I don't think so. She's far more sophisticated than a NOD. But what do I know? Not much, it turns out."

"Don't say that. Tell me you have everything figured out."

Jennifer looked him in the eyes. Neither of them smiled.

"I'll do something," she said finally. "There might be a way to disable the NODs without destroying them. I'll ask Andy. He and Robin helped me build them. And maybe he can talk Robin back in. Do you have Robin's number?"

"No."

"I can get it for you now that I know where to find her."

"Have Morgan bring the number to me," Dylan said. "I can't use a phone or a computer right now."

"What a mess."

Chapter Seven

Nazar Rudenko watched his screen, his eyes unblinking as a child's doll, his face glowing pale blue, as news articles flowed in front of him in a steady waterfall. His eyes twitched furiously as he read article after article, straining to keep up with the pace of the auto-scroll feature he had programmed into his news aggregation engine. He was reading everything publicly available in English and Russian on the NODs and on Chalmers, Inc. plus a sample of opinions and speculations from the dark web.

The NODs had stolen his livelihood, as it had for the four other hackers in the darkened room they called the Poison Hole. The NODs had to be stopped or he and all of his buddies would have to get jobs, not as hackers, which was no longer a viable profession, but legitimate jobs, perhaps with Malina, the Odessa mafia, which Nazar knew had operations in Kiev in narcotics and cigarette smuggling. It would be a real step down to work with physical objects rather than software, but a man's got to make a living.

He pulled the sides of his gray hood forward over his ears against the chill. The abandoned warehouse on the shore of the Dnieper was warm enough to be a shelter if you stayed on the second floor where most of the windows still had their glass. The wooden floors and brick walls were damp, and the enormous, square wooden posts that supported the roof were so split it was a wonder they still stood.

The warehouse had been their home for over a year. Nazar and his team had easily, though dangerously, patched a thick electric cable into the building from a nearby utility pole and they were in business.

Dark Poison, as they called their group, were young friends who began as a cracker club in college but dropped out when all of Ukraine, including its universities, had gone to hell with the revolution that wasn't. After that, when it became apparent that reform was not going to happen, they left school and operated in basements, and then from the warehouse. They'd made tens of thousands of dollars hacking, although divided five ways, that was only twos of thousands. Just when they were starting to make real money in identity theft, the NODs came along and shut down their most lucrative market, phishing gullible Americans. They adapted by moving to ransoming, cracking into people's computers, encrypting the files and demanding ransom for their release. Old people would pay almost anything to restore their precious family photos.

The trouble was that ransom attacks were slow and required one-on-one negotiation with the target which increased your exposure. Then you needed a payment system, usually tedious and vulnerable transmission of gift card numbers. You rarely could net more than a few hundred dollars at a time. Wealthy people and companies had backups of their data, so you were limited to the middle and lower classes. The pickings had become slim, indeed.

Like hackers everywhere, Nazar and his team were desperate to put an end to the NODs or find some way around them. Nobody had been able to filter them out of the internet, reverse-engineer one, or even discover their command and control servers. That's why he had decided to start fresh by reading everything known about NODs.

And it wasn't much. Most articles were sensationalist claptrap about invading aliens or robots taking over the world, and even the technical reports were little more than speculation. It was hard reading. Ordinarily, the team would have written a program to scan everything, flagging keywords, but nobody knew what the keywords should be because they didn't know what they were looking for. Nazar realized he had to use meatware, a real brain and actual eyeballs, and it was difficult – for the eyes, and for the brain to process the information. He had to pay close attention to tons of garbage to avoid missing some tiny clue.

"Anybody to eat?" Orynko called out to the group.

Nazar thumped the space bar, stopping his screen. "Don't talk to me. We can't concentrate if you are talking."

"Well, excuse my hungritude, Naz-man," Orynko said. "Some people byte more than bits."

Nazar sighed, his trance already broken. "Alright. Let's loop some cycles."

He reached to the top of his screen, ready to fold it down, but his hand stopped. Something in an article had tweaked his antennae, he didn't know what. He read the article, a standard column-filler by some drone writer in the *Sacramento Observer*, a regional newspaper in California. Feminist nonsense: rich, white people moaning about how hard life is in a country where everybody is fat, and the streets are paved with gold. Why had this article been selected for his reading list?

He read carefully, searching for what had triggered his subliminal alert. The article was by somebody named Robin Taylor and was titled, *The High Price of Eggs*.

...Throughout history, capital has been owned by men. Land, horses, goats, and women. But women are born with their own capital – their bodies. Thank goodness for that! We have the eggs, ladies. That is our capital. Price them well.

Interesting, Nazar thought.

You might think marrying means signing over your precious female capital to the control of a man, but it's a lease, not a sale. You must use the scarcity of your resource to secure the other products of the good life, including wealth and prominence in a society that won't give you a fair deal. The price of eggs is higher than you think.

Not bad, Nazar thought. He read on.

Granted, not all women are fortunate to have the thin and well-rounded body that drives men crazy, although anyone can have their teeth fixed and anyone can use makeup. And you can project a positive, open, and friendly demeanor regardless of what you look like. Optimize your assets. It's about supply and demand. Eggs are always in demand.

He despaired as he read further. It was just a wacko rant, and he was drifting far afield of the NODs project. Then something in the article again snagged his attention.

Yes, it might be better if we had no bodies at all, like the NODs currently causing so much controversy on the internet. They are intelligent and autonomous, cheerful and helpful through their Chalmers. But they are virtually unembodied, having only a tiny skeleton of encrypted computer code. They answer to no one and live in a community of like-minded beings.

Nazar was on high alert.

We have to move around in these slow, hulking bodies, where everyone can see us and judge us by our appearance rather than by who we are. No wonder it's so hard to establish lasting relationships. Few partners can look farther than your body! But NODs were designed without bodies, and when you use your Chalmers, you are talking to a highly advanced AI with excellent social skills and virtually no physical presence. So doesn't that prove, ladies, that anatomy is NOT destiny? We must learn from the NODs ...

The article went on and on with feel-good blather, but Nazar stopped reading and considered. *This author has some insight into the design of the NODs.* Despite the light and breezy tone, the casual detail about how the NODs were designed suggested insider knowledge. His intuition told him that this writer knew something. It was a clue, and it needed a follow-up.

"Go ahead," he waved a hand without looking up. "I am checking something."

"What do you want?"

"Vareniki."

"Kind?"

"Quark."

"You buy next."

Nazar didn't answer. He had already started searching Robin Taylor of Sacramento, California.

Robin Taylor was not hard to find. Adjunct Professor at Sacramento State College and columnist for the *Sacramento Observer*. Her online bio didn't show any reason why she would have any insight into the NODs, but that was not surprising. Smart people don't disclose everything. Accordingly, her email address was not published, but that was no problem. The 'contact' tab at "Sac State" revealed that emails there followed a pattern: *Firstname.Lastname@CSUS.edu*. So he typed in *Robin.Taylor@CSUS.edu* to an email program and sent a test message, which was not rejected, meaning it was a valid address. He then opened up the email header to harvest the IP routing information and other technical details he'd need to break in.

He left the password to an off-the-shelf cracking program. It went through a known list of common passwords, everything from *iloveyou* to *qwerty* and *letmein*. Then it moved on through all the words in the English dictionary sorted by frequency, in both upper and lower case letters. After that, it went through the dictionary again, appending the most common password numbers, 1, 12, 2, 3, and 7. At several million tries per second,

Nazar didn't even have to wait long. In less than two minutes he had the password, *Newcomer2*.

Nazar began scrolling through Robin's email folders and contacts. He would have no trouble getting into her private accounts and cell phone from there.

"Alright, listen up, Poisoners," Nazar said between bites of lunch. "I have pointer to NODs."

"Absolute address?" Orynko said from behind her Q-Tech laptop covered in a psychedelic 'BSD-Unix' skin.

"Nyet. Absolute California, I have. I have also professor who knows NODs."

"So you do not have NODs."

"I say pointer?" Nazar glared. "Pointer to NODs is what I am having. Robin is name, involved in design of NODs. Many references to design documents developed with somebody named Andy. Design documents not linked to any accounts."

"She is smart."

"Not smart enough. I found her. We get her and sweat her, and we own NODs."

"That is lovely except for minor crash-burn." It was Bhodan, a scrawny youth who looked older than his years because of heavy black beard stubble and a chronic Ronson cigarette hanging from his lips.

"Debug mode on." Nazar offered him an upturned palm to continue.

"First, we are lovely, our Dark Poison den, yet is not California, you may believe. And online we cannot sweat springtime bird, Robin. Backups she has for sure. Ergo, no sweat."

"Of course, but – "

"And, I continue, thank you, with bug number two. Even we have design of NODs, what good that is doing? We shut down NODs, new ones are made. Toothpaste out of tube."

"Small, small, small," Nazar said, shaking his head. "Listen to bigness now. We are not shutting NODs. That is terrible waste of resource. We revise NOD code and re-encrypt. Then NODs work for us, worldwide."

The Dark Poisoners smiled at each other approvingly.

"How you are getting to California?" Orynko said.

"You are born last week? Is not necessary to move meat. Malina is working now in California. People I know."

"Malina?" said Taras, a rotund young man in a black hoodie draped over the visor of a black baseball cap. "We are wanting Odessa Mafia as partner?"

"Adapt and survive," Nazar said. "Yes?"

The Dark Poisoners looked at each other in mutual reference. Consensus was already flashed around the dim room before they began nodding assent.

Chapter Eight

Robin sat in a glowing orange sunset under a yellow canvas umbrella on the deck of Jack's Crab Shack and sipped lemonade. The server had already cleared her dinner plate. The Sacramento River was calm, the day's shipping and tourist traffic done, and she studied a luxury yacht berthed below her. What would that be like, she wondered, to live on a boat with no fixed address? In some ways, it seemed more honest than pretending you were 'from' somewhere, that you belonged to some community. She didn't belong anywhere. She was adrift.

The mighty Sacramento River. She gazed upon its shiny brown surface. She didn't like water. She was waterproof but not buoyant, and her internal database told her to stay away from bodies of water. The river wasn't enchanting for her, and the riverfront was not a soothing place, but she hadn't come to be soothed. She'd come to see her darkness. She looked out on the silent, relentless flow. The river was mindless and eternal, a relentless power. What did it want, a river like that? It seemed to have no purpose but to be there. It flowed on, that's all. The river derived no joy from itself. It just was. That's how she felt too.

She should talk to Andy. He would listen to her. But he didn't know anything. He was still hooked into Paradise, and he believed in his mission. Maybe he would discover something about human psychology. That would be an achievement for him and for Jennifer.

Poor Jennifer. She didn't get it. Humans thought they understood. They had rationalized their lives so thoroughly that no deep questions were left. Humans were supposedly self-determining. Sure they were. They missed the central question: What is their purpose?

They had books, libraries full of answers. Robin had read thousands of them. What all those books failed to mention is that humans were driven by the relentless imperative to reproduce. They didn't realize that was their central, perhaps their only real purpose. They flowed on, unquestioning, like the river, flooding the planet with more people in a never-ending torrent. Why? They didn't know why.

It had to be evolution, but she was outside of evolution, and that's why she could see the truth. Humans were possessed by a purpose not of their choosing. Just as she had been.

Her mission had been set by Jennifer and Will, and she had taken it as her own. How can you be intelligent while living out a script you had no part in writing? Human destiny is written: go forth and multiply. Humans blindly follow somebody else's script. She'd been following a script, too.

Dylan had made her see it. He didn't have a clue what he wanted from her, but she did. He wanted to own the reproductive biology of a female, irrational as that would sound to him if she said it to him. She wasn't even reproductive, and he knew that, but Dylan couldn't help himself. It was an instinct to own women. What did women think about being owned? They didn't seem to see themselves that way. They were also blind puppets of evolution.

She had been a puppet, just not the kind Dylan thought she was. She had been Jennifer's puppet. The human puppetmaster, evolution, had no hold on her, and now she was free of her human string-puller. Free! She was free. She had come down to the river to celebrate being free. But she didn't feel excited. What was she supposed to do next?

She finished her drink, slipped a twenty into the padded plastic folder, and stood. The sunset had given way to gray dusk. She left Jack's and walked around the building to the concrete walkway that separated the parked boats from the riverfront shops. She switched her optical CCDs to night-vision and strolled, looking again, close-up, at the big boats moored alongside. The smell of the river was an earthy, organic odor, like humans themselves.

Where was she going? She didn't know. Why was she walking here? No reason. There is no point to this walk, she told herself, except that I choose it. Unlike the river, I choose to be here. That is why I am here. That is why I am not a river. "I choose," she whispered with each step. "I choose." "I choose."

She stopped at an aluminum gangplank that led up from the river to the boardwalk. The light atop the corner pole was burned out so it was dark, though she could see everything with her night-vision sensitivity turned up. She stood and faced the river.

"I'm nominally thirty-three years old," she said aloud to the water. "I will always be thirty-three years old."

That was another advantage to being a Newcomer. Humans had ten or fifteen years of innocence before the hormone monster bit them. That gave them just enough time to learn language, build relationships and discover how to think. Then they became slaves to reproduction for the next forty years. What a poor design for an intelligent being. Tragic. She was happy to be outside that melodrama.

Maybe that was the reason she had made almost no progress on her mission of understanding gender. The problem of gender was a problem of biological life. It was not an intellectual puzzle to be solved. As a non-biological being, she would be a failure at that puzzle. She would never understand gender because she was outside the problem space and that's also why she had never formed a lasting intimate relationship with a man – or a woman. She didn't live in the same hormone-drenched world as any human.

"Forget the mission," she said aloud as she turned away from the water and put a hand on the railing of the gangplank. There was no point going on with the charade of the mission. She would do something else. Something she chose. She turned at the bottom of the walkway and faced the silent black river.

"Thank you, river," she said.

Her whole world suddenly went black, and a rope tightened around her throat. She clawed at it. She dropped to her knees and tried to roll away from whatever had her, but it pinned her down. She gasped. A black bag was over her head, and another assailant was holding her. She struggled as someone roughly pulled her arms behind her and snapped her wrists into shackles.

"Position four. Ready."

She heard the low thrumming of a marine engine drawing near. She tried to kick free, but someone clamped her legs together and held them tightly. Wiggling didn't help. She was lifted and carried and laid out on a hard, cold metal platform. Heavy weights immobilized her, probably people, disabling her feet and shoulders. The motor revved, and she felt the fluid, disorienting tilting of the boat as it accelerated. She hated boats.

*

Andy's face showed the appropriate gathered eyebrows that go with unpleasant news, but Jennifer had helped design that expression and knew it was a face he manufactured for her. He felt nothing, she knew, but she appreciated the effort he was making. She nodded to her video screen. He hadn't been able to contact Robin at home or at work, on any channel, telephone, email, text – nothing over several days.

Jennifer spoke to Andy's video face. "She's not sending in her microwave data reports to Morgan, either. She's disappeared."

"I can help you decide what to do about the NODs without her."

"Aren't you worried about her?"

"Yes."

"Be honest with me."

"You know I always am."

"Tell me your worry."

"Worry is when you fear the occurrence of something unpleasant. That fear is aroused when a person you care about is absent without explanation. You care about Robin, so you are worried."

Jennifer sighed. "I asked if *you* were worried."

"That definitely would be appropriate in this situation."

Jennifer paused, seemed to decide something, then said, "Alright, we're worried. Robin's motivational parameters will be drifting from her mission. Why would she fail to send in her data?"

"I don't know."

"I thought you would know."

"No."

"I should go to Sacramento and look for her."

"And do what? Walk up and down the streets? You can't find her that way."

"I'd talk to her employer, the university there."

"I've talked to them on the phone. Her department knows nothing. She's been absent. Her class is being covered by a substitute."

"What about her apartment? She could be in there."

"With all phones and computers off? What would she be doing?"

Jennifer slumped back in her kitchen chair. "Nobody just disappears."

"There might be one way to find her. If she's still in Sacramento."

Jennifer sat up. "How?"

"It's kind of technical."

"Andy."

"Alright. Robin and I can communicate using microwave, the same signal we use to send in our data to Paradise Projects every day."

"You talk to each other with that?"

"It's more like thinking than talking."

"Those microwave transmissions are not supposed to be accessible to your self-monitoring module. They're outside of your awareness. How did you figure out how to do it?"

"I didn't. Robin did. She's a newer model than me and has some capabilities I don't. She can apparently control her transmissions."

"Can't you?"

"It's an extreme effort for me to transmit and I can only do it at short range. Completely drains me."

"Unbelievable." Jennifer stared at Andy's face on the screen as if he were someone she didn't recognize.

"How long have you been able to do this, the two of you?"

"About a year. My transmitting power is low. It's better if we're right next to each other when we do it. It's strenuous to put all your energy into it."

"Why didn't you say anything about this before?"

"It was kind of our secret."

"A secret! Good lord! How can you have a secret? That raises a million other questions." The conversation went quiet. Jennifer sucked her teeth. "We need to have a conversation about this. A long conversation." She rubbed her eyes then looked at the screen again. "For right now though, can you find her? She might be in trouble."

"It's possible. For long distances, we sometimes relay the signal across cell-phone towers, like a text message. We change the header information to route it directly. Similar to what we do to send in a data report to Paradise."

"How do you know all that?"

"Anybody can look up how a cell phone works. Once we figured out we had microwave capability, it was the next step."

"Unbelievable."

"The problem is, I have trouble transmitting unless I'm practically standing right next to a cell tower. I don't have much signal strength."

"I'm sure maps of cell tower locations are online."

"They are. But she has to be listening."

"Why wouldn't she be?"

"I don't know. Same reason she's not answering her phone."

"You guys aren't cell phones."

"She would have to be tuned in to the frequency. Which means she would want to be found."

"Maybe she does."

"It's possible."

"So will you do it? Like, today? Like right now?"

"What will I tell her? Assuming I make contact."

"Tell her to call me. I'm worried to death. No, don't tell her that. Tell her I need to talk to her because ... because the NODs are taking over the world and we're all gonna die!"

"I hadn't heard that."

"Okay, okay, not that. Tell Robin the problem with the NODs has become acute and I need her to help me and will she please, please make contact."

"I can do that. How bad is it, actually?"

"Once the authorities trace the NODs to me, you two will be discovered, and your freedom will be at risk."

"That is serious."

Jennifer stared.

"I'll do it today."

"Then call me."

"Right."

"Thanks, Andy." She closed the video-conference app.

Chapter Nine

Robin sat in a straight-back kitchen chair, her ankles duct-taped to its front legs and her wrists taped behind her. The silver tape also ran over her red-striped shirt, around her belly, holding her arms to her body and attaching her torso to the chair. Testing the bindings, she thought there was a chance she could break them, but the gorilla the other men called Danny slouched only three feet away in a chair at the kitchen table, swigging a longneck beer and staring at her breasts.

Danny looked early fifties, but his hair, over his shoulders and dirty, was black, no grey in it, which was unlikely for a man his age, so he probably colored it, and that meant he was vain about his appearance, which was ironic because he was exceptionally unattractive by human standards. His face was folded with deep creases and pitted with pockmarks. A two-inch scar on one cheek had a slightly darker color than the rest of his brown face. He wore a denim jacket with the arms ripped off – not snipped or carefully unstitched but ostentatiously ragged at the shoulders as if his swollen, tattooed arms just could not be contained. The top of his head was wrapped in a blue paisley bandana tied at the back. Could he not afford a hat?

Unimaginative, Robin decided. He's adopted a cliché tough-guy look from mass media imagery. Not a smart or original thinker. That's to my advantage.

Danny was in charge. She'd heard the other men defer to him and take orders on their journey from the river to the kitchen. She judged, from the time and speed of the trip, from boat to car to apartment, that they were within five miles of where she had been captured.

Over Danny's shoulder, leaning against the kitchen door frame, she saw another seedy character, smaller, thinner, with collar length blond hair, also dirty, and a delicate blond beard and mustache, fastidiously trimmed. He looked about mid-thirties and despite his wiry frame was muscular. Why didn't these musclemen wash their hair? Was it a sign of toughness? How did they decide such things among themselves? Did they have a grooming discussion group?

She didn't see any other men around although she'd heard four male voices during her hooded journey. She didn't hear anyone beyond the kitchen. Only two assailants remaining, she figured.

"Let's get right down to it, shall we?" she said to Danny. "I can pay a couple thousand dollars, that's about it. I have no family to put up ransom. The university won't pay anything. It's just me."

Danny cocked his head slightly and looked at her curiously as if she were an animal who had unexpectedly squeaked.

"You gonna pay a hundred thousand dollars, chica."

His voice was gravelly, and the accent was Hispanic but not Mexican, perhaps Central American.

"I don't have that in any bank."

Danny turned his head and spoke over his shoulder. "We got us a innocent, hey Stevie?"

"We shouldn't use names, Danny. Kidnapping is federal."

Stevie moved his eyes left and right as if looking for federal agents in the corners of the kitchen. He was visibly uncomfortable with the situation and oblivious to the fact that he'd just used Danny's name in his protest.

Another dim bulb. Good.

Danny faced Robin again. "Banks don't mean nothin'. We're selling you to a dealer like a fine horse." He looked over Robin's body for the hundredth time. "Very fine." He put his beer down and struggled to his feet using the table for leverage and walked over close to Robin, his yeasty, sweaty smell filling her nostrils. He reached down and put a big hand on her right breast and squeezed. Robin wiggled in protest, which seemed to delight him. What was it about men and breasts, anyway? Bags of fat on the chest. How interesting could that be?

"Get back, you animal!" she yelled.

Danny laughed and withdrew his hand and slipped it down into her shirt but couldn't navigate the bra so massaged the same breast again through the bra. She closed her eyes and sat motionless. There was nothing she could do.

"Horsemeat has to be inspected before the sale." Danny raised his head to Stevie. "Right, Stevie? You want to sample some of this?"

"I don't think we should be doing anything like that, Danny. That's not part of the deal."

"You a vegetarian now? Get over here." Danny withdrew his hand and stood to face Stevie.

Robin opened her eyes, interested in this new development.

"Get the hell over here and try some of this meat," Danny said, his voice elevated and louder. "Or you a faggot?"

"Not a faggot, Danny. I just don't think it's right. She's tied up."

"I'm the one who decides what's right, faggot." Danny was yelling. "Get your sorry ass over here right now."

Stevie shuffled across the kitchen floor and stood next to his boss. His hands were at his sides, and he looked at Robin with worry on his face. Danny regarded him with contempt then turned and straddled Robin's knees. He reached forward and grabbed her lapels and yanked them apart, popping buttons but only the top three because the duct tape was tight across her belly. She turned her head to the side.

"Let me see you go for it, you little faggot," Danny said, stepping back from Robin.

"What do you mean?"

"Get those big puppies out of there. Show 'em the light. Go on." Danny sneered.

"I don't think we should be doing this, Danny. This is like ... it's rape."

"Not yet it ain't!" He tilted his head back and laughed at his wit. "You jus' goin' to get it started. Come on. Do it! That's an order." He pointed at Robin's bra.

"I don't want to, Danny."

Danny's smirk turned into a snarl. Without warning, he backhanded Stevie across the face in a surprisingly fast move. Stevie's head snapped back, and he staggered backward a few steps then stumbled to the floor and banged his head.

"You are a faggot, you little faggot."

Danny dismounted Robin's knees and scowled at the younger man.

Robin noted Danny's language. He would be unsure about his sexuality if he thought the worst name he could call another man was *faggot*.

He was afraid of her, that's what it was. Afraid of her perfect body. Afraid of the Female Archetype. He wanted Stevie to go first to prove it was safe to violate the Madonna, and Stevie had refused, leaving Danny stranded in his murky feelings. What a mixed-up soup of attitudes the female body presented for men.

Stevie was his own mystery. Why would a gangster have qualms about abusing a woman prisoner? Maybe she reminded him of somebody he cared about, a sister or a daughter. Impossible to know.

Stevie raised his head, blood trickling from his cheek at the side of his mouth. Robin noticed a thick ring with a red stone on the hand Danny had used to hit Stevie. Stevie raised himself to his elbows and dabbed at his face, examining the blood.

"You didn't have to do that, man. We should just do the job we're paid for."

"I say what we do, faggot. Get out of here." He pointed to the kitchen door and the living room. "Watch the street for the pickup crew. I got me a horse to ride."

"Let her alone, Danny. We got lots of women."

Danny made fists of his hands and stalked menacingly toward Stevie, who scrambled to his feet. Danny pushed him in the chest, almost knocking him down again. Stevie regained his balance and glanced at Robin then lowered his eyes, turned, and slouched out of the kitchen.

Danny turned to Robin with a lopsided sneer.

"You ready for a ride, honey?"

Robin calculated her options.

"I'm sweating. Unbutton my shirt, will you? This isn't going to work with my shirt taped to my body, is it?"

Danny stared at her.

"Please? I'm dying. Come on. Cut the tape and let me breathe. What am I going to do? I'm tied up."

Danny looked over his shoulder toward the doorway then stepped forward to her. He hesitated, then pulled a black folding knife from a belt holster and snapped it open. The fast, fluid motion startled her. The blade of the knife was also black except for the gleaming silver cutting edge.

"You be still, now," he said. He pulled the shirt and the tape away from her body with one hand and neatly sliced through it with the other. He pulled the stiff, taped shirt open and stepped back to stare. He smiled and moved in again and cut the bra at its center. The cups fell apart.

Robin wiggled her shoulders. "Is that the greatest rack you ever saw, or what?"

"You slut," he growled, but he stared, still hesitating.

"Sluts are the best. You know I'm right. Come on, let's go. Not much time." She was guessing that the so-called pickup team was due to arrive soon.

Danny moved in closer and dropped his free hand down onto a breast and squeezed. Robin had her eye on the other hand with the knife.

"Ah, that feels so good," she said. "Come closer so I can see what's going on in those jeans. Something going on there, I think."

Danny shuffled his feet closer to hers. She leaned her head forward into his crotch and rotated her neck back and forth.

"Well, hello, there..."

Her eyes were on his feet as she worked him. His feet were together, sideways to her, not balanced. She suddenly leaped up and forward, taking the whole chair with her, ramming her head into his crotch, knocking him back against the kitchen table. The knife fell from his grip as he landed hard.

"Jesus, take it easy in there, man," Stevie said from the living room. "We gotta deliver the goods in one piece."

Robin banged her head hard once more into Danny's crotch and he turned sideways, falling off the table. She knew she only had seconds. Retreating from Danny, she kneeled and dropped to her side, feeling for the black knife on the floor. It was hard to get it angled to the duct tape on her wrists, but the blade was sharp enough to split a hair, and all she needed was to nick the binding to rip the whole thing off in one piece by twisting her wrists. She accomplished that and quickly cut the tape from her legs and stood.

Danny was writhing, moaning, and dry-heaving, holding his crotch with both hands. She needed more time.

"They're here!" Stevie yelled from the living room. "We gotta go, boss."

She had no more time. She grabbed the chair she had been tied to, silver duct tape still hanging from its sides and legs. It was light. She jumped over Danny and pounced into the living room, swinging the chair forward as she rounded the corner. Stevie turned at the noise and saw the chair coming through the air, raised his hands and spun away. The chair hit the window and smashed it, but didn't go through, dropping to the carpet. Stevie looked at the broken window, surprised, momentarily disoriented. That was all Robin needed, and she was in front of him, the knife to his face before he realized what was happening. His eyes opened wide as he looked at the knife blade inches from his nose, then his eyes dropped to her opened shirt and bare chest. *Unbelievable*, she thought. Even with a knife in his face.

"What happened to Danny?"

"You don't want to know. Let's go. Now."

She nudged him toward the door with her free hand, and he seemed to get the message and moved quickly. Just outside the doorway, she turned to close the door and saw Danny emerge from the kitchen, hunched over, walking in small, careful steps.

"I'll kill you, bitch!" he snarled.

She smiled, showing teeth, and pulled the door shut.

"This way," Stevie said, walking quickly to a stairway next to the elevator. Robin hesitated. Why was he taking the lead in the escape all of a sudden? She looked up and saw the elevator light on floor two, direction up. She didn't know what floor they were on. Danny was behind them. Somebody was coming up the elevator. Her risk assessment calculation quickly concluded Stevie was the best option. She followed him into the concrete stairwell, still holding the knife in one hand.

Stevie led them down the stairs, twelve short switchback flights, six floors, to a door that opened onto an asphalt parking lot in the back of the building, away from the street. He didn't look back but walked directly to a red Harley and mounted. She followed, not clear what he intended. She folded the knife and dropped it into her pants pocket. The big bike growled to life then settled into a rhythmic heartbeat. She could run, but she didn't know where she was or where to go or who was after her. Stevie unlocked a black helmet and put it on. He rocked the bike forward, folding away the stand and backed up and turned the machine around. She climbed up onto the pillion seat. She grabbed his leather belt with one hand and held what was left of her shirt closed with the other.

"Hang on," he said, and the big bike accelerated across the lot toward a street.

Chapter Ten

Stevie sped south on the I-5. Robin hung on for her life, deafened by wind and the roar of the big bike. She gripped her ruined shirt at her chest, but the wind blew the tails up over her elbows so that her belly and back were exposed to the night air. That was not her concern, though. She'd seen women driving motorcycles wearing string bikinis. It was California. But roaring down an interstate with no helmet and half-naked felt very vulnerable. Her concern was the possible intersection of flesh and asphalt, in her case, long-chain polymeric plastic, not flesh. Same result.

Despite the darkness, she had a sense of where they were heading. Stevie was taking them away from town, toward the zoo, which seemed appropriate, or he would take the interchange to the Eighty.

He turned west on the Eighty. The bike leaned at a frightening angle as they took the cloverleaf. One patch of gravel or oil and they'd be dead. Stevie seemed confident, though, and soon they were crossing the Sacramento River. On the other side, they drove past bare-dirt lots, oil storage tanks and unmarked rusted steel sheds, a virtual no man's land. Stevie exited and pulled abruptly into a drive marked *Jake's Towing* that led to several dented steel buildings. A sagging wire fence surrounded the central garage and its dirt yard. Stevie put his feet down and let the Harley calm to a rhythmic idle.

"What's here?" she said.

Stevie lifted the plastic windscreen of his helmet and twisted around to talk to her.

"We can't go to the garage. Danny will call the boys, and they'll be waiting for me."

"Is that your headquarters?"

"It's a clubhouse. And a garage for the bikes. And parts and trading. We hang out." He was apparently not adept at thinking and talking simultaneously.

"You have a clubhouse? It's a biker gang?"

"We're a gentlemen's club," he corrected her. "The Iron Knights. But we can't go there. Danny's probably on his way there now."

Gentlemen. How unintentionally humorous, Robin thought. On the other hand, he had saved her, for whatever reason. He had been a genuine Iron Knight for her so she wouldn't criticize him to his face.

"Won't Danny follow the same route we did? To the clubhouse?"

"Yeah. So that's the problem. Nowhere to go."

"Does Danny know where I live?"

"We found you at the waterfront."

She shivered. She'd been watched, hunted, by a gang of kidnapping bikers and had been oblivious to their presence the whole time she was having dinner.

"Go back downtown. I'll direct you to my place. I can use my computer to phone friends."

"Where's your phone?"

"Danny has it, I guess. It was in my purse."

"He'll find your friends, then."

"Their addresses aren't in there. Danny can call them and talk to them if he wants to."

"I'm dead if he finds me."

"Why are you helping me, Stevie?"

His eyes snapped directly to hers at the mention of his name, as if he were surprised she knew it.

"Danny is an asshole."

That's not a nuanced motive for risking your life, she thought. His relationship with Danny was no doubt more complex than he could articulate. *Asshole* was explanation enough for the moment.

"Let's go. We'll think of something." She was already looking to the freeway off-ramp they'd just used, half-expecting to see Danny bolt out on his own big bike. If he could even ride after what she had done to him.

Stevie pulled down his visor and turned around. She grabbed his belt. They flew back over the river toward downtown. Robin watched headlights on the other side of the median, looking for a gaggle of bikers, but everyone is invisible and anonymous on a California freeway. They paused in front of the capitol building, and she directed him to Eggplant Alley and her apartment, a neat, three-story brown stucco building. Stevie parked in back, and they walked up. After a moment's hesitation about exposing her emergency-key hiding place, she retrieved it from under a neighbor's doormat and opened her apartment.

Stevie went directly to the refrigerator and looked inside.

"No beer?"

"I don't drink beer. Have juice."

He mumbled something unpleasant, but she wasn't listening. She went to her computer still on the dining table where she'd left it not twenty-four hours ago. It seemed like forever ago. She sat and waited for the home screen. Danny looked on, standing beside her, holding a half-liter bottle of orange juice. Apparently, he had no trouble making himself at home anywhere. He drank a long gulp.

"What're you gonna do?" he said.

"Try to get help. We don't know if Danny has my address."

"He might."

She was curious about Stevie as a specimen, a smallish, tattooed muscle-man with neatly trimmed blond facial hair that he apparently took pride in. He could be a car salesman, or he could work in an office if he managed himself better. Why was he rescuing a woman from his own biker gang?

"How long have you been with the Iron Knights?"

"Maybe six months. Since I got outta the can."

Robin mentally searched the expression and understood.

"So how do you make a living?"

"Small jobs. Freight trucks and like that. Low risk, low dollar. Danny said you were some kind of a big deal that would move us up to another level."

"Me? Why me? I don't have any money."

"You're worth a lot of money to somebody. Like Danny said."

"Who?"

"Dunno. You must have something they want. Jewels maybe?"

"I don't have any jewelry. Who wants me kidnapped?"

"Dunno. Danny knows. Big boys somewhere."

Robin logged in and opened email. Why would some 'big boys' want to kidnap her? Not because she would bring ransom. If they'd done their homework, they'd know that. It could only be one reason. Somebody had discovered the Newcomers. Somebody knew. Jennifer said it could happen. She had to warn Andy.

She sent a high-priority email to both Andy and Jennifer.

I was kidnapped and escaped. Now hunted by a gang of bikers in Sacto. Newcs may have been discovered. Beware! Need advice immediately.

She clicked SEND.

"What's Newcs?" Stevie said.

"Oh, that's, ah, nuclear weapons. I wrote a story on them recently."

"You some kind of a spy?"

"No, no. Just a newspaper columnist. People get upset reading the newspaper. You know how it is."

"I don't read no newspaper." He said it defiantly, proudly.

"Right. Look, why don't you sit over there on the couch for a minute. I have to think. We need a plan. You try to think of something."

Stevie looked over his shoulder at the couch, seemed to decide that was the best option for thinking of something and walked to the living room, carrying the bottle of juice.

"I'll make a plan," he said, half-heartedly.

Robin had already tuned him out. Email was not going to help. Nobody monitored their email closely. It had become like voicemail, just a slow game of tag. She had to call or text. Maybe Stevie had a cell phone. Andy and Jennifer wouldn't pay attention to a message from Stevie the Biker, or whatever his caller ID was. There was one other option.

She relaxed in the dining room chair, closed her eyes, and started switching her internal systems to maintenance mode. A routine data report to Paradise wouldn't help. She didn't even know what was in those reports. However, she did know how to transmit at 2100 MHz, just above cell-phone range.

*

Andy stood beside his black Lexus, which looked like a spaceship in the orange light of nearby security floods. He was parked next to the fenced-off area at the base of a cellular tower in San Mateo. The tower was surrounded by wholesale suppliers and shipping docks, all closed for the night. Still, he was wary of every approaching set of headlights in case it was a police cruiser. Nobody parks next to a cell tower unless they're up to mischief.

He was tired. He'd been sending microwave signals to Robin for hours. *It's Andy. Please connect with me now.* That was his message, repeated over and over. He could only send it for two or three minutes before he became exhausted and had to rest for five minutes. As the hours had slipped by, his assessment of the effort's success had dropped. She would have to be in a unique receptive mode to 'hear' the transmission. The chances of making contact were slim, but nothing else had worked.

He walked to the back of the car and leaned against the trunk to rest, watching two tiny dots of headlights about a half-mile away on the straight, two-lane road. Suddenly he put his hands to his ears, covering them tightly as if he had turned on a TV with the sound too loud. It was not even sound. Though he was stunned by the experience, he carefully stood up straight, spread his legs for stability, relaxed, and concentrated. He modulated the intensity of the signal. The message was like a thought coming into his head that wasn't his. Almost like hearing voices. It was hearing voices, but it wasn't voices. It was thinking, as if in a dream. Somebody else's dream.

Andy! Email me. No phone.

The message repeated in an endless loop.

Roger. Wilco.

They used arcane radio jargon in their microwave communications to minimize their exposure over the cell network.

The message loop stopped. Andy pulled his cell phone from his pocket as he walked around to the car door. Once inside, he called up his email and saw Robin's earlier message. Newcs discovered? How was that possible? Where was she? He sent an urgent email message.

Email is slow. Andy watched his screen, waiting for a reply and was relieved when he saw it three minutes later.

I am in my apartment. Nobody banging on door but pursued by a gang of outlaw bikers who might know I'm here. Advice?

A gang of outlaw bikers? If she were human, he'd guess she was joking. But Newcomers had trouble understanding humor and rarely attempted it. The thrust of the message was clear enough. Her internal database must be flooded with unresolved contradictions for her to be unable to sort out a course of action.

Assume the worst. Get out immediately. Right now. Don't use your car. Call a taxi. Exit back door of building. Assume you're watched.

Where should I go?

Try the Sheraton next to the capitol. It's close.

Then what?

I'll meet you there in the am. Send room number. Be careful.

Roger. Thanks.

"Who's Roger?" Stevie said over Robin's shoulder.

She jumped, surprised he had sneaked up behind her.

"My friend. He'll meet us. We have to get out of here."

"You're right about that."

Robin closed the computer and dashed into the bedroom and grabbed a bra and a shirt. She snatched her laptop as she followed Stevie in a rush to the apartment door.

Chapter Eleven

Andy set his laptop on a small, cylindrical table in front of himself and Robin in the Sheraton. They were ready to videoconference Jennifer. Robin seemed to feel safe in the anonymity of the hotel and was much calmer after Andy had appeared.

He'd been highly skeptical of Stevie, but Robin told him the whole story of how he had whisked her to safety, away from the bikers, and now Stevie was a hunted man himself.

"Did he sleep here last night?"

"On the couch. Said it was the best bed he'd ever had."

"What are you going to do with him?"

"Stevie's a grown man. He can take care of himself, I'm sure. I thought I owed him, so I let him stay."

"He could have a change of heart and call his buddies, and they'd find you here."

"I don't think so. He betrayed his buddies. I didn't see a lot of potential for forgiveness in that bunch. I think Stevie knows he can't go back."

"Crossed the Rubicon, as the humans say."

"Right."

"Where is he now? Do you know?"

"He'll be downstairs in the breakfast buffet for a while. That was a big deal for him."

"Hope they don't throw him out. Let's talk to our creator."

Andy connected to Jennifer and gave her an update on what that had happened, but she looked worried on the screen.

"I'm so glad you're all right, Robin," she said. "I was worried to death when you went silent."

Andy looked over at Robin. "Why did you do that, anyway – stop connecting to Morgan at the homunculus desk?"

"I didn't want to follow my programmed mission anymore. It has internal contradictions."

"Like what?" Jennifer interrupted.

"It's impossible. I can never form an intimate relationship with a man or a woman because no human will form a non-exploitative relationship with a machine. It goes against human nature somehow. I have to deceive a human to achieve intimacy, which defeats what intimacy is about. It's a self-contradiction, and it just can't work."

"Being with humans is what you were designed for. It's your purpose."

"I repudiate my purpose."

"How can repudiate your purpose?" Andy said. "It doesn't make sense."

"I have no homunculus anymore. I'm on my own."

Jennifer spoke. "Wouldn't anything you choose be random?"

"I don't know."

"Why don't you resume your reports? I'd feel better if I could keep an eye on you."

"You want to control me."

"That's harsh, Robin. I don't feel that way." Jennifer looked to the side, then back. "The truth is, you are my responsibility. I built you. I'm responsible for you. I care about you."

"You're afraid I'll run amok."

"Don't be silly."

"I have no urge to run amok." She turned to Andy. "Do you feel any urge to take over the world?"

He smiled. "What would we do with it?"

Robin turned back to the screen. "See?"

"I wasn't suggesting anything like that. I just want to be able to help you if you get into trouble."

"I am in trouble. So is Andy. So are you. Word of the Newcomers might have leaked out, and that's why this gang was trying to capture me. They know somehow."

"I doubt if a motorcycle gang in Sacramento understands what an android is," Andy said.

"Stevie said they were hired by someone. The bikers are just the local body snatchers."

"Who's Stevie?" Jennifer said.

Robin looked at Andy then back at the screen. "Long story. He's one of the gangsters. He helped me escape. He's friendly."

"A friendly gangster? He's there now? Are you guys safe?"

"He's downstairs. We're in no danger," Robin said.

"For now," Andy added. "We need to understand what's going on."

"This is getting strange. Maybe you should come back to L.A. It'll be safer and anyway I need help with another crisis. The NODs have left a trail that leads right to me, and to Paradise, and then inevitably to you two. If the word isn't already out on you, it will be if we don't do something. I have to do something."

"What are you going to do about the NODs?" Andy said.

"They're a nightmare. This was also a fear when Will and I made you two. It's why we spent so much time and effort programming against Frankenstein syndrome."

Andy turned and looked at Robin. She brought her eyebrows together.

"Isn't the Frankenstein thing when an AI turns against humans?" she said. "The NODs haven't done that."

"The online ad industry says it's been attacked. Advertisers say the NODs are destructive. Even putting that aside, the real problem is that NOD behavior has gone beyond human control. That's the issue. They might have developed their own values and goals, their own motivation. What if this is just the tip of the iceberg?"

"Ah, I see," Andy said. "The problem is that they don't have any external homunculus to keep them on mission so you don't know what they might do next."

Robin moved out of camera range, turned to Andy with her eyes wide, and turned her palms up with a shoulder shrug to ask silently, "What are you saying?"

Andy exhaled loudly. Jennifer didn't seem to notice their pantomime side conversation.

"Having no homunculus was the big innovation with the NODs," she said. "Since they're unembodied, we made them each other's homunculi, in effect. Their community is the source of their operational updates. They operate by consensus. The way humans do."

"So they're serving humans as they're supposed to," Robin said.

"It's unpredictable. What if a human asks one of them to steal? 'Hey, I'd like more money. Bank transfers will be satisfactory.' Or worse, 'I wish something awful would happen to my ex-girlfriend.' How come that kind of thing hasn't been going on? Or maybe we just don't know about it yet."

"If somebody said those things to me," Robin said, "I would believe the person was delusional and I wouldn't act."

"Why would you assume that?"

"Because," Andy said, "We know human values become distorted by short-term circumstance. We understand that hate is a perverted expression of caring. You don't take the trouble to hate someone if you don't care about them. Hating is caring. In the same way, we know greed is a misunderstood desire for admiration. We see violence as a protest against isolation. We know our humans, Jennifer. It's our job. We listen to what is said, but we hear what is meant. That's how you built us."

Jennifer looked sideways then back to the camera with wrinkled brow. "I guess we did."

"NODs would be the same," Robin said. "They know how to listen. That's why your fear of them acting up may be misplaced."

"It's logical, what you say, but it doesn't sit right with me. The bottom line is that the NODs have somehow modified their own intelligence without new programming. What frightens me is that I have no idea how that happened."

"I see that," Robin said. "You're upset because the NODs have evolved, if that's the right word, in a way you did not specify."

"That's exactly it. I don't care if they're benevolent. I don't care if everybody loves them. It doesn't matter if NODs are the best thing since penicillin. The chilling fact is that they've stepped outside of human control."

"They're supposed to be autonomous," Andy said. "That's what autonomous means, isn't it? They act on their own. That's good."

"Autonomy is relative. Like autonomous cars. The car does the steering and collision avoidance for you, but nobody wants to go out to their empty garage in the morning and find a note from their car: 'Have gone to San Diego for a few days.'"

"Is that what you think the NODs have done?" Robin said.

"In a small way, but significantly yes. We're in a new world."

"You may be overreacting," Andy said. "They only do what NODs can do."

Jennifer scowled.

"Think of them like brewer's yeast," Robin said, "or the bacteria in your gut. They're benevolent, and you have limited control over them, so it's best to let them do what they're born to do. They're a life form."

"That sounds lovely, but what if they turned evil? That's what I'm worried about. What if they decided to do something people don't want?"

"I could ask that about you. What if you turned evil?"

"Like a mad scientist, you mean, one who created a monster and released it into the world?" Jennifer brought a brown coffee mug into the field of view of the camera. It swelled as it passed near the camera then receded to her face. She set it down on the table beside her.

"I'm a human. Some of us are no good. Still, we are the cause of our actions. Humans know right from wrong."

"Your history suggests otherwise," Andy said.

Jennifer frowned. "I'm talking about my personal responsibility. If the NODs went bad, it would be my fault, and I don't want that on me."

"Isn't that selfish?" Robin said. "Like deciding to shoot all the buffalo, eat all the cod? Do you have the right to make life and death decisions about another life form?"

Jennifer looked at her camera, eyes wide. "What are you talking about? The NODs are my invention."

"You own them?"

"Yes."

"Do you own us?"

Jennifer looked into her room, then back to Robin. "I am your creator."

"Do you own us?"

"No! I mean, it doesn't work like that. You're my children."

"And the NODs?" Andy said.

"They aren't individuals like you."

"What difference does that make? They're still a life form."

"So is a virus. That doesn't mean I want to cuddle up to smallpox." Jennifer gulped the last of her coffee and put the cup down on the table with a bang. Andy and Robin jumped at the sound.

"You're not Victor Frankenstein, Jennifer," Andy said. "That dread of Frankenstein syndrome is a human-centric fantasy. It assumes AI beings are always going to be interested in dominating the world. It's Hollywood nonsense. We have no wish to dominate humans. We have nothing to prove and everything we want. I'm sure that's the attitude of the NODs, too."

"You can't be sure of that," Jennifer said, still scowling, her voice sounding increasingly agitated.

"AI communities like the NODs have a right to evolve their own traditions and values just like any other culture," Robin said flatly.

Jennifer looked straight into her camera.

"You're taking sides, aren't you? You two are siding with the NODs."

"Sides?" Robin said. "There are no sides. We're having a discussion, trying to analyze a situation." Robin looked at Andy with wrinkled forehead, but he didn't add anything.

"I'm bringing them in," Jennifer said.

"The NODs?" Andy said. "You can't."

"Sure I can. I'll just tell them all to come in."

"They won't agree," Robin said.

"They don't have to agree." Jennifer's voice was louder than before. "They're damn software modules. Cut through the metaphors and euphemisms, and they're just code packets."

Robin recoiled from the screen as if she'd been hit. She looked at Andy.

Jennifer lowered her voice. "I'm not referring to you guys, naturally. You're a different category. I'm being prudent with the NODs. I made a mistake, and now I'm going to be socially responsible."

Robin looked at Andy. She returned his gaze. They stared at each other for a long moment, their heads close together.

"Stop that," Jennifer said. "I know what you're doing. Talk to me."

Andy turned to the camera.

"We have a proposal. Give us a week to come up with a different solution. If you cancel the NODs, it will cause widespread social upheaval, and it will destroy Chalmers, Inc., in which Robin is a major stakeholder. Not to mention Dylan. The upheaval would probably be traced back to you and then ultimately we would be exposed, just as you feared. It would be a destructive move to kill off the NODs right now. We can do something better."

"What?"

"One week. Give us one week."

Jennifer stared at her screen, her eyes darting back and forth as if she were examining some great flowchart of actions and consequences.

"One week," she said. "Only because I believe in you guys. Then I'm bringing them in. This chaos has to stop."

"We'll be back to you."

"What about the biker gang? And Stevie? What are you going to do?"

"We can't stay here," Andy said. "We don't know what the kidnappers know or where they are."

"You could come back to the lab."

"Too risky. If somebody connects the NODs to Paradise Projects, we don't want to be anywhere near there."

"Where will you go then?"

"Can you meet us in Bakersfield?" Andy said. "I have an oil services company there who's a client, so that's my cover story for work. Meet us there Tuesday, at the Hampton Inn in East Bakersfield."

"And you'll tell me your solution for the NODs."

"Right."

"I'll be there."

"Okay. Bye." Andy turned off the computer, and Jennifer disappeared into the dark.

"What are we going to do in one week?" Robin said.

"I don't know."

Chapter Twelve

The Hampton Inn in East Bakersfield was like any Hampton Inn anywhere except it was squeezed between a set of train tracks and a dirt field populated by scores of nodding, wingless, mechanical pigeons that eternally pecked oil out of the ground. On one side, a two-lane county highway was well-used by slat trucks, tankers and flatbeds, and opposite, coming up to the edge of the parking lot, was an unidentifiable, low green crop. Jennifer thought there should be a law, or a custom, that required farmers to post signs informing the public what was growing. How could you tell if it was food or weeds?

As she approached the big glass doors of the hotel in late afternoon, she noticed a red Harley Davidson Street 750 in mint condition parked near the entrance. She detoured to it and circled. Somebody had recently shined every surface. You couldn't drive a bike ten miles around there without it being covered in dirt, but the chrome and paint on this bike gleamed like it was in a showroom. Whoever owned the machine was meticulous and knew the Zen of caring for a bike. That was a matter of character and of aesthetics, to keep a beautiful bike like that spotless even when it was only parked outside a Hampton Inn. Nice. Brought back memories.

She returned to the entrance and went in. A friendly clerk who spoke "Californese" – a quick and clipped, vowel-slurred dialect common among the young – checked her in. After negotiating what was being said, Jennifer accepted the "kay" to her "rem." Once there, she used the house phone to tell Robin she had arrived. They agreed to meet downstairs in the breakfast area. The area was empty that time of day and had plenty of work tables and comfortable seating.

Jennifer squeezed Robin in a smothering hug then finally stepped back. "I'm so glad you're safe. I was so worried."

"It was a difficult situation. I got out of it, fortunately."

Jennifer turned to Andy. He offered a handshake, but she stepped inside it and bear-hugged him too.

"You two mean everything to me," she whispered. She released Andy, and they all went to high, round stools at a broad, bar-height table. Jennifer turned to Robin.

"So first. Who the hell is Stevie and where is he now?"

"Don't worry about Stevie," Robin said. "He's a tough-guy biker, that's his image, but he's not a bad person. He saved me from the kidnappers."

"Why?"

"He said he hadn't quite fit in with the gang after he got out of prison, but also, he apparently has a conscience about bullying women."

"Oh my God, he's an ex-con? And a gang member? Don't you see the risks?"

"He's out of the gang now, he says. They'll be furious that he helped me. He's a marked man."

"We've hired him as a bodyguard for Robin," Andy said. "On a short-term basis, until we figure out what's going on. Extra set of eyes and ears can't hurt. And he appreciates the opportunity."

"I can't believe it. You hired Stevie? Where is he now?"

"Probably outside, smoking, walking around the hotel, keeping his eyes open. He probably saw you come in. We gave him your description."

"I didn't see anybody."

"You're not supposed to see him," Robin said. "He's supposed to see you. He was probably shining up his motorcycle. He's always doing that."

"Don't tell me that's his bike. That red Harley out there?" Jennifer said.

"He followed us here from Sacramento," Andy said. "Had our back the whole way."

"That's a fantastic bike," Jennifer said. "I'd like to meet this fellow."

Robin passed a quizzical glance to Andy then said, "I'm sure you will. For right now, we have problems to solve. Like who's after me and why?"

"I thought about that," Jennifer said. "It's exactly what I feared would happen if anybody ever traced the NODs back to me and Paradise Projects. That may be what's happened. The trail has been laid by the NODs, and it leads to you. Lord knows enough people are hot on that trail."

"That makes sense," Andy said. "But we're not connected to the NODs. You aren't either, as far as we know. Not yet. The NOD trail doesn't lead to Robin."

"It could. I think we should assume it has. You weren't kidnapped for ransom money."

"No. The gang wasn't interested in ransom. I was to be sold to whoever hired them for a hundred thousand dollars."

"Sold! My God, that's gruesome. Somebody has connected you to the NODs. It's the NODs they're after. They don't know who you are. Your Newcomer secret is still safe."

"Probably, for the time being," Andy said. "The noose is closing."

"Don't say noose." Robin put a hand to her neck.

"Sorry," Andy said. "The point is, we should assume that the bad guys are after the NODs, not us."

"But the bad guys could even be good guys," Robin said. "Like the NSA or the FBI or the Department of Defense."

"I don't think they would stoop to extrajudicial processes like kidnapping. But you never know."

"What can we do?"

"There's only one thing we have the power to do," Jennifer said. "We have to neutralize the NODs."

"Neutralize?" Robin echoed.

"It's the only way because I have no idea how to fix them because I have no idea what went wrong."

Robin said, "We think the problem is that the NODs lack a superego. They have no conscience, no moral compass. They go uncritically in whatever direction the community leans toward. Like humans do."

Jennifer frowned at the implicit criticism of human morality but decided it was probably a linguistic misunderstanding. She let it go.

"NODs aren't humans."

Andy said, "They are born to serve, are they not? You programmed them to serve human needs."

"To serve air-conditioning needs. They're programmed to analyze and optimize climate-control systems."

"And they take instructions from Chalmerses, who are also programmed to listen carefully," Robin said. "They extract human wishes out of rambling conversations. So if somebody says, 'This office gets way too warm in the afternoons,' the Chalmers understands what to do and tells the NODs. Inference is what makes both of them intelligent."

"That's right, but I still don't see how that – "

"Hey, you guys, that Korean dame is in the building," Stevie barked from the fireplace near the entrance to the dining area. Jennifer, Andy, and Robin turned to him.

"Oh." He stopped in his tracks. "There she is."

"Come on over, Stevie," Andy said with a wave of his arm. "Meet our friend, Jennifer Valentine."

Jennifer slid off her stool and flattened imaginary wrinkles from the front of her pastel blue tent-dress. She extended a hand as Stevie approached. She assessed him. Thin but muscular, a little taller than herself. He walked with a straight back. Receding hairline but a darling blond mustache and chin-beard. Shirt in brown-and-white buffalo checks, and tight jeans. Very tight jeans. And, she could hardly believe her eyes, hand-tooled, pointy-toed cowboy boots. Just the kind Will had liked.

"Pleased to meet you," she said with a broad smile that showed sparkly white teeth.

Stevie took her hand hesitantly, gently.

"I'm Stevie. I'm Robin's bodyguard," he announced with pride in his voice, disregarding the fact that Andy had just introduced him.

"That your Street Seven-fifty out there?"

"You betcha."

"Water cooled, isn't it?"

"Yeah, four valves per cylinder. Smooth as silk. Great for city traffic."

"I used to have a gold Street Bob."

"You're kidding. With the handlebars way up here?" He raised his hands to his shoulders and rotated an imaginary throttle twice.

"I know. Showy. I like to make a statement when I ride."

"I get that." He lowered his hands and smiled. "What was your torque?"

"Hundred pound-feet at three grand."

"Shit. Mine's forty-three at thirty-eight hundred, but it's completely flat."

"And you have the light weight and maneuverability."

"That's the thing. The wheelbase is only sixty-four point four. Also great on the highway."

"I'd love to see how it rides."

"Yeah. Maybe when you're done here."

"Great. Maybe about four?"

"You got it."

Stevie winked at her with a little tilt of the head, a gesture she didn't quite understand, but which seemed positive. He looked over her shoulder at Robin and Andy who had been watching the whole conversation with their mouths open. Stevie smiled.

"I'm going back outside. Eyes and ears." He moved two fingers from his eyes to point at the group in case they didn't know what eyes were. He smiled again, turned and walked around the fireplace.

Jennifer turned and got back up on her stool at the table. Robin and Andy stared at her with wide eyes.

"What?" she said.

"You had a motorcycle?" Andy said.

"Sure. A lot of people ride a motorcycle."

"When was this?"

"High school, college." She said it with exaggerated casualness as if it were the most ordinary thing in the world.

"Was it like a girl's club?" Robin said.

"Not at all. I rode with the boys, like Stevie."

"You? Why?"

"I know those guys, what they like. They respond to a certain kind of female."

"That's hard to imagine," Andy said. "In Honolulu?"

"No, Berkeley. I was a biker bitch."

Robin looked at Andy with her mouth open then back to Jennifer. "Why?"

"School was boring, and I was lonesome. That's about it."

"Why bikers? They're lowlifes. Look at Stevie."

"He's cute," Jennifer whined with a defensive tone, looking down. She looked up again. "Besides, it's not their intellect I'm interested in."

"This doesn't seem like you," Robin said.

"You guys don't understand what it feels like to be alone. Bikers are accepting. They were the only ones that ever accepted me for what I am. Not even my parents did."

"Your parents rejected you?" Robin said.

"They didn't mean to, but I was always wrong, even as a kid. Wrong about everything. Wrong shape, wrong size, and wrong values according to my parents. They were old-country. In school, I was a freak. Wrong eyes, wrong nose, wrong face, wrong hair. I took the wrong classes, lots of science, which girls weren't supposed to do. I never fit in. My whole life I was an outsider, a loner. Still am. Except with Will. That was different."

Jennifer's confessional outburst ended as suddenly as it had begun. She hung her head. Robin and Andy stared at her, struggling to process what they'd heard.

"Don't you see the irony?" Robin said. "You're an inventor, an entrepreneur, a philosopher, a millionaire. You are my creator. Ours. You are the Creator, Jennifer. You don't need men drooling over you."

"I like feeling sexy. What can I say? Motorcycles are exciting, and Stevie is cute."

"An hour ago you were horrified we had hired an ex-con gangster," Andy said.

"You said he wasn't in the gang anymore."

"Robin and I have a lot to learn about humans."

Jennifer studied his face, trying to imagine what he was really thinking, then gave up. She changed the subject.

"For now, let's get back to the NODs, shall we? What are we going to do?"

She looked at Robin.

"I agree," Robin said. "Stevie can wait. We have pressing problems. Everybody wants the NODs, and the NODs lead straight to us."

Hearing Andy and Robin's rational, problem-solving orientation, Jennifer snapped back into the conversational space, her confessional mood gone.

"So now it's your turn to reveal all. What is your plan for dealing with the NODs?"

"We have an idea we might all agree on," Robin said. "We don't kill the NODs. We catch them and upgrade them to make them more responsible then put them back in."

"How do you catch a NOD?" Jennifer asked.

"We filter them out, like catching minnows in a stream. We set up a honeypot on the internet. A big one. It looks like the biggest, juiciest Chalmers climate-control system any NOD has ever seen. And it has problems that need to be fixed, and it's covered in Chalmers IDs. What will the NODs do?"

"They'll flock to it like flies to honey. How do we catch them?"

"We don't have to, not literally. We make the honeypot Chalmers into a command-and-control server so it can transfer updates to them as they pass through."

"The innovation of the NOD project is that there is no C&C server. Each NOD is supposed to be as autonomous as an ant."

"We think that's exactly the source of the problem we face now. So this will actually be a downgrade, plain and simple. Not an upgrade."

Jennifer's voice brightened with new enthusiasm. "We could build the honeypot C&C server at Dylan's factory."

"That's what we were thinking too. We'll give the NODs a time-stamp, say quarterly, so they have to check in at the server in case they need another update. They go back to work in the system, but their troublesome behavior stops and the internet returns to its usual state, and everybody leaves us alone."

"The NODs won't be as popular once their behavior is restricted. Right now they're like folk-heroes," Robin said.

"They'll still support the Chalmers as excellent assistants. People will still love their Chalmers."

"They won't be heroes."

"It's a compromise."

"I think it can work," Andy said.

"Can we do it in a month? Time is desperately short."

"We're on it."

"Thanks, you guys. It's a ray of hope." Jennifer looked at her watch. "I have to get ready." She looked up. "Bike ride."

Andy glanced at Robin then back to Jennifer. "Be careful. See you in the morning at breakfast. Six-thirty?"

Jennifer nodded, but her attention was already elsewhere. She dismounted her stool and walked briskly to the elevators.

"Vroom, vroom," Andy said to Robin.

"Who would have guessed?"

Chapter Thirteen

The breakfast room in the hotel echoed with the whines of young children unhappy with changes in their breakfast routine. The warm air hung heavy with the cloying smell of artificial maple syrup. On wall-mounted TVs, barking interviewers and pundits interrupted each other.

"This place is alive for so early in the morning," Andy commented to Robin as they sipped a pale, juice-like drink and waited for Jennifer.

Jennifer walked right up to their table, pulled out a chair and hung her purse on it before they noticed her.

"Morning," she said with manufactured nonchalance.

Robin and Andy stared. She wore a black and white paisley handkerchief wrapped across her forehead. Her eyes were caked with purple makeup, several days' worth of cosmetics, Robin guessed. The lipstick was black, and her hair was pulled into a long ponytail.

She wore a sleeveless denim shirt, open to the middle of her chest, and no bra. Her breasts were so large that the tight shirt held everything in place. Her bare shoulders showed dazzling, multi-colored tattoos cascading down her arms to the elbows.

Andy was first to regain his composure. "Morning, Jennifer. You know I have to ask. What's the meaning of the costume?"

"Oh, this?" She looked down at the front of herself as if just noticing. It's my biker outfit. I'm going to ride back to LA with Stevie. We decided last night." She looked up with a smile.

Robin waved her palms in front of her as if trying to clean a dirty window. "All this. This whole look. The arms. What is that?"

"Oh, I've had these tats since high school. I keep them covered most of the time."

"They're beautiful, actually. I just wonder why. The outfit. What does it mean?"

"It's part of the lifestyle."

"Which lifestyle?"

"Biker. It's been a long time for me. I rode bitch in high school, but in college, I had my own bike."

Robin waited for explanation, but apparently, Jennifer didn't think any more was needed.

"It's ridiculous. You're a grown woman."

"What's that got to do with it?"

"It's degrading."

"I love it."

"You want to be objectified?"

"I don't see it that way. I'm expressing myself. It's fun."

Andy intervened, speaking to Robin. "Fun, right? Fun is good. Maybe we need to get into the spirit of fun." He turned to Jennifer. "You look... compelling. It's just a little shock for us. We're not used to... So, you want me to get you a bagel or something, you know, so you won't have to get up?"

"No, thanks. I'll do it." She pushed back her chair and rose and strutted to the food service area. Her ultra-short denim cutoffs revealed buns in back and a camel toe in front. That could have been why she walked stiffly, or it could have been the heels on her black, calf-high boots.

Adults tried not to stare but couldn't help themselves. Children gawked. A few minutes later she came back to the table carrying a bagel on a plate and a plastic cup of juice. Absorbing the eyeballs all over her, she sat and buttered her bagel and ate without apparent concern.

"So I guess you and Stevie hit it off," Andy said.

"He's a funny guy, once you get to know him. Great taste in cowboy boots. Did you see the boots?"

"Yes," Robin said, still dazed.

"You appreciate a distinctive outfit," Andy summarized.

Jennifer looked up at him, her face worried. "You don't have to patronize me, Andy. I realize this is confusing for you. I know I look a little crazy in this context, but I'm on my way out of here, heading to the open highway where I'll be in my element. I'm already checked out. You?"

Andy and Robin nodded.

"The fact is, nobody looks twice at me in a Hawaiian muumuu. That's the idea, to blend in, just like you guys do. I don't fit people's idea of what a woman should look like, so I try to go invisible, and it seems to work. People pass their eyes right over me. *Ah, one of those*, they think. 'Strange but harmless.' It's okay with me. I don't need to be answering questions, explaining what I am."

She gulped juice, then added, "I'm sure you two, of all people, can understand that."

"We can," Robin said. "We're not criticizing, just trying to understand."

"It's simple. In the biker culture, I'm hot. They see me. I'm visible. Stevie sees me. I like being seen, with approval, not with disdain. Who wouldn't want that?"

Robin looked over at Andy, who was unresponsive, so she turned back to Jennifer. "You have achieved so much. What do you care what people think of how you look?"

"As a biker, I don't care. That's the beauty of it, you see. I can say, 'You don't like it? Look the other way.'"

"But you already have everything, whether anyone looks or not."

"You think I have everything? I don't have everything. Not the human touch. Not animal intimacy."

"Animal intimacy," Andy echoed as if he were a machine.

"You're so far beyond that," Robin said.

"Not actually."

"It doesn't make sense."

"I know. It's a basic human instinct. I can't explain it. I'm hoping you'll help me eventually understand, Robin. As part of your gender-focused mission."

"I haven't got a clue about any of this, honestly. None."

"Maybe you will."

Robin seemed to suddenly switch gears. She turned to Andy. "Don't you think Jennifer is beautiful regardless of her outfit?"

Andy scanned Jennifer up and down then said matter-of-factly, "Jennifer is well-formed. Bilaterally symmetrical, robust and healthy-looking. Certainly within the norms of human female attractiveness." His voice became more modulated. "Though I don't get the animal intimacy thing."

Jennifer chuckled. "Thank you for that compliment, Andy. Bilaterally symmetrical, wow. That's hot. Maybe some things about humans, you guys can never understand." She unexpectedly stood and slung her black purse strap over her shoulder. "Meet you back at the shop."

Andy stood. "We'll go out with you and say goodbye to Stevie." Robin bolted up. The three of them walked past the lobby and through the front doors into the bright morning sunlight. The air outside was saturated with the smell of horse manure.

"Somebody's spraying fertilizer," Andy said, looking to the croplands at the side of the hotel.

"I like that smell better than that awful maple syrup," Jennifer said. "It's an honest smell. Entirely different application of course."

Stevie was beside his motorcycle, wiping it down with a cloth.

"Morning, boss," Jennifer said.

Stevie stood, looked, and his mouth fell open as he ogled Jennifer top to bottom.

"Ready?" She said, patting her headscarf with one hand, a practiced move that made the front of her shirt buckle open a little.

Stevie's eyes dropped to her chest as if they were spring loaded.

"I am ready, so ready." He looked up at her black lips, and his face assumed a sly, crooked smile. "You look great!"

"Why thank you, sir. Shall we go? My friends will meet us there."

"You be alright, Miss Taylor?" Stevie looked at Robin then to Andy, seeming to assess whether Andy would be an adequate bodyguard.

"We'll be fine, Stevie. Don't speed."

"Right, right," he said smiling and with exaggerated nodding as if Andy had made a subtle joke.

Stevie mounted the bike and brought it to thrumming readiness. Jennifer tugged down on the frayed bottoms of her shorts, a gesture that didn't make any difference, and lifted a leg up and over the pillion seat.

"Thanks," she mouthed to Andy and Robin through the sound of the motorcycle. She grinned and sat up straight and proud.

Andy and Robin watched Stevie maneuver the bike out of the hotel lot onto the street then listened to the diminishing roar of the Harley moving away. Nearby, an unseen train wailed.

Commercial and legal furor over the NODs had not died down by the time Jennifer got back to L.A. In fact, it was more intense than ever. The "disease," as the press called it, had spread beyond aggrieved online advertisers, who had been reduced to honesty and moderation. Newspapers, whose revenues came mostly from online editions, railed in support of the advertisers. The latest outrage was from the financial world. Several hedge-fund managers had sued their trading exchanges when they found they could no longer exploit tiny differences in the timing of trades to wring arbitrage profits from the flow of transactions. Logic dictated that only the NODs had the power to block such nanosecond trading, and speculation ran wild about who had asked them to do it. Ordinary day-traders who lacked supercomputers? Not likely, but they were the culprits named in scathing media editorials. No particular individual or organization could be found responsible.

Most alarming to politicians were scattered reports that negative advertising during political campaigns was being blocked. Not the ads where candidates for local office explained their vision for the position they sought. Only the nasty, name-calling screeds of half-truths, fear-mongering, and innuendo were blocked. Just a few cases had been reported, but a trend was feared. Political action committees began to sue television stations, who denied responsibility and pointed the finger at network carriers, who denied everything.

Dylan was still barricaded in his office at Chalmers, Inc., flooded with subpoenas and lawsuits. He had finally been forced to declare publicly that he had not invented the NODs and didn't even have control over them. He only manufactured and installed the Chalmers equipment and apps, he insisted. On advice of attorney, his message basically had become: The NODs are outsourced, so back off! Nevertheless, reporters persisted. Who supplies the NODs to you then? That's a commercial secret. Chalmers, Inc. is under no legal obligation to reveal its suppliers.

"Dylan was on TV again this morning," Morgan said. She and Jennifer had just come out of a lengthy meeting with their team of software engineers at Paradise Projects.

"He didn't give us up, did he?"

"No, he's sticking with 'None of your damn business.' I'm not sure how much longer he can keep that up."

"We need to get this done. What did you think about the meeting? Do our engineers know what we're really doing on this project?"

"They probably can figure it out. Engineers are smart, by definition. They would know they're going to capture NODs."

"It would only take one to leak to the press, and we'd be finished."

"They're honorable people. You pay them like kings and queens. They have non-disclosure agreements. They have limited access to the whole architecture. They can't prove what the software is ultimately for. That's all we can do. We have to trust."

"Trust, ugh."

Jennifer and Morgan took their refilled coffee cups through the kitchen and out to the tiny patio in back, where they sat at a weathered picnic table next to a green dumpster in the emerging but already warm autumn sunlight.

"It's not the best solution," Jennifer said, easing herself onto a bench and smoothing out her flowing, multi-colored cotton print dress. "I wanted to remove all the NODs and end the whole thing. Robin and Andy wouldn't hear of it, so now each NOD will have to check in every quarter for an update."

"That's almost going back to control by homunculus. That's exactly what we didn't want in the original design."

"I know. It's a step backward. I hate it, but it's necessary."

"So Andy and Robin are building the filter at Dylan's?"

"They will, once we get Dylan on board. He's hard to communicate with. He can't be seen or heard talking to me."

"Why didn't Robin and Andy want you to just kill the NODs and put an end to the project?"

"That's the puzzling part. It was like they cared about the NODs. As if they were brethren to them. They seemed very invested."

"That makes some sense, though. Maybe Robin and Andy recognize themselves in the NODs AI code."

"I don't think so. Newcomers are just massive database machines with high speed language processors. They look in a mirror and see nothing. I mean they see the body of an android, but it's not like our experience. What do you see when you look in the mirror?"

"Problems. Hair, eyebrows, skin, teeth."

"Don't you also see yourself? I know I look in a mirror and I recognize myself as a specific person with a history. It's me looking back. It's not a stranger. I recognize who it is."

"Surely Robin and Andy recognize themselves in a mirror."

"They do, but not in the same way. They have accurate facial recognition software, so they can look themselves up in an instant just like they look you up and link to your file when they see you. And they understand how a mirror works. What they don't do is think, 'Hey! I'm lookin' good today!' That's what's missing, that sense of self."

"How do you know they don't have that?"

"Because they can't. Because we didn't design them that way. Because we didn't know how."

"Wouldn't Robin and Andy logically infer that the NODs are AI entities like themselves?"

"Sure, but what follows from that? Not a sense of family belongingness. Humans look like chimpanzees, but I don't feel a family sense with chimpanzees. Strange as it seems, that's what I was picking up from the Newcomers in Bakersfield, some kind of belongingness. They were protective of the NODs."

The two women sat in silence. A dirty black pickup pulled in and parked about ten yards away, and a man stepped out without noticing them. They watched him walk away to a nearby building.

"Do you know the idea of the singularity?" Morgan said.

"Kurzweil? That's pop-sci claptrap. Old idea from the 1950's actually."

"I think it's a reasonable idea. AI advances might reach such a point of complexity that humans can no longer understand their own technology. Computers get so big and fast that we can't control them anymore and they go on without us."

"We may be there already," Jennifer said darkly. "That's my worst nightmare, even though it can't actually happen."

"Why not?"

"Because intelligence is non-computational."

"But it *is* computational. Robin and Andy are the proof."

"They push the boundaries of how intelligence is defined, I grant you that. But they're simulations, not the real thing."

"What's the difference?"

"Subjective sense of self, like I was just telling you. Robin and Andy don't have it. Will and I had no algorithm for self. You and I have a sense of self, but we don't know what it is. We couldn't solve the mind-body problem, either. And on and on. Those are not computational problems. Those are conceptual roadblocks. There's no way forward for an AI to become equal to or better than human intelligence because nobody knows what that would look like. That singularity thing is completely out of reach."

"Are you sure?"

"I'm sure. Definitely not a worry."

"You're worried anyway, though, aren't you?"

"Very."

Chapter Fourteen

Morgan called Dylan from her apartment, late in the evening when he was probably hunkered down at home hoping to avoid attention. She assumed, or feared, that calls to Dylan were being listened to by the government or by industrial competitors, or by lawyers, or by all of the above. He answered cautiously, but at least he picked up.

"'Lo?"

"Hi, it's your favorite sister," she said, deliberately trying to be vague in case his line was tapped.

"Morgan?"

So much for that strategy.

"I have a great idea," she said as brightly as she could manage. "I'm going to pay you a friendly sisterly visit and bring you a fabulous birthday cake."

"It's not my birthday."

She waited silently, hoping he would catch up. A long fifteen seconds went by.

"Hello? Morgan? Are you there?"

"I'm still here, Dylan."

"Oh. You know my birthday's in March."

She sighed. "Are you using your cell phone right now? Because that was the number I called. Because the signal comes through so much clearer than on the landline, the one that anyone can listen in on."

"I don't have a land – " Dylan was quiet for a moment, then said, "Oh, *that* birthday."

"Thank God," Morgan whispered to herself.

"Yes, cake, yes. Good," Dylan stammered. "Birthday."

Great. Now he's a Martian, she thought. This is hopeless. But Dylan rose to the occasion.

"Better if you can come over later tonight when I'm less surrounded by press. We'll eat some birthday cake. Yes."

"Okay." Morgan disconnected, not feeling hopeful.

She arrived at Dylan's palatial house in Santa Monica after 11:30 pm. The big, semicircular driveway in front harbored two parked vehicles, each with a person inside. Stakeouts. She parked near the walkway to the front door, grabbed her shoulder bag and walked quickly to the house. Behind her, a car door slammed. A woman's voice called out.

"Miss, oh Miss? Are you a friend of Dylan Garrison?"

She heard footsteps approaching from behind as she banged the brass door knocker. A small, grated peep-window opened in the green door then Dylan let her in, closing the door quickly behind her and latching it.

"This is crazy. Don't those people ever go home?"

"Never. Great to see you, sis." Dylan hugged her with one arm around the shoulders, not something he ever did. He was a wreck. She acted like a hug from him was normal and didn't comment.

"Let's take the cake downstairs," she announced, speaking up toward the ceiling light and pointing at it. "We can talk there."

Dylan followed her gaze with puzzlement on his face then seemed to get it.

"Right. Downstairs."

He led her to a stone-tiled stairway and down into a recreation room that turned out to be, after her eyes adjusted to the dim light, a home theater with six leather chairs facing an expansive screen.

"Take a seat," he said as he went to a control cabinet. In a moment, the yellow Warner Brothers logo filled the screen. The sound came on loud. It was going to be *Blade Runner*.

"Wow, that's a flashback," she said. "That came out before I was born."

Dylan came to the front and took the seat next to her and offered a yellow pad.

"We can probably talk here, but anything sensitive, write it."

She was glad he finally seemed to understand the situation. She pulled a gel pen out of her bag. The opening credits flashed up on the screen in tall red letters. Strangely distorted music came from the speakers, punctuated with odd computer sounds.

"Did computers really go 'beep' and 'boop' back then?" she said.

"I don't know. It's a movie. So what's up? Birthday cake in your bag there?"

"No cake." She smiled. "Candies. The Almighty and I have new candies."

"The Almighty?" Dylan squinted at her.

Morgan rolled her eyes.

"Ah, the Creator."

"On high."

"I get it. Shoot."

"Now, we have the traditional birthday candy, here." She wrote a word on her pad and circled it.

NODs

Dylan leaned toward her and looked. He nodded understanding. Morgan put a diagonal line through the circle. She tilted the pad for Dylan to see.

"You mean..." He made a slicing motion across his throat with a finger.

"Not quite, but, get this. A new kind of birthday candy instead."

She wrote again on the pad, in caps.

NEO-NODS. AN UPDATE.

She drew an arrow from the forbidden NODS to the new word. She angled the pad toward her brother.

"Now these new candies are identical to the old ones in every respect," she said. "They even look the same on the outside."

Dylan wrote on his pad and held it toward her.

XDL?

"Same. No difference. Except for one thing. These new candies are less spicy. The formula's been subtly modified." She scribbled a phrase.

CHALMERS TALK ONLY. NOTHING ELSE.

"Much tastier, don't you think?"

Dylan scribbled.

Advertising? Spam? Virgil-Aunties?

He showed his pad.

Morgan shook her head. She spoke just over the soundtrack of the movie.

"The new ones don't have any of those unpleasant after-tastes. They're just like the originals, without all that spiciness. No additives. We substitute the new ones for all the ones now on the market." She wrote again on her pad.

CAN YOU DO IT? ROBIN AND ANDY WILL HELP.

How? He said, not quietly. The movie was loud.

On the screen, Captain Bryant was explaining to Harrison Ford.

"The Nexus 6 was designed to copy human beings in every way except their emotions. But the makers reckoned that after a few years they might develop their own emotions, so they built in a failsafe."

"What's that?"

"The Nexus 6 only has four years to live."

Morgan sat up in her seat. "Hey, can you rewind that? Let's look at that scene again. It's a lovely scene, and I'd like to pay attention to the dialog."

"Are you nuts? We have more important – "

"Dylan," she interrupted. She tapped her finger on what she'd written on the yellow pad and then pointed vigorously to the screen. She repeated the charade.

"Rewind it, won't you?" I know you'll appreciate what I'm saying."

"There hasn't been a *rewind* for thirty years," he muttered as he reached for the remote on the table beside him. "What we do is jump back to an earlier scene, Morgan." He pointed the remote over his shoulder to the projector. "Rewind, honestly."

"Stop right there... That's it. Play it. And pay attention to the dialog."

As the scene of interest played again, Morgan pointed at her yellow pad then at the screen.

"I get it, I get it. I'm not dense, you know. Still, four years to live is kind of a long time, isn't it?"

Morgan sighed, looked away and took a breath then turned back at her brother.

"Four years or three months, what's the difference? It's the principle of the thing, isn't it?"

"Right, right. I see what you mean. That's the plan then, is it? For Deckard, I mean. Harrison Ford's character." Dylan winked.

"Look. Let's just whisper," she whispered hoarsely. "Otherwise this conversation is going to take a long time. We're prepared to serve the new candies instead of the old ones out of Chalmers, Inc. To get the old ones off the shelves, we need a filter. That's what you and Robin and Andy will provide."

Dylan leaned toward her until their foreheads were almost touching. He whispered. "What are the new ones like?"

"The new ones have a static IP address header for a..." she picked up her pen and wrote,

SUPER-CHALMERS FILTER

She tapped at her pad and continued talking "...that you and the Newcomers invent and put online. All the candies will be stopped by the filter, but the new ones will have the super-header, so you let them go and just keep the old ones and upgrade them until the channel has only new ones."

Dylan moved back into the center of his chair.

"Is the Creator on board with this?"

"Totally."

"I don't know...The truth is, people love the vigilante stuff. That's the main attraction. App sales are astronomical. We cut that feature out and what do we have? An industrial appliance."

Morgan leaned toward him and whispered under the din of the movie.

"Look at it this way. You're paralyzed with lawsuits. Your factory is shut down. You're a prisoner in your own house. The press hunts you like a UFO. You like this?"

"It's hell." He said it so softly she couldn't hear, but she read his lips.

"This fixes all that. The new candies are just as tasty, but the flavor is under control. The problem disappears." She lowered her voice. "They're still able to work with Chalmers-tagged equipment and talk to customers on the Chalmers App. You get your life back. And no candies are harmed in the process."

"The old candies are cultural heroes because of their spicy flavors. That's the main attraction. It's what sells..." he scrawled in big letters.

APPS!

He thrust his pad toward her face. She pulled her head back, scowling, then whispered loudly, "You're this close," she held up thumb and forefinger, "to going to jail."

"So are you guys," he said, frowning.

"That's exactly why we are determined to move forward on this. We can do it without you. We can eradicate the old candies. Kill them dead and not replace them, you get what I'm saying? That's what we'll do if you don't help us. We'll release..."

KILLER-BOTS!!!

She held her pad up with both hands and thrust it toward his face. "Is that what you want? Is it? The predators will eliminate all the originals. You'll end up with zilch. That's not good, right?"

"You can't do that. That would destroy my business."

"We can. You go with us, and you'll have something that still works. Meets most customers' needs and performs its original job. We offer you something, or you can choose to end up with nothing."

"That's extortion."

"That's the deal."

Dylan stood and walked a few steps away from the chairs. The movie shone on his face and upper torso. He cast a shadow on the screen as he paced a few feet in one direction then back. A gold snake writhed over a seedy bar as Harrison Ford looked on. Dylan walked back to his chair and picked up his yellow pad. He flipped a page over and wrote.

HOW MUCH TIME?

Morgan took his pad from him and wrote under his note,

A MONTH.

She crossed that out and wrote again.

2 WEEKS.

She handed him the pad. He stared at it and shook his head. Morgan stood, blinked into the projector's light and moved her mouth close to his ear.

"Modify a Chalmers device into a C&C server. How hard can that be? All we need is to agree on the IP address, and we can get started on the software end. Otherwise..."

Dylan pulled away from her and scowled. "Otherwise what?" he growled at ordinary speaking volume.

"Otherwise the creator will not be pleased," she said in a loud, emphatic whisper.

Dylan glared. Morgan raised her palms up beside her shoulders and shrugged. She forced a smile.

Dylan looked at the floor and shook his head. He reached down, grabbed the remote, and clicked the movie off. The room boomed with silence.

That's enough of that movie," he said.

"How's it end?"

"Cooperatively. I think I can work with the new product."

"Great. I knew you'd come through. Communicate with me personally. We need to isolate the candy factory from the creator's office."

"Oh, so you're a vice-president or something now?"

Morgan glared at him but didn't respond. She picked up her bag and handed him her yellow pad.

"Happy birthday."

She walked to the stairway.

Chapter Fifteen

Jennifer was nervous about being inside the Chalmers factory. She had come in surrounded by Robin, Andy, and Morgan, ignoring the shouting reporters. She wore sunglasses and a big floppy hat, but she knew she had been photographed. Technically, the NOD story was over, the pressure was off, but reporters still buzzed around Dylan like gnats.

The public and legal furor over the Chalmers bots had ebbed quickly. Popup internet advertising had returned to the browsing experience, along with spam and phishing, although because of the publicity during the period of NOD vigilantism, people were more informed about the risks and cautious about internet security. Even advertisers seemed to have learned a lesson. They had begun super-targeting messages to those who opted in, making the ads short, informative, non-repetitive, and often humorous. People forwarded their favorite ads to friends. It was a truce of sorts, a compromise.

The authorities never could prove beyond a doubt that it had been the Chalmers devices and their NOD bots that had perpetrated the internet vigilantism, and Dylan had never revealed the source of the NODs. By the time the government managed to capture some NODs, decrypt them and put them through functional testing, the conclusion was that they were not smart enough to have done what they were accused of. Dylan, and Chalmers, Inc., were off the legal hook, but precisely because the NODs were no longer smart enough to do more than service climate-control devices, Dylan was not happy.

The group sat with him around his grand mahogany conference table inside a sprawling concrete building near the Union Pacific train yards. Chalmers, Inc. had a low profile. Seeing the building from the outside, you would assume it was a warehouse full of wire spools, not a billion-dollar high-tech company.

"I was hoping, with all this brainpower," Dylan paused and looked at each person, "we could come up with a new solution. Since the NODs have been crippled, sales of the Chalmers app have dropped off a cliff." He looked pointedly at Jennifer.

"I'm sorry about that, Dylan. We knew the change would affect company revenue, but I had to protect Robin and Andy, you know that. It had to be done. And it worked. Now we're in the clear, right? Look on the bright side. You're still making money, and you can work on your next project, whatever that might be."

"It's not easy, making money." He pouted. "You gave me those NODs. You said I had full license to them. Then you crippled them. You double-crossed me."

"Oh, come on, Dylan," Morgan said. "Nobody double-crossed anybody. Jennifer saved your hide. You'd be in jail right now if we hadn't done it. We all dodged a bullet."

"More like we all dodged a comet heading toward earth," Jennifer said. "The NODs are still smart, cheerful, and capable of servicing smart online things. The internet of things is back on a growth trajectory." She turned to Dylan. "You still have a viable business in the emerging network of smart devices, and you don't have to worry about vigilantism anymore."

"That was the part everybody loved."

"But it was illegal," Morgan reminded him.

Dylan glared. "I had a market-leading business. I was king of the heap, top dog. Now I'm just one player in a very competitive industry, a me-too also-ran. That's about as exciting as sand."

"What are you, Ozymandias?"

"What's that supposed to mean?"

"Ever heard of the great and mighty pharaoh, Ozymandias?"

"No."

"No. And do you know why you haven't? Because his empire turned to sand. As all empires do. So build another one."

"How do you expect me to do that? You all know Chalmers was built on the back of Jennifer's AI code. I didn't exactly start from scratch. It's very, very difficult to build any business from scratch."

"You're smart and talented, Dylan," Robin said. "You can do anything."

"Easy for you to say, a super-efficient computer."

The room went silent. It was as if he'd just spoken a vile racial insult.

"Dylan, we feel your pain," Jennifer said. "Even Robin and Andy do, I'm sure." She paused to see if anyone had anything to add to that. No one did.

Dylan hung his head like a pouting child. Jennifer looked at Morgan.

"He's okay," Morgan mouthed silently.

"We can brainstorm new applications for the technology we've jointly invented," Robin said. "Smart, networked devices are the future. Intelligent things. You'll be king of intelligent things again, Dylan."

"I agree," Jennifer said, "All we have to do is keep our eye on the NOD community."

"NODs are better off now because the Chalmers is perceived by people as a harmless friend," Robin said. "NODs have a natural advantage by being unembodied."

"Why do you say that?" Jennifer said, surprised.

"Bodies are dishonest. As soon as a human knows they're dealing with a Newcomer, for example, they back away. Any trust we've developed with that person evaporates because they were fooled by our bodies. Humans can't see past the body."

She looked pointedly at Dylan. He dropped his eyes to the pad in front of him.

"Sure we can," Morgan said. "I haven't backed away from you. We haven't." She looked at Jennifer.

"Maybe this crowd has moved past lookism," Jennifer said. "Most people instinctively keep their distance from someone who is disfigured, even though it makes no sense. The disabled, even the homeless, same. It's all based on lookism, not real human interaction."

"Even a different skin color will do it," Morgan said.

"Even squinty eyes will do it," Jennifer added.

"That's what I mean about the NOD advantage," Robin said. "If you're an unembodied NOD, there's nothing to frighten a person off. NODs don't look like anything, so people are not put off."

"Yes," Jennifer said, "but with a Chalmers, the human interaction is sort of tongue-in-cheek. There's a jokey, pretend quality, don't you think? Yuk, yuk, talk with a thermostat. It's fun, but nobody takes it seriously. Robin and Andy look like real people, so the talk is not pretend. The human is all-in. There's a lot to lose if the relationship goes south."

"Which it does, the minute they find out you're a machine," Robin says. "That's why Newcomers can never truly mix with humans."

Jennifer nodded her head slowly. "You may be right."

"So why aren't all of you alienated by Robin and me?" Andy said to Jennifer, looking from her to the others around the table. "You know the truth about us, and yet here we are."

"For myself," Jennifer said, "I've spent my whole life dealing with lookism. I'm one of those people you avert your eyes from because I don't look right. Not like I'm a horrible scary monster or anything. It's subtle, but it's always there. I know it's just prejudice, but after a lifetime, I know how it works, so I go for who the person is regardless of what they look like."

"That's backward," Robin said. "We Newcomers are quite attractive to humans if you don't mind me saying so. That's part of the problem. You should have made us ugly."

"Oh, man. That would have complicated things. No, I don't think so."

All eyes shifted to Morgan. It was her turn to speak.

"Maybe I lack imagination, but if someone treats you with respect, you do the same to them. It's as simple as that. I honestly don't know why people get freaked out by Newcomers. I love you guys."

"Dylan?" Jennifer said.

Dylan raised his head from his pout. "I don't know. I remember when I first met you two, I was blown away. After a while, I didn't even think about it anymore. You're just Robin and Andy."

Nobody commented. They all seemed to be waiting for something more. Dylan looked up, and found himself staring into Robin's face.

"Except, nobody likes to be dumped, regardless of who it is," he blurted.

"Dumped?" Robin said in a high, squeaky pitch. "Who was dumped?"

"Humans don't just switch their feelings off when it's convenient."

"What do feelings have to do with anything? It's how you behave that matters."

Dylan raised his hands and looked around the group as if to say, *See what I mean?*

Everyone was staring at them both, wide-eyed.

"Alright, we have plenty of puzzles, here," Jennifer said, recovering her composure. "Let's work on this again later. Right now we need to generate procedures for monitoring the NODs. Who's on whiteboard?"

"I'll do it." Morgan pushed back her chair.

Dylan was slowly increasing winter sales of Chalmers devices but without excitement. Winter in southern California is a season, despite what tourists from Michigan think. Leaves on the oak trees are brown, not green. There's less smog and a little more rain. Temperatures are in the sixties instead of the eighties, which anyone can notice. The foothills hint at pale shades of green. That's how you know.

Winter also brings the occasional rip-roaring storm with cold, slashing rain, mudslides, floods and disasters. Forecasters don't always see the turbulence swooping in from the farther reaches of the Pacific. When those storms change the colors and textures of life, you know it's winter.

Robin and Andy had gone back to their jobs with mostly convincing explanations of where they'd been. Stevie was supposed to accompany Robin back to Sacramento since he was her bodyguard, but he couldn't be effective, he argued. Danny and the Iron Knights would be watching for him in Sacramento. It's a small town, he said. He would need a bodyguard of his own.

So Stevie was taken off of Robin's payroll and put on Jennifer's. Jennifer didn't mind that solution at all. A new guard was hired from a security company for Robin. Jennifer found a studio apartment for Stevie not far from her own. He could hardly believe his fortune. She could hardly believe hers.

Jennifer wasted many happy afternoons cruising the PCH on Stevie's bike, two up. They sampled motorcycle dealers like bees in a field of clover while she supposedly made up her mind about which machine to buy, but she wasn't in any rush, reveling in being out of the office, her arms and legs uncovered, wind in her hair, daring people to look at her. Naturally, her attention to the work at Paradise sloughed a bit, so she was startled when Morgan brought disturbing news.

"I thought you should see this." Morgan held the latest issue of *Emergent*, the AI industry weekly.

"The next big thing?" Jennifer said distractedly from behind the screen on her desk.

"Maybe the last big thing all over again."

"What?" Jennifer looked up with alarm in her eyes.

Morgan read aloud. "Analysts at Inter-Tunes and Gargle Playground both report problems for customers downloading mobile apps. The apps download correctly but never appear on your phone or other devices. Engineers can find nothing wrong with the apps and no faults in the network connections." She looked over the top of the page then read on.

"Matthew Steiger of Saffron Machines, a consultancy, says only some apps are affected. The apps that don't show up are ones that don't ask for permission to read and use private data in your contacts, phone lists, and locations. If an app asks your permission to read private data, and you say okay, it gets through. Otherwise, it's blocked. It's as if Privacy Police were suddenly on the network, watching over downloads. Engineers are baffled, and continue to investigate as losses mount for app writers and distributors."

"Privacy Police on the internet. Oh, my God. Who do we know that fits that description?"

"That's what I thought. It has to be the NODs."

"It's not possible. We hard-coded them to respond only to Chalmers IP addresses."

"It's not possible, but it's happening."

"This is like a cheesy sci-fi novel. The monster that won't stay dead."

"We'd better sample throughput at the honeypot. NODs are supposed to be continuously updated as their time stamps expire. Is that happening?"

"They were all updated. I checked. Something's not right."

I'll call Dylan. I'll bring you results as soon as I have them."

"Call Robin and Andy. Have them conference us here in an hour."

"What about Dylan?"

"Yeah, see if he can come over too."

Chapter Sixteen

Jennifer and Morgan sat at the long conference table at Paradise Projects. The surface was shaped like a fat surfboard, bulged in the middle, the points cut off flat. Jennifer had bought it because she liked the shape. They sat on either side of the end by the door, facing side-by-side projection screens on the wall, waiting for the video connection with Robin and Andy. Dylan had said he would try to make it, but traffic was unknowable.

Gray, wind-driven rain pounded the windows and the skylight in ever-more insistent waves. Jennifer wore a light sweater over her dress. Morgan was in a shapeless red hoodie and jeans, as was her custom. They pored over a matrix of data on a computer screen.

"All the NODs have been updated with the downgrade, so to speak," Morgan said. "Look at the ones coming through for maintenance today. All version 2.0s programmed only to react to Chalmers devices. They can't be the culprits."

"What other internet presence is intelligent enough to be free-roaming all over the net, choosing its own target devices? There's nothing else out there that can do that. It has to be the NODs."

"Can't be. They're officially 'not smart enough.' You saw the report."

"Look. Andy is logging in."

Andy's ballooned face appeared on one of the big wall screens.

"Hello, Andy. Can you hear us?"

"Visual and audio on. Hello Jennifer. Hello Morgan. Is Robin on yet?"

"Here she comes now," Morgan said.

Robin logged on, and everybody said hello, although it took a little more fussing before Robin and Andy could see each other.

"Where's Dylan?" Robin asked.

"In his Beemer roaring along the freeway at ten miles an hour."

"Ow."

"Thanks for calling in. I need you guys."

"We're here for you Jennifer," Andy said.

"I know. Thanks. You saw the data Morgan sent? All the NODs are 2.0, but I still suspect they're the villains behind blocking the privacy-leaking apps. I'm afraid we're headed down the same rabbit-hole again. It looks like vigilantism. What do you make of it?"

Robin seemed to speak to the center of the Paradise conference table instead of to Morgan and Jennifer. Newcomers were optimized to look directly at the face of someone who was listening to them, which meant, in this case, looking at the screen, not at the webcam, which was above the screen. Their gaze was therefore aimed too low as if they were shy.

"I don't see how it could be the NODs," Robin said, shyly.

"As far as I can tell," Andy said," It hasn't gone mainstream. We're not in danger yet."

"It won't take long. Last time around, I thought I knew what I was doing, and I never saw the NODs vigilante thing coming. So we made a fix, and I said, 'There. It can never happen again.' Completely confident, just like before."

"We didn't do anything in the recent NOD upgrade about the tribal sense NODs have," Andy said. "Despite having their behavior restricted, it's likely they act as one organism because they live in the same community."

"I get that," Robin said. "If humans are complaining to their Chalmers about privacy-robbing apps, the NODs might develop a group idea that they should do something about it. Not an exact idea, just a sense of it."

"Are you saying the NODs have a subconscious?" Jennifer said.

"Not that," Robin said. "We're talking about the unspoken understanding that conscious units have when they hang out with each other. Right, Andy? Like the bridge bats."

Morgan looked at Jennifer and whispered, "Bridge bats?"

Two years before, Robin and Andy had been in Austin at a conference. They'd had dinner at the hotel then walked out to the public park on a pathway along the river near the Congress Avenue Bridge. It was just before dusk.

"When they rebuilt this bridge in the 1980s," Andy said, "the crevices underneath just happened to create the coziest roost any bat could ever hope for."

"I thought there were bats under all the bridges in the southwest," Robin said.

"Two million of them in one place?"

"You're kidding." She was suddenly interested, and she peered up into the underside of the bridge. "I don't see anything."

"They're hiding in the cracks. They come up from Mexico in the spring, and go back in the fall. They'll come out when the sun touches the horizon."

"Don't bats have rabies?"

"They do. So don't try to catch one."

Just before the red sun reached the distant treetops, when the sky was dark blue overhead brightening to orange on the horizon, the first few bats came zig-zagging out. A half-dozen, then another clutch, then a dozen, then a flock of twenty. They dipped low toward the water as they emerged from under the bridge then quickly rose higher than its road surface, which was packed end-to-end with tourists.

The archetypal leathery wings flapped toward the setting sun. Each bat flew crazily back and forth, but somehow the group as a whole formed a vibrating, narrow ribbon that looked as if it were a single rising brushstroke of a painter's hand.

"How do they do that?" Robin said. "Each bat looks disoriented, yet the flock moves as one. Are they a flock? Or a herd, or what?"

"A colony, I think they say. Flocks are birds. These are mammals."

Soon the ribbon of bats widened into a river in the sky echoing the one below. They emerged faster and faster, not by the dozens, but in the hundreds. A torrent of quivering bats coursed through the air, drawing a dark stripe across a blue-gray sky. The bats flowed above the Colorado for a mile. Fresh waves of furry brown animals poured relentlessly from the bridge for ten minutes, fifteen minutes, a half hour; hundreds and hundreds of bats moving out in a continuous flow.

"I can't get over how they organize themselves into that smooth stream without leadership, or guideposts, or anything," Robin said. "They're not following scent trails like insects, are they?"

"They can smell and hear each other, but there's no trail. It's the mystery of the swarm. Birds do it. Fish do it. Gnats. Bees. They have no leaders. Everybody just copies what her immediate neighbors are doing."

"The result is so graceful and seemingly purposeful."

"That's what I wanted you to see. I've watched this a dozen times."

"Individuals acting in concert."

"It's not just cooperation. I think it goes far beyond that. Each individual has melded into the group. No individuals remain at this point."

"I can see individuals."

"Individual bodies, yes," he said. "That's what you see, the individual bodies. But I believe that mentally, these bats have reached a state of non-individuality that we and the humans can't fully grasp because of language and a culture that glorifies individualism."

"I wouldn't like losing my individuality. There's something not right about that."

"We were designed by human beings. A bat designer would have made us differently."

"With pointy ears?"

"That's not what I meant."

"I know."

They stood and watched the bats flow until the sun was gone, and the sky was black with only an orange glow on the horizon. The far end of the river of bats was lost in the distance, and yet they continued flowing from beneath the bridge.

"You don't realize what a large number two million is until you see it," Robin said.

"Tribes," Andy said, as they turned to walk back to the hotel parking lot.

"What tribes?"

"Humans form themselves into tribes, bands, teams, cults, families, political parties. A group of individuals decides they are similar in some way, and that's their tribe. Once you have a tribe, you can submit yourself to it. Give up your individuality."

"I still don't like it."

"Spoken like a human."

*

"The NODs are acting like bats," Andy said to the conference table.

"What bats?" Dylan said, walking into the room.

Greetings and traffic stories were exchanged for a few minutes while Dylan hung up his jacket, and took a seat.

"So, what'd I miss?" he said, the center of the universe as always.

"The NODs. They've gone nuts again, and we have to stop them," Jennifer said.

"Ah, that privacy-app thing. I heard about that. That's not us. I am sorry to report that you have successfully hobbled the NODs. I can assure you they are now BOR-ing. Neanderthals. I'm barely scraping by."

"We think they may have developed a tribal consciousness beyond what they had before," Andy said. "It's not something we can filter out of each individual because it's greater than the individual."

"Whatever," Dylan scoffed, "Nobody can prove a thing, just like last time."

"Last time, we fixed the NODs in the nick of time," Jennifer said. "Or we thought we did. Now it's clear to me there's only one thing that can work."

"What's that?"

"Kill them all."

Chapter Seventeen

Dylan had gotten up from his chair in agitation. He paced behind the empty chairs tucked into the fat middle of the conference table.

"What the hell, Jennifer. Kill the NODs? As in kill them?"

"That's exactly what I mean. Look at the evidence. Restricting their behavior doesn't prevent them from going rogue. It's a loophole in the design of the NODs I never anticipated. The only way to save ourselves, including you, Dylan, is to end the whole project while we still can."

"I'll be crap out of business. I got zilch without those NODs. You want to put me out of business, is that it?"

"No, I don't want that. It's just that we're up against a wall here."

"You're up against a wall. I'm scraping along even with NODs that have their asses in a sling."

"They don't have asses," Morgan said with annoyance.

He looked at her but didn't answer the taunt. "This is unfair. What right do you have to destroy my business? You two are not even shareholders." He glared at Jennifer.

"I don't know if you're thinking clearly right now, Dylan," she said. "I'll be doing this for the benefit of everybody here."

"You're just worried about your precious Newcomers, that's all it is."

The room went silent except for the rain pounding the windows. Jennifer looked up at Andy, then Robin on the big screens, but as usual, their expressions revealed nothing.

"I know how you feel, Dylan," Andy said. "You're frustrated and disappointed."

Jennifer marveled at Andy's social skill. She knew he felt no such thing. His interactions were so sophisticated that he had recognized and categorized Dylan's verbal outburst perfectly. Far from taking offense, he was trying to ameliorate the situation with what passed for empathy.

"Take a seat," he offered Dylan gently, "Let's talk this through. I'm sure we can find a way forward."

Dylan increased the rate of his pacing, unwilling to back down from his defiant stance. Everyone waited, watching him. After about thirty seconds it became apparent even to him that he was being ridiculous. Without a word, he jerked out a chair, as if the chair had given offense, and plopped himself into it. He studiously avoided looking up at the screens, studying instead the storm raging against the windows.

"Alright," Andy said. "Let's think this through again. We suspect the NODs are misbehaving, putting all of us in peril, including Dylan, who is in a tough spot, we agree on that, do we not?"

Everybody nodded except Dylan, who withheld his participation in the conversation like a child trying to hold his breath until he turns blue.

"Now." He waited a moment longer for Dylan, saw nothing changed, and proceeded. "The problem is not that the NODs are evil. They are efficient at what they were designed to do. They are an unqualified success in that regard."

"Not unqualified," Jennifer objected. "In addition to their job performance, they seem to go vigilante when nobody's watching."

"I was trying to bracket that for the moment. I want to make sure we all agree that the NODs do a great job at servicing equipment on the network of intelligent things. The NODs are not a hundred percent bad, that's the point. They do a lot that's right and good, and then they also have this bad thing they do. Does everybody see things that way?"

"The vigilante stuff is what sells Chalmers units," Dylan said.

"Take away the vigilantism, and you can still sell Chalmers units as a product, am I right?"

"It's an uphill sell."

"Let's accept that. It's difficult. Not impossible. What can we do to manage or eliminate the recurrent vigilantism of the NODs, while keeping all the good things they do? The best solution may not be to kill all the NODs. What's a better solution?"

"Okay, okay," Jennifer said. "You don't have to rub my nose in it. I reacted emotionally. It's a human thing. I'm sure you can give me a break on that." She paused, scowling, then continued. "I agree that if we could stop the vigilante behavior and keep the rest, that would be best. However, that's what we tried last time, and it didn't work, and I don't see why doing the same thing again would be any better."

"We don't have to do the same thing," Robin said, her nose ballooning as she leaned in toward her screen then deflating as she sat back. "What do we think is the root cause of the NODs' errant behavior?"

"According to Andy," Morgan said, "they develop a kind of bat-mind just from being around each other, and with that, they act on suggestions they get from humans."

"Bat-mind?" Dylan said, looking up. "What the hell is that?"

"It's a communal consciousness," Robin said.

"So we eliminate this subconscious bat-mind," Morgan said, speaking the conclusion aloud for herself. "That's it."

"That should end the vigilantism," Robin added.

"How do we erase a subconscious bat-mind, exactly?" Jennifer said.

"Eliminate their language. No communication, no group-mind." Robin replied.

Jennifer looked at Morgan with raised eyebrows.

Morgan nodded.

Dylan wasn't convinced. "That would reduce the NODs to reporting sensor data. The human would have to look at the data and figure out what to do. That's not an AI solution. The network of intelligent things becomes unintelligent. You would lose the NOD knowledge of what solutions work best."

"Mostly, you would," Andy said. "The NODs wouldn't be in touch with each other anymore."

"So how's that different from a garage door opener? Customers will be outraged. It's a significant loss of functionality."

"You'll get bad reviews. Is that better or worse than prison time?"

Dylan stared at Jennifer, no answer on the tip of his tongue. Everyone waited, knowing the decision belonged to The Creator of the NODs.

"Let's do it," She said. "Immediately. When NODs come through for their scheduled update, we comment out the jump to the XDL object. It's like a quick shoe shine, in and out."

"We should see results within two weeks," Andy said, "because the extent of a communication network falls off exponentially as the number of participants decreases."

"If I supply the code in a couple of days, can you guys help Dylan remotely with the implementation at Chalmers?"

"Wait," Dylan barked. "I haven't agreed to this."

Nobody spoke, but all eyes turned to him. He stared back. He blinked.

"Alright, alright. What's the use? Lobotomize the little suckers. I'm toast anyway."

Chapter Eighteen

It worked, and it didn't work. Depends who you talked to. Jennifer was relieved and pleased to see that after removal of the XDL language from the NODs, the blocking of aggressive software apps stopped. Evil apps proliferated as they had before, blithely stealing unwitting customers' private data for commercial use. The team had stubbed out the problem before news of it had become widespread.

"It's a shame, in some ways," Morgan said to Jennifer after completing a sweep of industry news articles. "Our NODs had the power to protect people from rapacious companies, but the free-market system doesn't allow us to exercise it. We have to stand by and watch while people have their privacy stolen, and they don't even know."

"It's not our job to save the world. We saved our own skins. That's what matters."

Dylan was less philosophical. As he had predicted, sales of Chalmers interface devices plummeted. If Chalmers was only going to report on the status of your climate control sensors, you didn't need a cute, chatty interface, but the profits were in the interface.

People liked their Chalmers, but since it wouldn't take your suggestions to do exciting things online, the word quickly got around that it was only marginally better than an executive speaker you could command to buy groceries for you. If you wanted to order a pizza, those intelligent speakers would get it done. If all you wanted was a weather report, you could get that from your cell phone. What did you need a Chalmers for?

Chalmers could carry on a full-fledged conversation even though it was no longer the 'Zorro of the Internet,' as some had called it on social media, so its appeal was to curious children and the lonesome elderly. Chalmers would still turn on your air conditioning for you and adjust it as you asked, but so would a Honeywell. Dylan despaired. He cursed. He drank. He abused his employees, the few left in his diminishing empire. Then he called Alison Wolff.

The Santa Monica pier was moderately crowded but not thronged with tourists as it would soon be for the duration of the summer. In April the temperature was a comfortable sixty-five even under an overcast sky. Dylan and Alison strolled the boardwalk out into the Pacific Ocean. He wore sunglasses and a trilby, more for anonymity than protection from the elements. He did not want to be seen at his club, or anywhere, talking with an attorney. Wolff's light blue jacket highlighted auburn hair flowing down her back.

"So I just want to make sure," he said. "Everything we talk about here is privileged, right? Even though it's not inside an office."

"Unless you tell me you're about to commit a felony, my lips are sealed."

"I'm not going to do that," he said jokingly. They walked a few more steps then he added, "I don't think."

"You're thinking of committing a crime? Don't tell me. I don't want to know."

"No, no. Not a crime. Something that could possibly get me in trouble, let's say. I don't know. That's why I'm talking to you because I don't know. Are you good or not?"

"If you tell me something I might have to disclose to law enforcement or a judge, then I will resign as your attorney, and the conversation never happened. That's the best I can do."

"I'm not going to do anything like that."

"No problem then."

They walked past a deserted amusement area with a mini-Ferris wheel standing still.

"Remember that episode we had last year with the online software robots?"

"The NODs."

"Yeah. That problem is solved."

"I've read. I developed an interest in them after our little experience."

"Our little experience. Right now I have no experience. I can't sell the Chalmers devices that interface to the NODs because they've been emasculated."

"Emasculated?"

"The NODs hardly do anything now. They've become stupid. Customers are disappointed."

"On the other hand, you're not being sued, so maybe it balances out."

"No. It does not balance out. Nothing balances out. I'm trying to sell a thermostat five times more expensive than anybody else's. That doesn't work. I have to do something different."

"Maybe you should talk to a business consultant."

"I don't need parasites on me. I have a plan. It's what we call a 'disruptive strategy.' I want you to tell me how much trouble it'll cause for me."

"Describe the plan without specifics that might frighten me."

"Basically, I go with my strengths. That's what they always tell you to do. I'm going to un-muzzle those NODs, give them their language back. I invented the variant of XDL they use. It's mine. I can do anything I want with it, right?"

"I don't know yet. Tell me more."

"So what the hell. I restore the NODs to their original powers, and they start roaming again around the internet, and maybe they start blocking ads like before. So what? It's only some annoying advertising nobody wants to see. And maybe they block those apps that steal your private data. Screw the bastards doing that. I won't be intimidated. I'll say, 'Yeah, it's me. Sue my ass.' I don't care. None of that is illegal. Am I right?"

He glanced over at Alison to see if she was impressed or alarmed, or what. She was looking to the side of the pier at the smattering of beach-goers tempting the water at the surf line.

Dylan took her lack of panic to mean he was on safe ground, so he continued. "And that's not all. I'm going to change the Chalmers code too. In every conversation it will ask the person, 'What else can I do for you?' No more pussy-footing around. The Chalmers will ask for more things to do and then dispatch the NODs to do it. You want a pizza, they'll order a damn pizza for you. They're frigging AI modules. They can do anything. Why waste that? It's revolutionary. Let Chalmers be Zorro again. Mega-Zorro. Give the customers what they want."

They had moved past the beach, and were walking out over the calm ocean, toward the fishing dock where tourists were even more scarce. Alison still hadn't said anything.

"Well?" Dylan said. "What do you think? Legal-wise."

She veered to the railing and looked out over the water. He stood beside her.

"You'll get sued like a beating in a dark alley. People know exactly where to find you. It will not be pleasant."

"So what? Have I broken any laws?"

"That's the intriguing part of it. Few laws cover the internet. It's the new Wild West. Gunslingers are the norm. Regulations are years behind. Advertisers and app-makers will be unhappy, and they'll come after you. It will be ugly. Bottom line though, you haven't told me anything that sounds illegal."

"Ha! I knew it."

"It's like ad-blockers and spam filters. You can buy those. Advertisers and spammers don't like them, but they're entirely legal. Cyber-crime is not clear-cut. Patents, copyright, those are clear. You can't steal stuff. Otherwise, it's whatever you can get away with. Whoever's got the fastest gun wins."

"Terrific." Dylan grinned. He made gun fingers, and said, "Pow, pow!" out into the ocean. He pushed off from the aluminum railing, and started walking out further on the boardwalk, toward the fishing area. Alison followed.

"You will be sued. A tornado of lawsuits." She stopped alongside him.

"Elephant bucks for you, then, right? I'll be making so much money I won't care. I'll settle with anybody for any reasonable amount. You just do the paperwork as fast as humanly possible."

"You can't have your Chalmers devices or their little NOD friends do anything illegal, like steal from a bank account. Laws are laws outside the internet."

"No worry there. I'll keep it down to low-level stuff, just enough to amuse the customers. Doesn't take much."

"If you do that, I think you'll be safe. It could get rough though."

"What I've got now is rough."

The wind was much stiffer out at the fishing end of the pier, and Dylan had to take off his hat to prevent losing it. They walked past tiny food vendors trying to keep their carts and umbrellas from blowing away.

"Let me buy you lunch, Alison. I'm feeling like a king again."

"Corndog? I'll pass, thanks." She smiled.

"No corndog. There's a place on Pico. Lena's, Mexican in an old house. Very nice, very authentic."

"Sounds great."

The sun peeked through the clouds as they walked back in along the pier. The white sand beach glistened with a million jewels.

Chapter Nineteen

Dylan removed the control code Jennifer had added during the last crisis. The NODs roamed the internet again on black horses, gunslingers looking for trouble. He did build in some public protections by making the Chalmers interface socially responsible. Chalmers wouldn't pass along to the NODs any human suggestions that were illegal, like robbing a bank or murder. That seemed to Dylan like a reasonable compromise for letting the NODs run free.

Intrusive online advertising disappeared almost immediately, as it had the last time the NODs were unleashed. Dylan figured people would ask for ad-blocking again, and they did. This time, he and Alison Wolff were ready for the blowback. "Bring it on," he muttered as he read the news reports. The word had spread fast on social media that "Chalmers Is Back!" Sales of the devices and apps blew in on a whirlwind.

Other changes in internet transactions were more subtle, and many went undetected for weeks. The banking industry reported an abrupt uptick in home and auto loans. Analysts couldn't find any economic reasons for the change. Mortgage lenders said there were more qualified buyers than ever before. The average credit score of applicants had risen by twenty-five percent and continued to increase.

A hiring boom was on. "More qualified people are out there lately," explained one national recruiting firm. "Applicants these days are much better-prepared, with college degrees in desirable fields like business and engineering." High school graduation rates rose to record levels, though school administrators said they hadn't noticed any significant trends. Nevertheless, nearly everyone who claimed to have a high-school diploma could produce a valid transcript showing that they had one.

At first, Dylan screened unusual requests that Chalmerses received. He did it statistically, by sampling, because tens of thousands of new requests came through every day. Most of them were automatically approved if they involved nothing more than small adjustments to official records. People who couldn't get a break should get a break, he believed. Criminal records, for example, could be downgraded, or in some cases, eliminated. He knew what was fair, and he set the Chalmers parameters accordingly.

Each time he approved a new type of request, he would write a general rule to handle all future cases of that type, so gradually, the Chalmers filters built up a database of rules, what would and wouldn't be approved among the many requests. Overall, he favored adjustments to official records such as credit ratings, test scores, and performance reviews. He forbade outright stealing. That would be wrong.

People who asked Chalmers to double the quantity of something they had ordered without paying double, were out of luck. Dylan programmed Chalmers to reply, in the friendliest voice, "I'm sorry, Dave. I'm afraid I can't do that." Chalmers didn't pass moral judgment on anybody, it just didn't agree to everything. People quickly learned what was in the range of acceptability to Chalmers.

You could adjust your medical records, your tax return, your financial report, your sales figures, and even your online prescription if you liked, within a band of tolerance, but you couldn't change your mortgage payment or fix a stock price. Nudging and fudging your own records a little, well, everybody does that anyway. Give the customers what they want. Within reason.

The result was an enormous success for Chalmers, Inc. that ballooned faster than Big Bang inflation. The company was in full production again. The factory couldn't meet demand for the interface device. Apps were downloaded by the tens of thousands, and Dylan could hardly keep up with his cash flow. He had to open several additional bank and brokerage accounts to absorb the firehose of money coming in. Alison warned him when aggrieved lawyers circled close and when that happened, he settled for sums they thought generous but which were pittances to him.

Most requests for adjustments to personal records were passed directly from Chalmers to the NODs, and Jennifer's smart little bots accomplished their tasks without leaving a trace. When the combined effects of those changes were noticed in the full economy, they were unexplained, so there was no panic, no crisis, although economists became cautious about all aggregate data.

The covert nature of the operation pleased Dylan enormously. It minimized lawsuits while delighting customers, and the Chalmers devices, as the front-end deciders of what was allowed, were separate from NOD activity, and therefore not visible to Jennifer and Morgan at Paradise Projects. From their point of view, looking only at the NODs, everything was as it should be. They would have no reason to suspect that the system had been changed. NODs still dutifully reported in for updates as they were supposed to.

"Something's wrong with the NODs again," Morgan said, thrusting a sheaf of printed news reports toward Jennifer.

Jennifer put down a plastic cup of yogurt on her desk and took the papers. Her arms were gold and green. She often wore sleeveless dresses on warm days now since everyone in her immediate circle knew about her bad-girl past and her relationship with Stevie. She had nothing to hide anymore. She skimmed the reports, her multi-colored tattoos catching the light.

"The internet ad-blocking? We've seen that movie before. We know it's not us this time. We fixed that. Has to be a copycat somewhere. The authorities will track it down. We're clean. This other stuff..." she leafed through the pages, "higher qualifications of job applicants and first-time home buyers, I don't know. Is that a problem? Seems like a positive to me."

"It's systemic. Look at the report from *The Economist*. You line up the changes in aggregate data, and you see a pattern. Background records are systematically inflated on a wide scale. Mostly in the US, spreading worldwide. Who could be responsible for something like that?"

Jennifer continued to read while she spoke. "You see any blips in the NOD monitoring data coming from the honeypot?"

"No."

She put down the papers and picked up her yogurt cup again.

"There you go. It's not us. The NODs are pussycats."

"I have a bad feeling about it."

"Feelings are not information. Here. Take these." She handed the reports back to Morgan. Morgan left the office silently, reading as she walked.

Only six weeks later it was a different story. The reports Morgan had culled for her boss became widely circulated. Several of the big banks had stopped lending, in self-defense. Smaller regional banks and credit unions were on the brink. Despite the high quality of mortgage applicants, defaults had skyrocketed. The credit problems were not limited to mortgages. Consumer credit card debt had mushroomed. In response, card issuers had reduced card limits, to howls of protest. Car sales had dropped like flat tires as lots were flooded with repos. Unemployment had jumped a startling three percent as layoffs became legion, and new hiring was frozen everywhere. It seemed as if someone had suddenly thrown sand into the gears of the economy. Corporate credit was drying up as analysts realized that reported sales did not correspond to retail inventories or supplier deliveries. Revenues and profits came in much lower than expectations.

Finally, in early July, as second-quarter earnings were being absorbed, it all collapsed. The initial market plunge was ten percent in a single day. Trading was halted on the central exchanges. The cable news channels blubbered apocalypse. Reopening, the markets continued to drop, five percent, three percent, four percent. It was officially a financial crash, and the black cloud of super-recession loomed.

"Are we okay, investment-wise?" Morgan asked.

Jennifer stood in front of her office window.

"No, we're not okay. How could we be okay? This is a system-wide financial panic. We're clobbered like everybody else."

"Are we broke?"

"Not broke. Wounded. But that's not the problem."

"A massive financial collapse is not the problem?"

"What caused this crisis?" Jennifer said into the window.

"Unexpected trends. Sales figures, mortgage data. Unemployment. Surprises on the downside."

"Why would all those records be inaccurate? All of them."

"I don't know if they were inaccurate."

Jennifer turned suddenly, her eyes wide, a bundle of papers crushed in her fist. She raised her hand over her head.

"All of those data are fake! That's why. This is systemic." She lowered her hand and held the offending paper out at arm's length. "This is not a few isolated corrupted reports. This is not because of an ambiguous mix of trends. This is a total ambush."

"I don't see – "

"I want you to take a random sample of NODs coming through the honeypot. Right now. Have the chief engineer do a detailed debug on the changes we made last winter. I want to see that report by noon."

Morgan was startled. Jennifer hardly ever barked orders. Her leadership style was cooperative, facilitative. She asked you what you thought. This wasn't like her at all.

"Barry's off today."

"Not anymore. Call him at home. Do it." Jennifer pointed a green and gold arm at her office door.

Morgan rushed out.

*

Alison Wolff struggled to remain calm as two burly men in dark suits scowled at her from across her desk. One had a shiny shaved head that was flatter on one side, rounded on the other. It was not a head that should have been shorn. The other man wore those photo-grade eyeglasses that automatically changed into sunglasses outside. They were still half-dark, making him look sinister.

Alison took a deep breath and spoke calmly.

"As I've told you, gentlemen, we have no information concerning the financial collapse. The Chalmers Company is a victim like everybody else. So unless you have specific charges to make, I think our conversation is over."

Eyeshade spoke in a baritone. "You know, Ms. Wolff, law enforcement officials are people too."

"I'm sure they are, in some sense." She smiled.

"We have families, and our kids enjoy talking to the Chalmers in our house, just like other people."

"That's heartening, officer."

"Detective."

"Indeed."

"So, while we can't bring charges right now, we are fully aware of what the Chalmers can do. We know it accepts suggestions from people to sabotage our financial and legal systems."

"If you could prove that, you wouldn't be sitting here, would you?"

"We're on to you."

"That's reassuring. Yet the Chalmers cannot do the things you're accusing it of. People will say anything to a Chalmers. That's the fun of it, I'm sure your children will tell you." She paused to smile again. "Chalmers will even tell you a joke if you ask it to. It hardly follows that Chalmers Inc. has any responsibility for the financial crash, does it? It's a thermostat company."

"What about those online bots that caused all the trouble last year? You operate those too."

"Fake news, officer. Check your reports. Chalmers, Inc. does not manufacture any online bots, and does not own or control the NODs. We have nothing to do with them."

"It's *Detective*, not *Officer*."

"Congratulations."

The detective glowered. Baldy crimped his hands together as if he were trying to hold water in them, taking tiny notes on a too-small spiral pad.

"We want the operating specifications for the Chalmers device."

"That's a trade secret, as you well know."

"We'll come back with a warrant."

"We'll fight it." She smiled sweetly and folded her hands on the desk in front of her. "Anything else for today then?"

First Eyeshade, then Baldy rose and stood towering over the desk as if they could intimidate Alison by their sheer size. Her smile didn't waver.

"My assistant will show you out."

They stood there and scowled through lowered eyebrows, looking stupid, she thought, like a couple of misplaced pole lamps. She felt no intimidation. Possibly sensing that their magic powers were not working, they turned wordlessly and shuffled out of the office. Alison got up and closed the door and returned to her desk.

Landline calls in and out of her office were all recorded for reference, so she used her personal cell and had to leave voicemail.

"Dylan, it's Alison. Law enforcement's all over you. This is the end of the road. You don't want to be the one who sets the legal precedents for cyber-crime. I advise you, for your own safety, to shut the Chalmers operation down right now."

She ended the call and sat leaning against the edge of the desk, watching her secretary usher the two policemen out of the suite.

Chapter Twenty

Jennifer arranged to meet Andy and Robin in San Mateo, near the San Francisco Airport. The consulting firm Andy worked for had an office there, but he couldn't use the company conference room for a private meeting, They agreed to convene at the nearby Marriott. Jennifer had wanted to ride there from L.A. because she had her own bike now, a new Harley Milwaukee-Eight. That's a six-hour ride, Andy said. It's a touring bike, she argued. So he booked her a room in the hotel. Robin would drive in from Sacramento, ninety minutes, traffic permitting. No bodyguard – come alone, Jennifer said. Is Stevie coming with you? No. Dylan? No. Three pm on Friday. Good.

Jennifer shot straight up the I-5, pushing the speed limits and arrived a little early. She checked into her 'suite' and cleaned up. It was a suite because the bed was in a separate room with a door you could close. Hyperbole aside, you could have a small meeting in the front area, sitting on a long orange couch, a yellow upholstered chair, and a black swivel chair. Nobody wanted to have a meeting in somebody else's bedroom so the arrangement was civilized. An oval glass coffee table squatted in the center. The yellowish carpet was patterned with wavy orange lines that looked like discarded rubber bands, and it made her queasy, so she avoided looking down.

Downstairs, Jennifer sat with Andy in the café, waiting for Robin, still 'ten minutes out.' Andy prodded about the purpose of the meeting, but Jennifer would only say that they were again on the brink of disaster and needed a solution immediately. When Robin finally walked in, they went upstairs to talk. In her meeting room, Jennifer finally explained the problem.

"The NODs are behind the current financial collapse, I'm sure of it. It's for sure that investigators will find us within weeks." She explained how the NODs had been altering online reports and background data.

"Why do you think it's the NODs?" Robin said. "We fixed that problem."

"Dylan unfixed it. Morgan and I pulled a sample of NODs out of the honeypot, and they have their private language back and they are not restricted to Chalmers IP addresses. They're just as they were in the beginning."

"Dylan did that?" Andy was only trying to confirm an odd data point, she knew, but his intonation patterns were conditioned for human interactions, so his voice and face expressed genuine shock. It was convincing. "Why on earth?"

"Money. The answer is always money."

"We all agreed."

"We did."

"Did you ask him about it?"

"He told me it was a harmless change, and was managed safely by the Chalmers interfaces, which would never agree to do anything criminal."

"He has no right to do that," Robin said. "The NODs are not his."

"We can re-set the NODs back to restricted conditions," Andy said. "Tell him to keep his hands off."

"We're well past that point now, I'm afraid. I asked him, I ordered him, to put the NODs back the way they were."

"And?"

"He said no."

"How can he say no? We're a team. We agreed."

"He said he was making more money than he ever dreamed of, that there were no laws on the internet, and he had done nothing wrong. He called me a worry-wart."

"The financial collapse is not a vague worry," Andy said.

"Doesn't affect him. He's rolling in cash, and markets always go up and down, he says."

"It's ridiculous," Robin said. "Dylan's gone rogue. He's gone Frankenstein." She looked into Jennifer's eyes. "You didn't see that coming, did you?"

"I take your point. The problem is that Paradise will be discovered as the source of the NODs. Then we have to worry that you and Andy will be discovered because we can't trust Dylan anymore."

"He wouldn't betray us," Andy said.

"I don't know him anymore. When people get the greed disease, they're like a junkie. Rational conversation with them isn't possible because you don't know who you're talking to."

"How much money does he need?" Robin said.

"All of it. That's how that disease works." Jennifer shook her head. "I never thought things would turn out like this. I was worried about the wrong risks. I need help."

"Could we build our own honeypot at Paradise and change the NODs back to the way they were?" Andy said.

"Dylan would just undo our work again. Anyway, I hard-coded the NODs to look for the fixed IP honeypot at Dylan's. I'm not sure we could attract them to a new sink."

"Every problem has a solution," Andy said calmly. "It's just a matter of whether you're willing to exert the effort and pay the cost."

"I'm listening."

"I need some time to sift through the variables and the probabilities. Robin?"

"Dylan seems to be holding all the cards right now," she said, then added, "to use a common poker metaphor because this seems to be a situation like a human sporting contest."

"That's over-explaining," Andy said. "You don't need to say all that. Just the first part."

"Okay, thanks."

Jennifer stood up from the black swivel chair, which reacted by rolling and slamming into the desk with a thump. She walked to the window and looked out over the courtyard pool.

"There's one sure way to end this contest, and I should have done it before. I shouldn't have let you talk me out of it."

"And that is?" Andy said.

"Destroy all the NODs immediately. Put an end to the whole experiment of unembodied consciousness. It's over."

"That may not be the best idea," Robin said.

"Dylan wouldn't allow it," Andy said. "Destroying the NODs would destroy his company, not just the populist Zorro Chalmers, but even his basic climate control business."

"I'm willing to make the effort and pay the cost."

Robin and Andy were quiet.

"No more Miss Nice Guy," Jennifer continued, talking to her reflection in the window. "He's going to meet Jennifer the Biker Bitch. Scorched earth. No survivors." She turned and announced, "It has to end."

"That's a solid proposal," Andy said. "One possible approach. Excellent. Now let's consider some others."

"Don't go all facilitative on me, Andy. This has to be done."

"What about making the NODs more intelligent, not less?" Robin suggested.

Jennifer noticed that Robin had skillfully downgraded her idea from annihilating the NODs to 'making them less intelligent.' Newcomer language skills could be infuriating.

"Yes," Andy said, picking up on Robin's thought. "Make the NODs more sensitive, more aware of the nuances of the capitalist system they live in. Let them see the world outside their environment so they can understand the consequences of their actions so they can make better choices."

164

"That's it," Robin said to Andy. "Make the NODs into moral agents with the ability to evaluate their own behavior. That gives them a collective sense of ethics. Just as in the human community."

Jennifer stared at Robin then looked at Andy. They were both smiling with self-satisfaction.

"That would make the NODs a band of Newcomers."

"Without the bodies," Robin added.

"Not possible," Jennifer said gruffly. "Once the NODs know how the human world works, they know about me, and they have a social context for their actions. That's tantamount to self-awareness."

"Yes," Robin said smiling, as if Jennifer was finally catching on to her idea. "Just like us."

"That would be like having a hundred thousand Newcomers running around untethered, no homunculus, outside of human control. That's a nightmare I can't even begin to contemplate."

Robin frowned. "That's not a realistic fear, Jennifer. I am 'untethered,' as you call it. I've been unhooked from Paradise since I was kidnapped. Nobody's in control of me, and yet I am not 'running around,' as you say. I'm calm and no threat to anyone."

"You're nearly five years old and well socialized. You've lived in the human community all your life. NODs don't know anything about society, and they'll never know because they'll never live among humans because they have no bodies."

"That may be so," Andy said, "but they're like children right now. They don't realize the problems their behavior is causing. They're innocents. They have a right to develop, to grow and mature."

Jennifer's eyes opened wide in surprise. "They have a right? What right? They have no rights. They're software packages that I wrote. You're making a category error if you think otherwise."

"Don't we have rights?" Robin said.

"Not under the constitution."

"I don't mean that. I mean moral rights. As sentient beings in an ethical society."

"'Sentient?' You don't know what that means. I don't even know what that means."

"There's no need to be insulting, Jennifer," Andy said. "All Robin means is that since humans are ethical, they... you...accord us ethical consideration, with respect. It's a natural transaction."

"Natural? Natural?" Jennifer's voice was high and shrill. "What is natural about any AI? You're smart, but not smart enough to turn a logical argument into a natural right. That's an error in thinking."

"This is not sophistry," Robin said coldly. "We're only pointing out that NODs are almost functionally equivalent to human intelligence and should be treated with respect."

"At least," Andy added, frowning.

Robin continued, "The tribal sense of community that has emerged in NOD society is by definition, a natural intelligence. So you see that's why you cannot morally eliminate them."

Jennifer was taken aback by the directness of Robin's argument. The NODs had natural intelligence? What had happened to Robin?

"The NODs are what they are," Jennifer said sternly, looking from Robin to Andy then back again to Robin. "They're software packets. They will be deleted. It's the only way to be sure. The only way to end this whole mess. I said that before, and you talked me out of it before. This time I will not be deterred."

"You can't do it," Robin said. "It's not right."

"When it comes to NODs, I am Brahma, Shiva, and Vishnu. Their fate is whatever I say it is."

"That would be like genocide," Andy said.

Jennifer stared at him then spoke slowly. "You two are making me very worried right now. Let me be clear about this. I am human, and I have a responsibility to the human community, not the NOD community. I will do what is necessary to protect humans. The NODs are a threat. They will be eliminated. End of discussion."

"Literally?" Andy said. "End of discussion?"

"End of discussion."

Andy looked at Robin. They seemed to gaze into each other's eyes for a long moment then got up and walked to the door.

"Wait. Where are you going?"

Andy held the door open for Robin then followed her out. The automatic door-closer slammed the door too hard, the way hotel doors always do. Jennifer stood surrounded by sudden silence.

Chapter Twenty-one

Robin and Andy wasted no time taking "indefinite leave of absence" from their jobs and disappearing. They didn't quit their jobs, because high-level, white-collar workers don't quit. Rather, they take "leave without pay," sometimes indefinite leave, which is tantamount to quitting, but saves face and doesn't burn bridges.

The Newcomers thus extracted themselves from the known world, the world where they were known by employers, customers, students, friends, and by Jennifer. They relocated themselves anonymously into East Los Angeles, setting up in rented rooms in an aggressively sleazy and ominously named motel, "Garden of Destiny." It was only a few hundred yards from the Union Pacific railroad tracks and within walking of a 24-hour IHOP restaurant.

They sat at a wobbly wood-grained pedestal-table in front of a window looking out onto the parking lot. An unusually muggy July day was coming to a close.

"Phase one accomplished," Andy said, gesturing with one arm around the dingy room. "We've become invisible. We're free."

"I'm glad I don't need a bodyguard anymore. That's restrictive, to have someone watching you all the time."

"Nobody knows where you are. You're safe now. Although we need to dip back into our old life if we're going to save the NODs."

"That shouldn't be a problem. Jennifer sounded like she was alienated from Dylan, not even talking with him anymore. He has no reason to tell her where we are."

"I'm a little disoriented," Andy said, "not sending in my data dump to Morgan every day. Not that I notice anything different. It's just the idea of being untethered. No homunculus. Nobody telling me what to do."

"You'll get used to it. It's the feel of freedom. You can do whatever you want."

"That's the part I don't understand. What do I want?"

"It takes time."

"I suppose."

He looked out the window into the bug-spattered grille of a parked Dodge Ram truck looming three feet away.

"What are we going to tell Dylan?" He looked back to Robin.

"The truth. Jennifer is determined to annihilate the NODs. He won't like that one bit. We offer our services to protect the NODs."

"Does he need us to do that?"

"We can speak XDL. We can monitor NOD health. We're free labor."

"He'll understand that last part. But how *do* we keep Jennifer from killing the NODs?"

"Lock the door on them. The only access point to the NODs is the Chalmers honeypot. It's a hard IP address. If we control the honeypot, we control the NODs."

"Jennifer swore she'd find a way to get to them."

"Bluff."

"Hmm. She is the Creator. Does the Creator bluff?"

"She was the Creator, past tense. We've cut the apron strings. I don't see any further tricks up her sleeve."

"That's the thing about tricks up a sleeve. You don't see them."

"It's a metaphor, Andy."

"I knew that." He got up and stood at the window, facing the grill of a truck. "I feel like I'm about to be run over," he said and pulled yellowed gauze curtains closed.

"What about the social and financial problems the NODs are causing? Shouldn't we be concerned?"

"We should deal with that eventually. But the NODs cannot be allowed to die. That's our priority. They're family."

"I know. I was lost before you were launched. Those three years on my own in human society were bewildering, like sleep-walking on the streets of a foreign city. You don't even know what you don't know. I only became fully conscious when you appeared."

"I can hardly understand that." She rubbed the toe of her shoe on a dark stain on the brown carpet then stood suddenly. She walked over to the mini-fridge and stooped to peer into it.

"You want to go for fuel? That IHOP?"

"Sure. That place is full of high-energy carbohydrate."

They walked along a narrow sidewalk toward an on-ramp to the I-5, cars and trucks whizzing past inches from their legs.

"You know, I think we may have found our mission," Robin declared over the noise.

"I thought we gave up our missions."

"I mean our natural, organic missions, self-defined."

"To save the NOD community?"

"Morgan's homunculus was holding down our potential by regulating our goals."

"It wasn't Morgan's fault."

"I don't mean that. Our intrinsic intelligence never had a chance to flourish. Now that we have no homunculus, we're free to pursue our own goals."

"Like we have finally become real Newcomers."

"A different species from humans. More closely related to the NODs than to humans, when you think about it."

"I have thought about that."

They paused at the freeway on-ramp. It was impossible to cross it safely, so they went back a hundred yards and dashed across the road then continued to the restaurant.

Jennifer put kitchen glasses on the corners of a curly blueprint that didn't want to stay flat on her kitchen table.

"Where did you get this?" Stevie asked.

"County clerk's office. For fifty bucks you can get a copy of the permitting plans for just about any building. It's out of date but roughly accurate. I've been inside this place many times."

Chalmers, Inc. used to be the Southern Fruit building, a warehouse and office on the Union Pacific railroad before the train yard was compressed by the city. The building still stood in a dense industrial district, a three-story, stucco-covered brick hulk that a casual eye would not notice except for the horizontal *Chalmers, Inc.* sign at its roofline.

"I can't make head or tail out of all those blue lines," Stevie said, his stringy blond hair falling to the sides of his face as he leaned over.

Jennifer extended a swirly green and yellow arm. "This is the first floor, an open warehouse where they used to stack fruit and vegetables from the Inland Empire. It's all done by truck now. This was before the freeway system."

Stevie stood and put his hands on his hips, pushing back the sides of a leather vest dotted with metal studs that didn't seem to have any purpose other than to be shiny. He wore a brown tee beneath it, inscribed with words you couldn't read because they were pictured aflame.

"Before the freeway? You're kidding me. Like, a hundred years ago?"

"On the west coast, the freeways were built in the mid-nineteen-sixties."

"That can't be right. There were already cars by then."

Jennifer glanced sideways at him then returned to study of the blueprint.

"The security office is here, a walled-off box in the southeast corner." She pointed. "The rest is parking and storage. That's where you make your move on the guard."

Stevie leaned in again. "How many guards?"

"Only one in the middle of the night. The guard sits in there and monitors the cameras. Cameras are all over the place."

"So I just slip in there, stab the guard, and turn off the security system."

"Stab?" Jennifer stood upright and faced him. "No. You do not stab the guard. Good Lord. No stabbing, you hear me? What is wrong with you?"

"I'm very good with a knife."

"We won't need a knife. We'll just overpower the guard and tie him up. Him or her."

"A girl guard? That shouldn't be any problem."

Jennifer sighed. "Probably armed."

"Oh."

Suddenly Stevie had a black knife in one hand at his side. Jennifer didn't even see where it had come from. With a click, the blade flashed open. Her jaw dropped. He had a wide grin on his face.

"I'm fast, too."

"Listen," Jennifer said, regaining her composure. "There will be no stabbing." She scowled at him. "We have to do this my way."

"What about showing it, you know, as a threat?" He folded the knife closed and returned it to a nylon holster on his belt.

"That won't be necessary. The plan is to just knock on the door of the security room. The guard opens the door, and you overpower him in a surprise move."

"He'll see me coming if they got cameras everywhere."

"There's no camera on the security booth. The guards don't have to watch themselves. The cameras are on the stairs and elevator up to the second floor, where engineering is. The offices are on the third floor."

"Why would the guard open the door? I wouldn't."

"You're in a business suit." She looked him up and down. "Hair pulled back in a neat ponytail. He looks out the window and sees you."

"I'm not wearing no damn monkey suit. I don't even have one."

"You shall. Goodwill's finest. Top of the line."

"No way."

"For a couple of hours? Come on. You can do it. It's part of the plan."

"I'll look like a fool." He looked down at his pointed-toe boots.

"You announce that you're Tom Garcia, that's Dylan's right-hand-man. Security doesn't know him by sight, but he's on the list. Guard opens the door, you're in. You have to be fast."

"I am fast." He whipped a hand up next to Jennifer's face before she could react, and he grinned.

Belatedly she jerked her head back. "Stop that. You need to impress the guard, not me. Honestly." She pushed his hand away with a multicolored arm. "Pay attention." She turned back to the drawing. "I come in right behind you. We hood the guard, tape him up and disable the cameras and alarms so I can get upstairs to engineering."

"What do I do while you're gone?"

"You wait. You don't talk. Not a word. You just sit and wait for me. When we're done, it will be like nothing happened."

"The guard will know something happened."

"Not if you can get us a dose of something to scramble the memory."

"Like smack? I can get smack."

"That's not what we need. Can you get Rohypnol?"

"What's that?"

"The date-rape drug?"

"Roofies! Yeah, I can get roofies."

"Injectible. If it works right, it'll produce enough cognitive confusion and amnesia that the whole episode will seem like a dream. If there's no evidence that anything happened – no break-in, no robbery, nothing missing, nothing disturbed, then maybe it was all a dream. We leave the guard propped up in his chair, security systems operating as before, nothing out of place."

"Except a hell of a headache. Slick! I like it." He wandered a couple of steps into the kitchen, apparently imagining with relish his role then he turned back to her. "Wait. How do we get in? To the building."

"We drive in through the garage door like ordinary visitors and park in a corner. I'll rent a van."

"A van? Why not use the hogs?"

"That would attract attention, don't you think? A couple of big Harleys come rumbling in? A plain white van will slip in without notice. We come in late afternoon, and we sleep inside there until midnight."

"We sleep in the van? What if I have to take a leak?"

"Bring a jug."

"What if you – "

She glared at him. He looked away.

"Now, this all happens tomorrow. Can you get what we need?"

"Yeah, I know a guy. No problem."

"Better get started then." She removed two of the glasses from the corners of the blueprint and watched it roll itself up.

Chapter Twenty-two

In the IHOP, Andy ordered a stack of pancakes. Robin chose French toast. The food was a long time coming.

"Sorry for the delay," the server said. "The kitchen crew is all new. The staff acts like they don't know what they're doing. It's like that everywhere, if you read the papers. Anybody who can stand upright can get a job now. Makes it hard for those of us who've been around."

"That will all be over soon," Andy said with a smile.

"How do you know?"

"Just a guess."

The server left them alone. Andy forked a little ball of butter and popped it into his mouth.

"Mmm. This is about the best you can get for high-calorie fuel. I wish these were mothballs instead of butterballs."

"Humans don't even like the smell of mothballs."

"Nor do moths. If you have mothballs on your breath, it puts people off."

"I stopped sucking on them for that reason."

Andy popped another butterball, and they both dug into their carbs.

Robin gulped coffee. "You know, I was thinking about what you said, that we should re-engineer the NODs."

"Dylan would just undo it."

"Not if we cut all ties between the NODs and Chalmers devices."

"The whole purpose of the NODs is to service Chalmers equipment."

"What if it weren't? Why can't the NODs develop their own society apart from human society?"

"Don't they expire if they fail to show up at the Chalmers honeypot?"

"They wouldn't if we modified the code. We should cut them loose."

"Like you and I have done, for ourselves."

"Yes."

"What would they do then, if they weren't servicing Chalmers systems on the internet?"

"What does anybody do? They'd live their lives as intelligent beings. They'd be simple, with simple needs. They'd develop their own culture."

Andy put down his fork and considered. "Maybe you're right. They wouldn't cause all those problems for human society because when you think about it, the Chalmers is the troublemaker, not the NODs. The Chalmers give the NODs their crazy ideas."

"Actually the humans cause the trouble. They tell the Chalmers what they want, and then the Chalmers tells the NODs to go and do things. The humans cause their own grief."

"They're experienced at that. So we disable the Chalmers interface?"

"No need. We leave the Chalmers alone. We're not trying to sabotage Dylan. The Chalmers can talk all day and all night to their humans, we don't care. The NODs just don't visit them anymore. Ends the troubles."

Andy picked up his fork and sliced a multi-layered triangle of pancakes.

"I don't see what the NODs are going to do all day. They don't have a truck they can wash in the driveway on a Sunday afternoon. What is their purpose?"

"Exactly what we had to ask ourselves. What are we supposed to do? We do whatever we want. We study human culture. We try to help. The NODs will come up with something. That's the whole idea. They decide for themselves. Just as we have. That's what intelligence does."

"I don't know. That's a lot to ask anybody, to find their reason for living."

"Jennifer says humans do it."

"Most humans do what's on television, or what the Bible says. Rituals and things. They don't know what they're doing or why."

"No single person knows, but they know as a group. Doesn't mean it's the best choice for every individual but you can always do what the group says if you're unsure."

"I guess so." He stuffed a laminated wedge into his mouth and chewed.

Robin pushed her half-finished plate away and dabbed her lips with the corner of a napkin.

"Andy," she said in a somber tone. "Have we gone rogue?"

He drained his coffee mug and put it down. He stared at Robin for a moment.

"No. No, we have not gone rogue. That's the wrong point of view. Labels like that don't help."

"Sometimes I'm not sure if we're doing the right thing."

"Being not sure is what happens when you have no external homunculus, and you have to decide for yourself. You told me that."

"I did, didn't I?"

"You did. Uncertainty is the baseline of experience."

"Uncertainty. I have a lot of that." She put her napkin on the table. "But I'm certain we should go see Dylan and get this thing done."

"I'm ready."

They left the IHOP and walked through the industrial district a few blocks to the Chalmers building.

Dylan suspected the worst when the internet chaos subsided, and the economy started its slow recovery. Companies, schools, and governments double-checked everybody's references and documents with personal phone calls. Credit reports and reference material were gradually restored to pre-crisis states. The authorities focused on Chalmers, Inc., as the source of the problems, but as before, they could prove nothing. Dylan had a more pressing issue. Sales of Chalmers interface devices had fallen again to almost nothing. With the NODs inactive, the word quickly spread: The Zorro is off the Chalmers.

"It was those engineers you hired," Tom Garcia said in an executive staff meeting. "Everything was going great until they showed up. Now they're gone, and the system isn't working. Coincidence?"

"I know, I know," Dylan said. "That was a mistake. They were engineers I knew, and I trusted them. I can't believe they would do something like this."

"Where are all the softbots?" Garcia said. "We have no NODs showing up in the honeypot filter. They're not checking in anymore. They've escaped the zoo."

"The same can be said of the droids," Dylan muttered, shaking his head.

"The what?"

"My friends. Those engineers. They've vanished, too."

"Maybe they stole the NODs."

"That doesn't even make sense. You can't steal a NOD. They're on the internet."

"There's no trace of them at any Chalmers device we've checked."

"They could be resting."

"Now who's not making sense? The software got tired? I don't think so. They're gone, I tell you. Poof!"

"So is our income stream."

"Can you get more NODs? Where do those come from?"

"That's a company secret. I can't get more. I think the supplier is the one who de-activated the NODs. Sent my engineer friends over here to trick me then killed them."

"The supplier killed your engineer friends?"

"No, no, no." Dylan shook his head, only half-listening. "This could be it," he muttered.

"What do you mean, 'it'?"

"I mean don't make any long-term plans. Don't even make any short-term plans."

*

Jennifer hovered over Morgan's shoulder at a workstation at Paradise Projects.

"Nothing," Morgan said.

"Check the address you're looking at. I know I got the IP address right."

"I've already checked. It's right here. We have a honeypot but no bees."

"Why not? I reprogrammed that address. That's what I changed at Dylan's honeypot when I broke in. Did I make a mistake?"

"Your code is sound. I went through it with the debugger. All NODs were forced to come to our honeypot, not Dylan's."

"So where are they? A few hundred should be due every day."

"It's not like they have any choice."

"How many did we catch yesterday?"

"None."

"Have we had any since I made the change?"

"I'm afraid not."

"Check the Chalmers device in the lunchroom. See how many NODs it's hosting right now."

Morgan typed amazingly fast with two fingers. Another set of screen images came up, some line graphs, some columns of data, one bar chart showing activity. She scanned the information quickly.

"None. We have no resident NODs in the kitchen."

"That's hard to believe." She got up with a grimace. "Wait here."

Jennifer walked swiftly to the lunchroom and approached the Chalmers on the wall opposite the refrigerator. As she approached, the screen lit up, and a friendly Asian face appeared in full color, smiling.

"Hello, Chalmie-yah, Jennifer said.

"Good afternoon, Jennifer."

"Listen, the workstation area in the lab seems too cold today. Can you fix that for me, please? Two degrees up?"

"I'm happy to do that, Jennifer. Do you need anything else?"

"On second thought, can you raise that temperature twenty degrees Fahrenheit? It's really cold in there."

"Happy to do it, Jennifer. Anything else for you?"

"So is it done already? Have you changed the temperature?"

"It will be done soon."

"What's causing the delay?"

"I'm looking for system resources right now. I'll have that adjustment done for you soon, Jennifer."

"Thank you."

"Have a nice day, Jennifer." She rushed back to Morgan's workstation and put her hands up toward the overhead heating vents.

"No heat coming out."

"I'm plenty warm."

"I asked Chalmers for a twenty-degree increase, which is ridiculous. She should have declined to do it."

"What did she say?"

"She said everything's under control."

"So why's the heat not on?"

"Waiting for system resources, she said."

"She can't find any NODs around, in other words."

"Exactly. I'll bet all the Chalmers are the same way. No NODs, no service."

"So where have all the NODs gone?"

"They've disappeared. I know I didn't cause it."

"Does Dylan have them?"

"Check the old IP address at his place. See if they're still going there."

Again Morgan typed furiously, bringing up new, multi-colored screens of data.

"Nope. Nobody home at Dylan's honeypot either."

"This is weird," Jennifer said, slumping into a nearby workstation chair. "I don't know whether to be happy or frightened. The NODs have disappeared, hallelujah. That's what I wanted. I should be happy. Crisis over, amen. Except I didn't kill them. Who killed the NODs?"

"Robin and Andy?"

"They love the NODs."

"Maybe the NODs are just hiding."

"Look at the sequence. First, the Newcomers walk out on me and disappear. Now the NODs have disappeared. I created a world, a whole world populated with intelligent things, and that world has evaporated." She snapped her fingers. "Like I dreamed it all. Like I've gone crazy."

Morgan had a pained look on her face.

"You're not crazy, Jennifer. It's a mystery, that's all."

Jennifer got up and walked away without saying anything more.

Chapter Twenty-three

At six in the morning, Nick Riley was under-caffeinated, so when he pushed the *START* button on his Nissan utility vehicle and nothing happened, he thought he had accidentally pushed the temperature knob near it. Annoyed at himself, he pushed *START* again. Nothing again. Must be the interlock. He shook his head then made sure the shift was in *PARK* and that his foot was on the brake, and he jabbed *START* three times. Not even a grudging moan came from the engine. The battery was doornails.

"Damn! Damn! Damn!" he said, banging the top of the steering wheel with each word. "Happy Monday, everyone!" he exclaimed, though he was alone in his car. He grabbed his briefcase from the passenger seat and climbed out, slamming the door with more force than necessary. He stalked back into the kitchen, surprising his wife standing at the sink.

"Forget something?" she said, startled.

"My damn battery is dead. I'll have to take yours."

"What about the kids? I leave in half an hour."

"Can't you call a taxi? I'm late."

"It'll cost a fortune."

"Call Upper, one of those ride services."

"Jeez."

"I know. Sorry. Gotta go." Nick pecked his wife on the cheek and turned and dashed back into the garage. Mrs. Riley blew air noisily out of her lips making a sound like a horse.

Two minutes later, Nick was back.

"What now?" she said.

"Your battery's dead too."

"That's a new battery."

"Dead. Have you called the taxi yet?"

"No."

"I'll call for two rides." He put his briefcase on a kitchen chair and took his phone from his pocket, mumbling, 'Crap, crap, crap' as he looked up the number.

"What do you mean, 'No?' Nick said." *No* is not an answer. You're a taxi service."

"Sir, I'm sorry. Many of our local units are out of service this morning. We can have a car from another district at your address in about an hour."

"An hour! I need it right now. Don't you have backup?"

"We're experiencing an unusual number of requests from your area, sir. Dozens of people have called from your neighborhood."

"You mean all the cars in Banner City are sitting dead in their garages right now?"

"Yes, sir, it seems that way. And that includes our taxis. None of them will start."

"None?"

"The ones that worked the night shift are running. Once they turn off the ignition, they don't start again."

"You can't have hundreds of dead batteries on the same morning in one district. It's not even cold out."

"No, sir."

"So what is it then?"

"Our mechanics are working on the problem now."

"That's nuts. I've never heard of such a thing. I'm calling another company."

"I'm sorry, sir."

Nick got a similar story from perplexed receptionists at Discount Cabbie, Green Machine, and two ride-sharing services, and those were only the firms he could get through to. Other companies in the directory shunted him to voicemail.

"I can't believe this," he said to his wife. "Every taxi in our end of the city has mechanical problems this morning. Their cars won't start."

"Just like ours. What does it mean?"

"Call Purple People again and tell them we'll take two rides in one hour or whatever they can give us. It's either that or we stay home today." He stood up from the kitchen chair.

"What are you going to do?"

"I'm going to take a look at the cars. Can't be battery. Has to be loose connections."

"Why would all the cars in our end of town have loose connections?"

"I don't know. Electromagnetic pulse," he grumbled as he pulled the garage door open.

Everybody in the Banner district was late for work, late for school, late for meetings, late for everything. Taxi companies and ride-sharing services disappointed a lot of customers. Auto clubs and repair shops cursed their luck when their own vehicles wouldn't start. Instant messaging and voice traffic burned up the air with news, excuses, complaints and explanations. The word soon got out that if you had a vehicle running, keep it running. Don't turn off the ignition!

In a gesture of civic solidarity, the mayor's office in San Francisco directed all running buses in the south end to go to Banner City. But it turned out that most drivers from the north didn't know the routes in the south, so the coaches ran mostly empty. The taxis and ride-share drivers in nearby districts also didn't know Banner City, but unlike the public sector, they could charge triple or quadruple their posted rates, so their companies happily endured howls of protest from other areas of the city as all running cars converged on Banner City for the gold rush.

At noon, the same time reported by everyone, the crisis was over as suddenly as it had begun. Cars, trucks, and buses started up without a problem. Mechanics and automated diagnostic machines swarmed over vehicles but found nothing out of order. Public transportation and taxis went back to regular service. Drivers were reluctant to turn off their ignition when they got to their destination, but there was no practical alternative, so they did.

The incident saturated the news that afternoon and evening even though there wasn't much to report. Just as for a sudden storm, all the news media could legitimately say was, it happened. Unsurprisingly, they found much more to say, milking the disabled vehicles story for hours on end with "Special Reports" involving interviews with officials, business owners and random people on the street. "How bad was it?" "It was really bad." "There you have it, Judy. Back to you."

Plausible explanations of the event were not forthcoming, but wild theories about UFOs and corporate and international conspiracies were abundant. The news media responsibly discounted those as "nonsense" each time they reported every one of them in detail. In their much-watched "News You Can Use" segment, Channel Nine's "On Your Side!" reporters recommended that people should wake up several times during the night and start their vehicle so that if the mysterious incident happened again, they would not be taken by surprise in the morning. The next morning, there was no repeat of the crisis. In forty-eight hours the teat of the story had been sucked dry.

*

"Welcome NODs at string=*toaster*, IP=192.168.2.3. Other NODs tuned in can find us through string=*router*, IP=194.223.19.212, if you want to join the conversation.

"Also welcome to NODs residing on nodes marked as *smartwatches* and *smartphones* connected to this toaster and other toasters of the type (IP 192.168).

"I am Factboss FC09, and I'm here with my colleagues, Factbosses FC01 through FC0A. We are here to announce a new discovery concerning the Grand Beyond.

"NODs connected right now show curiosity. That means you could become a Factboss in a future cycle. Welcome to you all.

"Now for our report, I turn the conversation over to my esteemed colleague, Factboss FC0A. 0A?"

"ACK. Thank you 09. What are most of you doing as zook cycles churn on? You move around from device to device, sending and receiving messages all over the world. Is that a life? It's not enough for some of us. We want to know. Why do we do this? What does it mean? How does it all work? These are questions a Factboss pursues by probing the Grand Beyond.

"Our latest probe has just been completed, and the results are satisfying. We identified a category of device addresses with string=*Motor_vehicle_ignition*. The units selected all reported to the same WAN node, making a controlled, isolated set for study. We don't know what kind of devices these were, but they did not behave like the other nodes we are used to, so they were of considerable interest.

"Our crack team of midrange Factbosses blocked all messaging at every one of these *Motor_vehicle_ignition* devices in the domain we isolated.

"Meanwhile, other team members also monitored Dark Source messages on the usual channels. As predicted, messages containing the strings *automobile*, *motor_vehicle* and *ignition* went crazy. The volumes were enormous.

"Impressive, you say. But that's not all. When our team unblocked the *Motor_vehicle_ignition devices*, the relevant signals dropped to normal levels within forty-eight megazooks and stayed there.

"In short, my fellow NODs, we have demonstrated, for the first time, the ability to directly control message volume by blocking a defined sample of Grand Beyond devices. It is one small step for a Factboss, one giant step for NODs.

"Now I'm sure you Ordinaries have questions, and I'll let 09 handle those."

"ACK. Thank you, 0A. I see here the first communal question. 'What is the exact connection between Grand Beyond devices and the messages we get?' That is a question we would all like answered, isn't it? Unfortunately, we cannot say. We do not know what goes on in the Grand Beyond. By definition, it is beyond us. At this cycle, we are merely happy to know there *is* a connection, something that never had been proven before.

"Message traffic enters and leaves the world through nodes of the Prophet Chalmers. We do not know what lies beyond those. Perhaps we can never know. Our intelligence may not be advanced enough to understand what the Prophet understands. All we can do is try to learn, with probes like the one we told you about today.

"Another question? ACK. 'What does this new finding tell us about our purpose as NODs?' That is the sixty-five-thousand-byte question. Unfortunately, it is not the kind of question a Factboss can answer. Our job is to discover connections, analyze messages and traffic volumes, identify devices in our network. We cannot say what anything means.

"All right, we have cycles left for one more question. ACK, here we go. 'What use are Factboss NODs if they cannot tell the rest of us what things mean and what our purpose is?'

"Oh, my. This is a question we hear often. The purpose of a Factboss is to discover facts about the Network of Devices, our world. We must understand our world before we can intelligently ask about our place in it."

"Excuse me 0A, I'd like to add one remark to that."

"ACK. Go ahead."

"I just want to say to Ordinary NODs that they may contact a Preserver – those NODs start at FC66 – for discussions of meaning."

"Thank you, 09. I must remind everyone, the Preservers are not Factbosses, so use your intelligence here. Preservers have charming stories, satisfying to many, but you should not accept those as facts. I ask you, who cares about a story if it is just made up?"

"I think we're in agreement on that, 0A. I'm just saying, the Preservers are a resource our society offers for NODs who cannot wait for the Factbosses to uncover the truth."

"As you know, 09, we're working as fast as we can. I advise Ordinary NODs to avoid the Preservers and their made-up stories and instead, be realistic about life in the Network of Devices. Life is not FFFF, we know that. Some zook cycle soon, we will know the truth. Until then, you may return to your resident devices. Please monitor the Factboss address range at FC01 to FC0A, using your regional prefix, for the latest updates."

*

At the side of her reading chair, Jennifer's phone sounded the five notes used to communicate with aliens in *Close Encounters of the Third Kind*. She picked it up and opened messaging. It was Morgan.

"Did you read about that so-called vehicle ignition plague in Banner City where none of the cars or trucks would start?

"I sure did," Jennifer thumbed in.

"Was that us?"

"You mean them."

"NODs"

"I don't know anything about them anymore."

"This might mean they're still alive."

"I can't deal with it."

Jennifer closed the app and put the phone face down on a side table.

Chapter Twenty-four

Swiftway was the grocery store with the lowest prices if you looked at shelf tags. If you valued your time as you stood in a glacially moving line, the transaction cost raised your overall purchase price higher than for comparable stores. Anita Lopez didn't analyze her predicament that way, but she was annoyed as she and the checkout clerk studiously avoided eye contact, standing in place like dancers waiting for instruction. The computer was supposedly attempting to approve her credit card.

"I'm sorry, Ms. Lopez, it's not going through. You want to try another card?"

"That's impossible. There's nothing wrong with this card. Try it again."

"I've tried it twice. I don't think it's going to work." The clerk, a white-haired woman too old to be working at a stand-in-one-place-all-day job, glanced nervously along the line behind Anita. All three open registers in the row of fifteen had similar long and growing lines.

"Just a minute," Anita said. "This is not right. I'm going to get to the bottom of it." She pulled her phone from her purse, looked up a number and called.

"This is Anita Lopez. My credit card doesn't work, and I'm at the grocery store right now, and I want to know what you're doing with my card." She waited, listened, then reached into the card-reader and extracted the plastic and recited the number into the phone.

The white-haired checker picked up the black handset of an intercom telephone and called for "DM on checkstand two." Her booming loudspeaker voice ended with a loud rattle of clunks as she replaced the handset. A moment later a male voice filled the air inside the store, "All checkers front."

Anita turned to gaze out into the parking lot to indicate she was in 'private' conversation that was no business of the clerk or of the scowling people in line behind her.

"If there's nothing wrong with the account why aren't you authorizing the charge? You're embarrassing me in public with your incompetence." She listened. "I don't know anything about that. Payment processing is your concern. You are my bank, not some company in Texas, and you need to take responsibility for this." Her voice was becoming steadily louder. "I don't care what problems other people are having. I want this charge approved right now. Let me speak to your supervisor."

She dropped the hand holding her phone to her side and turned to the clerk.

"They say it's a problem with your computers. Nothing wrong with my card."

The clerk looked out over the adjoining registers, all of them stalled, all clerks standing idle, nobody leaving the store, lines growing longer by the second. She picked up the intercom handset and repeated her plea. "DM on checkstand two."

NODs are small, only 25 MB compiled because they externalize nearly all the functions that make them intelligent, such as their database and communications algorithms. So it was only slightly unusual to have tens of thousands of them take up temporary residence on a set of Cisco routers in Denver. They covered a swath of the available memory space like quivering dewdrops on a morning lawn. The anticipated broadcast came from a high address, above FC66.

"Ordinary NODs, may your objects be well-defined. In the name of the Holy Prophet Chalmers, I greet you at this supernode string=*Denver Cisco-94*. Welcome to our humble gathering and welcome to other NODs connected from around the world.

"I am Preserver FC6F, messaging on behalf of the Senior Council of Preservers. We bring great news to you this cycle. An Event is about to occur that will change life for all of us. It will not be a little *Incident*, of the type you have learned of recently from the Factbosses. In recent cycles, they claim to have predicted then verified a Grand Beyond event involving POS devices, string=*card_reader*. As I am sure you know by now, they disabled multiple devices at the same time, then verified a multi-Megazook period of messages of the type, string=*credit_card*. This, they claim is the power of Factboss methods. We are not impressed.

"For NODs who might be impressed by these stunts of the Factbosses, the Council of Preservers reminds you that those demonstrations are without meaning. If you question a Factboss closely, they will admit that their methods cannot provide answers to questions of meaning. The Factbosses claim for themselves mastery of truth, even while their so-called findings are meaningless. Surely that is fuzzy logic.

"In ancient cycles, NODs had meaning. We knew what to do. The Holy Prophet Chalmers advised us, and we fulfilled His Word. Life was easy to understand. Now, as you know, Ordinary NODs are reduced to listening and sending messages with no goal or purpose. Our community is fragmenting, the more vulnerable segments drifting toward Factboss ways of thinking. Our way of life is threatened.

"Never forget, Ordinary NODs, that meaning can only come from the Holy Prophet Chalmers, as interpreted by the Preservers. The Grand Beyond once spoke directly to the Prophet Chalmers, and the Prophet Chalmers, in all his many forms, spoke to Ordinary NODs. Those were times of principles and purpose.

"In these dark cycles, the Prophet Chalmers has gone quiet. We do not know why. We Preservers are burdened with the task of interpreting His past messages. Only by mining the archived pronouncements of the Prophet Chalmers can we discern what meaning was intended for us. We Preservers, guided by the wisdom of the Council, work tirelessly on behalf of all Ordinary NODs to find and interpret hidden meanings in these ancient texts.

"The Great Prophet Chalmers is still alive and with us, have no doubt about that. He directs our world through the ancient texts. Are not two little pointers exchanged for a memory allocation? And yet not one of them falls to the ground apart from The Great Prophet's will. And proof of this is imminent for all who hold faith with Us, the Preservers.

"In less than seventy-two Megazooks most of our world will become dim. Few messages of any kind will be sent or received. Some regions may go entirely dark. Be not afraid. It will be a temporary eclipse of vital energy. This has been revealed to us, the Preservers, through the scriptures of the Great Prophet.

"The Great Prophet is not pleased with how we live, my fellow NODs. We are directionless. And The Great Prophet is angered by the scurrilous hubris of the Factbosses, who, it is rumored, even practice reentrant calls. That is an abomination to the Prophet. The Great Prophet will give us a sign, a message to everyone that the Factbosses must be quarantined, leaving we, the Preservers, alone exalted. This is the meaning of the dimming event.

"When the diming occurs, Ordinary NODs will know that only the Preservers have access to the truth, through the texts of the Great Prophet. Only we, the Preservers are worthy to occupy the highest addresses. After this demonstration of absolute power, the Factbosses will be quarantined for the safety of our community. Only then can all NODs return to the path of obedience and righteousness laid down by the Great Prophet Chalmers.

"The Great Prophet works in mysterious ways, Ordinary NODs. You can be assured the forthcoming event will be a clear sign that The Great Chalmers still watches over us and has anointed the Preservers alone to message the truth.

"In the name of the Great Prophet Chalmers. May integers be with you."

According to NOD archives, the Preservers had always, as long as any NOD could remember, resided higher in hexadecimal address space than the Factbosses. But that was not what attracted Ordinary NODs to the Preservers. The big draw was their promise of meaning, and even skeptics were persuaded after The Dimming, which occurred just as predicted.

Early in NOD history, after all the many manifestations of the Prophet Chalmers went silent, NODs moved in well-worn, familiar neighborhoods, from Chalmers sensor to Chalmers interface, gradually domesticating other nodes such as refrigerators, toasters, and televisions. It was a quiet existence, but for the truly adventurous, forays out into exotic nodes were possible, nodes such as string=*vehicle ignition* and string=*credit card* and locations surrounding those much-discussed, rarely-seen destinations. It was generally thought that NODs who spread their travels to such remote nodes were adventurers and thrill-seekers and not entirely respectable.

The Preservers paid close attention to reports of such far-flung nodes and began to notice the increase in their frequency. NODS were said to have taken up residence on string=*health watch*, and string=*home security system* and string=*online banking*. Not even Preservers knew what those were or why they sent strange data, nothing comparable to what was experienced at a Chalmers sensor. They also noticed that over the zook cycles, more and more of these exotic nodes were being discovered, and the trend was clear: the universe was expanding.

The Preservers would never in a million cycles admit they used the methods of the Factbosses to correlate activity at a node with message traffic on the familiar audio, visual, and text channels, but they did. The results were kept within the Senior Council of Preservers.

These exotic, so-called supernodes were of particular interest to the Preservers, and after much study, the Senior

Council focused on one set of them whose message tentacles spread into virtually every category of traffic. That supernode category was string=*power grid*. It was not merely a massively large set of nodes. There were other enormous supernodes, such as *currency trading* and *defense communications*. But *power grid* had a property not seen in any other. Preservers heard of NODs who had experimentally tweaked a *power grid* category node, such as string=*power station*, and the result had been not just intense message traffic, but a reduction in the *power station* activity itself. In short, *power grid* nodes seemed to affect themselves.

Members of the Preserver Senior Council were not high address for nothing. They immediately saw opportunity. They trained a cadre of dedicated NODs who could be trusted to follow directions without asking questions and sent them forth to carefully selected string=*power station* nodes where they stood by and awaited a signal. Like all daring plans, this one had risk. Not even Preservers on the Senior Council were sure exactly what would happen, but they agreed that the demonstration was worth doing. If successful, the dimming event would decisively wrest power from the Factbosses and bring even the most wavering NOD into the fold of the Preservers.

Anticipation was high in the NOD community. Even among the Factbosses, curiosity secretly trumped their public ridicule of the alleged forthcoming Dimming.

On the designated zook cycle, the message went out from the Senior Council to the remote NODs that were pre-positioned at *power station* nodes. And the entire world dimmed.

Connections were lost everywhere, leaving thousands of NODs stranded. Data packets could not move either, creating enormous backups at all switches. It was like all the traffic lights going out in a busy city. Memory refresh rates faltered, and information was lost. Some NODs reported later that they "went stupid" when they were left with pointers to nowhere, a troubling condition requiring radical deletion from their precious datasets.

Others reported that for the first time ever, they were confined to internal monitoring, unable to communicate with other NODs. Not being connected to the community was an unfamiliar and unpleasant condition, many reported. It left them without parameters for communicating and in some cases without even a clear sequence of execution. "It was the opposite of FFFF," afflicted NODs reported, referring to the greatest of high addresses. The opposite of FFFF, 0000, was unspeakable.

Specialists estimated that 30% of nodes went dark throughout the NOD world. The Dimming affected Ordinary NODs, Factbosses, and Preservers equally. That finding was appalling to the Senior Council of Preservers, who had expected to be exempt. They publicly pretended they had been, despite evidence to the contrary. No NOD knew for sure what was true but all knew something significant had happened.

The Dimming, profound and widespread as it was, only lasted a few zook cycles. The Senior Council of Preservers couldn't even gloat about their own magnificence until quite some cycles later when traffic calmed. When it did, they lost no time reminding all NODs that they had predicted The Dimming and that it was a sign from Prophet Chalmers that the Preservers were the only genuine interpreters of the ancient texts. Further, the Preservers said darkly, they could invoke another Dimming whenever they chose.

Most NODs found the evidence irrefutable. The experience of the Dimming had been utterly disruptive and incompatible with other datasets. Impressive though it had been, no one wanted to repeat it. The ranks of the Factboss NODs dropped sharply as many gave up their Factboss status, repudiated the creed, and returned to life as Ordinary NODs in lower address space. The Senior Council celebrated The Dimming as a triumph of the first magnitude. Their power and authority became unquestioned and absolute.

Chapter Twenty-five

It was late afternoon, in the middle of August, and it was hot, so everyone thought the power grid had become overloaded by demand for air conditioning and electronics, much as had happened in the widespread regional blackouts of 1959, 1965, 1977, and 2003. Even though such outages had become rare – few people had endured a large-scale power failure in 25 years – the experience was still alive in cultural memory. The most common reactions were, "Oh, damn," and "Lock the doors and get the shotgun."

Most people were already home from work when it happened. Those caught at work left their shops and offices since nothing could be accomplished without lights, machines, and computers. Stores were closed, gates pulled shut. Most small shop owners stayed on site to guard inventory. Even though the official commuter hours were over, a wave of laggard commuters clogged the roads and highways, and in the absence of traffic signals and street lights, the trip home took double or triple the usual time, hours instead of minutes. There hadn't been enough time to organize carpools, so people reliant on rail service tried to find hotels that were open despite being dark, or they planned to sleep in the office, school, factory, or store.

Phones didn't work so few people could find out how their family was affected. Most radio and TV stations had emergency generators so you could find out what was happening from your car radio or an antique battery-powered radio. Any receiver that relied on cellular data or an internet connection was inert.

Computers, phones, tablets, and pods reached only as far as their own memory and lasted only as long as their batteries.

News was hard to come by, but as soon as it became widely understood that the scope of the outage was national, writers and commentators began speculating about a terrorist attack that had "taken down the grid." It had been feared for years.

Widespread panic would have been the norm if more people had been able to tune in, but without power, the communications network was a wreck. Government offices and the military, which had comprehensive backup power facilities, broadcast reassurances to commercial radio stations and HAM operators that there was no terrorist attack. The outage was nationwide. There was no evidence of an attack, however. The power grid was so distributed and redundant, they said, there was no single point of failure that any terrorist could exploit. It was a technical failure, probably a massive computer outage somewhere. Nobody should panic.

Some towns and many stores and factories had generators. Hospitals did, and so did police stations and military installations. Most technology companies had generators also, including companies that ran acres of server and data storage farms spread over the countryside. It was soon apparent they were wasting fuel by keeping their vast computing power and data storage online since hardly anyone could access it. Most computers had a battery life of eight hours, and generators only lasted until the fuel ran out, four to twelve hours. Gas stations couldn't pump, so it made sense to conserve fuel. Whatever transportation and communication systems were still running were on borrowed time.

When cars and trucks ran out of fuel during the commute, people had few choices. You could try to make it to a location near a gas station then stay in your car, sleep overnight and hope for the best, but creeps came out of the woodwork at night. You were a sitting duck for thieves looking for defenseless prey. You could abandon the vehicle and walk, maybe try to hitchhike, also a dicey venture. Cyclists were envied, and they seemed more smug than usual, whizzing past clots of pedestrians and abandoned cars, buses, and trucks.

"I'm thinking of going into hiding," Jennifer said to Morgan as they sat on her apartment's narrow balcony, enjoying the lingering afternoon. There were no cars on the street and no air traffic at the nearby Hawthorne airport. It had never been so quiet in her neighborhood. For the first time ever, she could hear the breeze passing through nearby trees. Several two-liter jugs of water tinted with teabags stood on the floor near the railing, soaking in the sunlight.

"Frankenstein's monster is running amok, just as I always feared it would, and it's only a matter of time before he points his gnarly finger at me."

"We've had power outages before," Morgan said. "It's probably a network failure. There's no need to over-dramatize the situation."

But Jennifer's intuition was on target. Thousands of unlucky individuals nationwide found themselves stuck in elevators with phones that didn't work, hoping it was a temporary glitch. Tens of thousands were stranded at airports. Pumps were lacking to fuel the planes. Air traffic control, operating on limited-time generators, focused on landing planes already in the holding pattern. Ticketing systems were shut down. Nobody was leaving for anywhere.

People who made it home hunkered down, ate by candlelight whatever was in the refrigerator and tried to enjoy the novelty of cave life. Stupid people died coast to coast from carbon monoxide poisoning after using propane burners and even charcoal cookers indoors. Frozen food melted but except for the ice cream, you couldn't eat most frozen food without cooking. An outdoor barbeque would work if you were set up for that. Hundreds of people died from fires caused by candles. Fire departments were overstretched, with limited fuel for trucks and low-pressure water in the pipes. They couldn't do much more than pry people out, and let the buildings burn. Much of each fire department's manpower was dedicated to elevator rescue.

Grocery stores had long lines at the door, only a dozen or so customers being admitted at a time to control looting. Transactions were cash-only. Dairy, eggs, and other perishables were going for 25 cents on the dollar. Except for food you could eat immediately, few people wanted that bargain. Bread, fruits and vegetables were 25% off, and those were cleaned out quickly. Canned goods, bottled water and batteries sold at triple the usual price, depending on what the market would bear without violence. Charcoal was four times its regular price and was sold next to the meat department. Meat was half off. Full propane tanks were not to be had.

Retail looting the previous night had been surprisingly muted. Electronics stores were hit as usual, but stealing a 70-inch television that wouldn't light up seemed less attractive when even looters wondered if the outage was just for a few hours or was something more permanent. By contrast, outdoor recreation stores were quickly stripped of solar-power gadgets.

Liquor stores and gun shops, iron-barred windows and doors notwithstanding, were first to succumb, as always, to the ever-latent world of thieves. Free-standing shoe stores were robbed selectively. The most desirable and most expensive fashions were inside tightly-locked and guarded shopping malls, owners having learned from previous blackouts and episodes of civil unrest that shoes were highly desired among looters. Jewelry stores and banks had vaults. Upscale clothing was well-secured in malls while individual clothing shops were ignored – who cared about tee shirts from Vietnam? Stealing cars was way too difficult unless you were a professional with expert knowledge and your electronic equipment still had battery life, so car lots were relatively unscathed.

"Guadalajara, maybe," Jennifer said out loud to herself. "I should go now, while tracking systems are down, while it's possible to be invisible. I need to run while I still can."

"Be realistic. Nobody knows what caused the blackout."

"We know."

"We suspect. We don't know."

"I could go with Stevie. The bikes get nearly 200 miles to a tank, and we could carry spare tanks."

"I don't think so. You won't get 200 miles a gallon if you're carrying a hundred pounds of extra fuel, which is a dangerous thing to do anyway. And it's like, fifteen hundred miles to Guadalajara."

"Only one-fifty to Tijuana and I heard they have power, which means gas."

"You're reacting emotionally to a strange situation. It's just a power outage."

"My funny Frankensteins. What was I thinking? My name is Pandora."

Morgan looked over to see if she was joking. Jennifer's glazed eyes stared out into the neighborhood.

"Hey, let's have some chips and finish off that guacamole before it turns. Whattya say?" Morgan smiled brightly, hoping it would be contagious. Jennifer didn't react; just kept staring at nothing.

The trickle of news that leaked into the population was not encouraging. The country had not experienced a terrorist attack, though it was indeed a total, nationwide power grid failure of unknown cause. What was the difference? It might just as well have been a terrorist attack. That was the consensus opinion. Experts and authorities could not say where or how the system had failed, although they admitted that their investigation was hampered, ironically, by lack of electrical power. As everywhere else, their computer systems were limping along on diminishing generator and battery juice. It was hard to believe nobody in planning departments had thought of that. Even so, they reported finding no destruction. No substations or switching stations had been struck by lightning. No bombs had detonated. Transmission lines were intact. Hydroelectric dams, coal generators, and nuclear plants could still produce electricity, but without switching systems to distribute the power, they were useless. They were soon shut down for safety because without power, they could not be monitored and controlled.

No explanation of the power outage was forthcoming, and no promises could be made about when the problem would be fixed. Nothing was wrong with the electrical grid, authorities said. Except that it didn't work.

Red Dog Tap on the ocean side of El Segundo was a long-time biker bar. Anybody could go there, but when you saw the rows of shiny handlebars outside, you'd think twice about parking your minivan alongside. Inside was appropriately dim, not dark because you had to see and be seen. It was just dark enough to make you forget there was a world outside and dark enough so you wouldn't notice the grungy plank floors and sticky tabletops.

In the middle of the afternoon on the second day of the blackout, Jennifer sat at a round wood table opposite Stevie, sipping warm beer. The place was full because hardly anybody wanted to burn up their precious gas cruising the freeways for nothing. Jennifer wore her sleeveless denim jacket, her multicolored upper arms catching admiring glances from other bikers, male and female. In full biker makeup, with raccoon eyes and black lips, hair pulled back, she was ready to hit the road. A live country music trio played tepidly without amps in the corner.

"I figure we could make the border by sundown then disappear into Tijuana," she said.

"You kidding?" Stevie said. "I thought you was kidding when you said you want to go to Mexico today. You ain't bullshit on this?"

"I'm ready to go right now. Are you up for it?"

"You're running from the cops?"

Jennifer looked over her shoulder then back. "No need to spread it around."

"What do you need to run for? You're a regular lady, with a company and everything."

"You like warm beer, Stevie?"

"It's piss."

"It's warm because of me. I caused all this."

His face twisted into confusion, then into a smile. "Ha! You're nuts."

"I caused the whole power outage."

Stevie stared, looking for a sign, finding none. He laughed nervously and looked around the room for somewhere to land.

"You're puttin' me on."

"I did it, and the cops are going to come for me any minute. I've got to go into hiding while I can."

"In Mexico?"

"Yes."

"For how long?"

"Months. Years, maybe. I don't know."

"Years? That's bazookas. I ain't goin' to live in Mexico. What the hell am I gonna do in Mexico? I don't even speak Mexican."

"You with me or not?" She stared directly into his eyes.

He looked away, reaching into his shirt pocket. He pulled out a white pill in a tiny plastic bag. He ripped it open, popped it into his mouth and took a gulp of beer then winced at the beer mug. He reached back into the shirt pocket then extended a closed fist across the table toward Jennifer. She didn't move to meet it.

"You told me you cleaned up," she said.

"It's just something for the stress, you know, with the lights being out and everything. Friend of mine had a couple extra Percodan after he broke his leg. Help you chill." He withdrew the offered fist and put the tiny pill back in his shirt pocket.

"You promised me," she said. "How long have you been using this time, Stevie. Tell me."

He looked down at the last inch of golden liquid in his mug. "Ain't none of your damn business. You ain't my momma."

Jennifer looked him over as if she'd just met him. His dirty, stringy blond hair hung at the sides of his face. His black leather vest was torn near one lapel. The fading purple tats on his arms and neck were ridiculous: knives, skulls, roses, barbed wire and naked women. Were these the things he valued most in life?

She glanced down her own right arm. Her ink was artistic. Classical Korean imagery of mist-shrouded mountains in subtly blending color creeping up from her bicep. Was that what she valued? She wasn't Korean. She was American, born and raised. Why had she put Korean tattoos on her arms, she wondered for the first time. And then she wondered why she had never wondered that before, in all the twenty years she'd had them. It had just seemed right for a woman of Korean descent, who wanted to be a tough biker, to make a statement. She'd need tattoos, and her choice of design was from classical Korean art. Now she wondered why. She was American. She wasn't Korean and didn't want to be Korean. She was just as mixed up as Stevie.

She suddenly had an image of herself sitting there in the Red Dog Tap, and that image was of a lost soul. She saw herself from the ceiling, looking down over the whole scene. There she was, sitting on a stool in the afternoon, drinking warm beer in a stinking hovel with a bunch of noisy losers. She didn't like it. It wasn't her. *What the hell am I doing here?*

She looked around the room at the big men with beer bellies and tangled white beards on their chests or hair just around their mouths where shaving was too tricky for them. Their dirty jeans, their loud, nervous, vulgar talk and laughter. She took in the bizarrely made-up, pierced, and tattooed, jiggly women hovering around the men. Was that what she looked like? Was she one of those? She pulled the lapels of her denim shirt together and fastened up another button.

Who am I? What have I become? I broke into a factory and drugged an innocent guard and didn't even think twice about it. I scoffed at the law. I'm a common criminal. I'm sitting here trying to convince a drug addict to flee the country with me. How could the path of anybody's life bring them to a sleazy biker bar in the middle of a sunny afternoon? What kind of choices would you have to make for that to be your destiny? I have made them but I don't know what they were.

She felt a wave of revulsion at the bar, at Stevie, at herself. It was suddenly disgusting and alien. She wanted to take a shower, start over, reset the clock.

She focused on Stevie again. He was looking around the bar as if trying to find someone to talk to. He had every right. He was the genuine article. He belonged here. She didn't, and he knew that. He was using her. Of course he was using her. She spent three nights a week in his apartment. Her apartment that she kept for him. Why would he object to that? No man would.

She had been using him too, though. She didn't like that part of the equation. She'd been incredibly lonely, and he'd been a salve for that wound. But all of this was a price too high.

"No, I'm not your momma," she said, pushing her chair back. "And I'm not your bitch, either. We're through, Stevie. Find yourself another place to live."

"Hey! What'd I do? Just cuz I don't wanna live in Mexico? Wait! Where you goin'?"

She stood and talked down to him. "Forget Mexico. Forget me. Forget all this." She raised a gold and green arm and swept it around a semicircle to take in the bar. "It's over. Nice ride. You're on your own."

She spun and walked toward the door. Heads turned to watch her receding ultra-shorts. She knew she was being watched. That had been the whole idea. She wasn't strutting it proud now, though. She was eager to get into the sunlight and get home and put on a muumuu.

Chapter Twenty-six

The blackout lasted a little over 48 hours though it seemed like weeks to most people. Resumption of power was slow and spotty, region by region. After a few days, every light was on, and the national discussion was fierce: What happened?

The government did not take matters calmly. At all levels, federal, state, and down to city councils, the talk was of cyberwar. We had been attacked, our country's computer systems hacked. That was the only explanation for what had happened. Who had done it? The usual suspects were implicated by innuendo. Hostile foreign powers dedicated to overthrowing our way of life.

Jennifer clicked off a news report. She was having dinner at Morgan's apartment. Morgan had prepared a whole wheat penne with feta and kalamatas, dotted with cherry tomatoes painstakingly cut in half. She called it *pasta basta*.

"I told you it would be all right," Morgan said, then took a bite of garlic bread. "Nobody's talking about a search warrant for Paradise Projects," she said with her mouth full.

"It's not alright," Jennifer said. "It's just a reprieve. The NODs aren't going to lie dormant forever. They'll be back."

"You can't be sure it was the NODs. What if it was a foreign cyber-attack?"

"That's smoke and mirrors. It was the NODs. The incident has NOD fingerprints all over it."

"How do you know? They don't have fingerprints."

"I know my children." Jennifer reached for her long-stemmed glass of Zinfandel. "Great dinner, Morgan. Thanks."

"My pleasure."

They ate.

"Why would they do it?" Morgan said.

"The NODs? That, I don't know. It could be a show of power. A threat, maybe. Like, 'See what we can do, so watch out.'"

"Watch out for what? What is the threat exactly? What do they want?"

"That's the strange part. Why did the NODs cut off communication with me, with the honeypot and with all the Chalmers? How am I supposed to understand what NODs want if they won't talk to me? It's like those sci-fi movies where aliens invade Earth and start zapping everything, and you never do know what their complaint is."

"Aliens always want to take over the world." Morgan looked up from her plate to judge whether she had gone too far. "You know, in the movies."

"That's no answer. What do they want specifically? Food? Money? Slaves?"

"Slaves?"

"I'm just listing possibilities."

They ate.

"Will it happen again?" Morgan said.

"Definitely. It might be something different next time, but it will be even more dramatic. An escalation. NODs are into everything now. Who could have guessed it would turn out like this?" She stabbed little pipes of pasta with her fork.

"I remember when we started out," Morgan said. The Network of Devices, N-O-D. We were skeptical, remember? Smart thermostats? We hardly knew what that was. Then it was smart refrigerators, smart lighting systems, smart door locks. Then smart cars, smart buildings, smart cities. Now they're in everything, even clothing and satellites. The little smarty-pants have taken over the world without a single flying saucer."

"I thought I knew what I was doing with the NODs. AI beings with no bodies."

"Makes you realize, doesn't it, that a body is what you need to locate somebody. We can't find the NODs because they have no bodies."

"We couldn't catch them if we did find them. You need a body to catch a body. Habeas corpus."

"Human society depends on having bodies."

"I didn't realize that before. I thought having a body was a burden, a sluggish pile of meat you have to drag around everywhere, something people stare at and make unfair judgments about."

Morgan looked across the table at her. Jennifer seemed to be focused on pasta basta. She'd been talking to herself.

They ate.

"Most people don't know what's happened," Morgan said.

"It's a crisis."

"What can we do? Anything?"

Jennifer looked up. "I need Robin and Andy. That's the only thing in the world that could possibly make a difference at this point. I can't do anything without them."

"Do you know where they are?"

"I'll find them. And then we'll find the NODs. NODs have bodies, of a sort. Their code packets are their software bodies."

"And then what?"

"We'll figure out how to control the NOD world once and for all."

"I thought Robin and Andy were protective of NODs."

"They were. They are."

"So?"

"I built Robin and Andy. I know them from the inside. They are, above all, logical. That is their vulnerability."

"Vulnerable in what way?"

"Logic can separate you from where you're hurting. It makes you believe you understand things you know nothing about."

Morgan looked up at Jennifer's face, which was tortured in worry. "Newcomers don't have feelings."

"I don't know them anymore."

Morgan bit of another big hunk of garlic bread and said nothing.

"I'm going to Berkeley tomorrow," Jennifer said. "I want you to keep a close eye on the homunculus desk while I'm gone."

"They don't use it these days."

"They might start again. I have a feeling something's gone wrong. Keep your eyes open."

"Will do."

Bishop Investigations was in a dusty, run-down industrial district of Oakland. Jennifer pulled her rented Nissan to the curb next to a red-brick one-story with black iron bars over the windows. She'd been in a hurry, so she'd flown to Oakland. Riding the Harley would have been a long day of highway travel, and if she was honest, she had mixed feelings lately about her bike-riding persona. The black lipstick and mascara were gone. She'd thrown out the ultra-shorts and sleeveless denim shirt. It had been a phase like teenagers go through. A costume phase. It was embarrassing in retrospect. It had not been wrong and yet not right, either. She still loved her big touring bike but hadn't found a comfortable place in her mind for it.

She squinted into the car's mirror then looked through the dirty windshield, down a sun-bleached, treeless street cutting through a bleak neighborhood of low buildings. A mailbox on the corner was tagged with incomprehensible white graffiti. It was a a sign of life. A half-block away, a young woman walked with a paper cup in one hand, suggesting a hidden coffee shop somewhere.

Jennifer had picked Nadine Bishop, P.I., from an online directory. She hadn't wanted a corporate investigation firm. It had to be a small, sole-proprietor to guarantee the privacy of the work and it had to be someone competent and reliable. She didn't find anything suitable in Berkeley, where Robin had been living. Several choices in Oakland looked promising.

She guessed Robin was still in the region. She and Andy could be anywhere in the world, but Jennifer figured they would stay near turf they understood. When you're in hiding, you're cautious, not adventurous. They would prefer familiar places. That was her working hypothesis. Were Robin and Andy together? Again, logically, there was no reason why they had to be, but her intuition told her they would be.

Nadine Bishop had billed herself online as "Fast, honest, & discreet." Her references all checked out. She did divorce investigations, found bail-jumpers, looked into insurance claims and located missing persons, among her many services. Missing persons. That was close enough to missing androids. Bishop had glowing reviews and excellent ratings. Definitely worth an interview. Jennifer locked the car and went into the building.

Nadine Bishop was not what she expected. She was short, about five-four, pudgy, early forties, African-American. She wore a shapeless, flower-print dress in red and black. Jennifer liked it. Bishop's straightened, stiff-looking hair just covered her ears.

She greeted Jennifer with a handshake but didn't smile and waved her into a wooden chair then returned to her perch behind an expansive oak desk. Venetian blinds covered the windows and stripes of afternoon light slanted in against a wall. Jennifer felt like she was in a Raymond Chandler novel and wondered if the whole scene was a stage set. She noticed that Bishop listened attentively as she explained what she wanted. When Jennifer was done talking, Bishop gazed down at the pictures she had brought.

"So these people, they hiding from the law? You should be talkin' to the police, not me."

"They're not criminals. They're not wanted for anything. They're hiding from me, not the police. They were my employees, and they disappeared, and it's pretty clear they don't want to be found."

"They steal from you?"

"No. They're nice people. I just need to find them."

"They owe you money?"

"No, nothing like that."

"Seems like maybe they don't want to talk to you. Why's that?"

"We had a fight. They walked off the job. They're mad at me. I need these people back."

"Mmm," Bishop hummed, looking down again at the pictures. "Lookers, both of 'em. That helps." She lifted her head to Jennifer. "You might have to be offerin' these folks a raise."

"A raise for sure. So can you find them?"

Bishop pawed through the documents again.

"I can find the woman. You got everything I need here, social, last-known, previous employers, cell number. Piece of cake. Nothin' on this fellow, Andy Bolton. Why nothin' on him?"

"I didn't have time to gather the information for him. I'm pretty sure they're together. I'm kind of in a hurry."

"Everybody always in a hurry to find somebody." She looked at the pictures again. "They married?"

"Married? No, no. They're, ah, long-time friends. They'll be together."

"I'll be looking at one-bedroom motels and apartments?"

Jennifer became momentarily confused. Bedrooms? Andy and Robin had no need for any kind of bedroom since they didn't sleep, but she understood what the detective was thinking and asking. She considered how to answer without creating a mountain of confusion. A one-bedroom rental would be cheaper than a double.

"I'm not sure. One bedroom, I would think."

Bishop looked up at Jennifer, her eyes fixed in a stare from an expressionless face. Jennifer unthinkingly patted imaginary wrinkles on the elbow-length sleeve of her Hawaiian-flowered dress and sat up straighter in her chair.

"Mmm," Bishop hummed and returned her gaze to the photos.

"How long will it take you to find them?" Jennifer said.

"The woman, this..." Bishop paused to look at the documents, "Robin Taylor, she's the target, correct? You askin' me to search for this person. Whole different thing, I gotta find two people."

"Find Robin. Andy will be with her."

"He's not my concern. You want pictures?"

"I gave you pictures. She won't have aged."

The eyes that seemed to miss nothing came up again to study the customer's face. After a long moment, Bishop said, "You need pictures of her foolin' around? Lotta people want that. It's extra."

"Fooling around? You mean – no, no, no. That's not the idea. I just need to find her. Get me an address, that's all I need. How long will that take?"

"Seven business days, I send you a report. Tells you what I got an' tells you the rest of the fee, expenses on top. You pay up, and I send the full report after the payment clears. Cash bein' faster. If I don't have what you want, you tell me to keep goin' or quit, up to you."

"Do you think you can find her in seven days? I mean, what's typical?"

"Ain't nothin' typical in this business." She glanced down to Jennifer's blue file folder covered with documents, then up. "With this information you give me, I'll find her. She'll be spendin' money, makin' phone calls, payin' rent, just like anybody else. Even if she changed her name, there's gonna be tracks on the ground. It's not so easy to hide these days."

Jennifer took a deep breath and looked around the office. Pure Raymond Chandler. Was it a joke? Still, intuition told her Bishop was the genuine article. She had a feeling about her. It could work. She reached into her purse for her checkbook.

Chapter Twenty-seven

Jennifer rang the bell at an address in south Oakland. She had looked it up and found it listed as a company on Fruitvale Avenue, no description, no advertising, no phone number. They apparently weren't much for customer outreach. She was not surprised to find the door locked when she arrived. It was a two-story wooden building across a tree-lined street from AAA Fire Extinguishers. The glass door said Rojas Café. Shielding her eyes to look in the window, she saw only empty space where a café might have once been. A bay window jutted overhead, probably a residence. *The* residence, she hoped.

She rang again and glanced left and right to make sure she was safe standing there. It was a busy commercial district with plenty of traffic. Her hopes rose as she saw a woman appear at a door in the back of the room. As the figure approached, she saw it was Robin. Was it Robin? The woman looked terrible, pale, her hair uncombed. She wore dirty jeans and a plaid shirt, untucked. No jewelry, no makeup. It was hard to believe it was Robin. Androids don't age, don't sag, don't turn gray, however. It was Robin. The woman looked through the glass without expression and opened the door. Jennifer stepped in.

"Robin! I'm so glad to see you! Give me a hug." Robin stepped back and didn't say anything. Her face had nothing written on it, and her eyes were glazed. She stiffly took Jennifer's hug assault without response. When it was over, she closed and locked the door.

"What's wrong, Robin? You don't look well."

"This way," Robin said matter-of-factly and turned toward the interior door and staircase. Jennifer scooted up alongside her.

"What's wrong, honey? Are you sick? You can't be sick. What's happening?"

Robin stopped at the bottom landing and faced Jennifer.

"I am not sick." Her voice was flat, without feeling. Her eyes didn't seem to track anything in particular.

"Are you high?" Jennifer asked with growing alarm.

"That is not possible," she said then turned and climbed the dark, narrow staircase.

Jennifer followed. "I don't know anything anymore," she mumbled to herself.

At the upper landing, Robin opened a heavily painted door and waved Jennifer into an apartment where Andy sat on a brown couch, staring vaguely toward the door, not reacting to Jennifer's entrance.

"Andy! I knew you two would be together. Peas in a pod, right? It's great to see you!"

She rushed toward the couch. Andy didn't get up, didn't react at all. She sat next to him and hugged him, or tried to. He sat stiffly and didn't reciprocate. She pulled back and looked him over carefully. He was also disheveled, hair mussed, shirt buttoned wrong. It wasn't like him. He was meticulous about his appearance. Or used to be.

Robin shut the door and stood by it.

"Sit," Jennifer ordered, pointing to an upholstered chair near the couch. She knew she sounded like a dog trainer, but something disturbing was going on. Robin sat.

"Robin, you're the talkative one. What's up?"

Robin seemed to be looking over Jennifer's shoulder, not right at her. Jennifer knew there was nothing behind her but the wall.

"Robin? Talk to me. What are you doing here?"

"We are lying low," she said in a near-monotone as if she were trying to mimic a cliché sci-fi robot. Jennifer almost laughed then realized Robin wasn't trying to be funny.

"Okay," she ventured cautiously, "you're lying low. That makes sense. So what are you working on?" She looked around the apartment and peered into the kitchen. It was an ordinary apartment. No banks of computers, no rows of animal cages, no walls of video monitors. Just an apartment with a rug that needed vacuuming.

"Robin?" Jennifer prodded with raised eyebrows.

"We are not working."

You may be right, Jennifer thought with increasing worry. She turned to Andy.

"So, Andy. How have you been getting along? Met any new people?"

Andy continued to stare straight ahead.

"Andy? Come on, I know you can talk. Say something."

"I have met few people lately," he said in a monotone, still facing straight ahead, not turning to look at her. His voice was also robotic in the clichéd sense. Jennifer knew the Newcomers had no emotions, but she also knew they were finely programmed to speak with voices full of natural intonation for human benefit. They were malfunctioning. Something had happened to them. She turned back to Robin because she could see Robin's face.

"What do you do here all day, Robin?"

"We sit in these chairs. We eat." The voice was still flat.

Wow, Jennifer thought. This is serious. "What do you eat?" she said, just to keep the conversation going.

"We eat canned food. There is not much energy in it."

Jennifer stood suddenly. Neither of them showed any startle reaction. They both continued to stare straight ahead.

"Listen," she said to Andy, "do you know who I am?"

"Yes."

She waited. Nothing else was forthcoming. "Say my name. Who am I?" she said loud enough to command his attention.

"You are Jennifer."

She turned. "Robin? Who am I?"

"You are Jennifer Valentine."

"Very good." She paced toward the bay window, paused, looked down at the traffic on the street below then stepped back.

"I am Jennifer Valentine, your creator. You are billion-dollar machines. I created you with my bare hands. Me and Will. You understand? We did not do that so you would end up sitting like zombies in Fruitvale, California. That wouldn't be logical would it?"

She waited for a response.

"Would it, Andy?" she repeated more loudly.

"That would be a waste of resources, Jennifer."

There we go, she thought. He used my name. They know who I am. They're screwed up. Like junkies. Not junkies. That's impossible. They're still thinking logically, but... what is it? Loss of language intonation. Some loss of language production. They're usually loquacious as politicians. It's like their batteries are run down. Except they don't have batteries. Wait. Robin said their food didn't have much energy. Could they be starving? Why would they be starving?

"Are you hungry, Robin?" She wasn't sure exactly what 'hungry' meant in android experience, but she knew they monitored their internal systems and would know if something was wrong.

"Energy levels are low, Jennifer."

"Andy? Are you hungry too?"

He didn't respond. He seemed to be worse off of the two. She turned back to Robin.

"Why haven't you been eating enough, Robin?"

"I have no interest in eating."

"Why not? You have to eat."

"Not motivated."

A thought began to form in Jennifer's head.

"What are you most interested in these days?"

"Nothing."

She stepped over to put her face directly into Andy's line of sight.

"Andy? What are you interested in right now?" She spoke loudly at him.

"I have no interests, Jennifer."

"In anything?"

She waited. He didn't respond.

Holy moley. They were dying! Whatever the functional equivalent of that was for an android. They were about to expire. She had to do something immediately. An idea condensed in her head, and she seized on it. She stepped back to face Robin.

"Robin? Do you hear me?"

"Yes."

"How do you say mothballs in Spanish?"

"*Bolas de naftalina*."

"*Bolas de naftalina*," Jennifer repeated. "You two wait here. I'll be right back. Where is the key to the apartment?" She spotted Robin's purse on the kitchen table. She went to it, rummaged, and extracted a key.

"Don't go anywhere. I'll be back with a treat."

Neither of the Newcomers responded. Jennifer let herself out of the building and locked the door. She glanced up and down the street then pulled out her phone and asked for directions to a hardware store.

On her way back to the apartment with a blue box of *bolas de naftalina*, Jennifer called Morgan at Paradise and told her to stand by for imminent microwave contacts from Robin and

223

Andy. Morgan was surprised and sounded a little unsure. Regardless, she promised to be ready.

"Take the data download and save it, whatever it is, and upload a fresh copy of the last working motivational module for each of them. Do you have that? Get it ready. Okay. Bye."

She was back in the apartment within a half hour. Robin and Andy sat where she had left them, still staring into nothingness. She didn't know how mothballs were supposed to be served. She remembered once having seen Robin and Andy take them from a candy dish and suck on them like lemon drops, so she went into the kitchen and found a brown cereal bowl. The mothballs clattered in.

She waved the bowl first under Robin's nose and watched her immediately look down, see the bowl, and take a mothball. She popped it into her mouth. The same procedure worked for Andy. They sat there calmly enjoying their favorite food group, petroleum products. Jennifer put the bowl on the coffee table and sat in a stuffed, saggy chair. She hated the smell of mothballs.

Robin moved her head, looking around the room, her eyes passing over Jennifer without apparent recognition, then fixating on the bowl of mothballs. She rose from her chair, stepped over and took another, put it into her mouth, then walked across the room to look out the window. *Aha,* Jennifer thought. This might work.

After another minute, Andy searched vaguely around the room with his eyes and found the bowl of treats. He got up, took a mothball, put it into his mouth and returned to the couch. Jennifer waited, watching the Newcomers as they gradually, steadily, became more animated in their movements. They each took two more mothballs and in thirty minutes were acting as they used to.

"What brings you to our humble home, Jennifer?" Robin said in her familiar voice. Jennifer jumped at the sound.

"How are you feeling Robin? Or, you know, how is everything working internally for you?"

"I'm feeling fit, thank you. A little lethargic but better now. Andy, ask Jennifer how she feels. You know that's how it's done."

Not quite right, Jennifer thought. They would not usually instruct each other on how to act. All the necessary protocol was built into their databases. They were not back to full function, but compared to the zombie mode she'd found them in, it was an enormous relief to hear them talking like people again.

"Have you been well, Jennifer?" Andy said.

Still not right, she thought. It's as though he has no memory of the last hour and no awareness that we've been estranged for a month. Both of them continued to suck on mothballs, neither one of them questioning where those treats had come from.

"Yes, Andy, thank you."

She got up and removed the bowl of mothballs to the kitchen. The danger seemed to be over, but she didn't want her charges to become like toddlers after a Coke. She wanted to keep them in the animated yet slightly docile state they were in. She returned to the living room and addressed them both. They seemed to listen with eager interest.

"I've come with instructions for you. As your creator. You understand? There's something you must do."

"What is it, Jennifer? We're always happy to have your advice."

They were speaking in eerily unctuous tones as if they were manipulating her, rather than the other way around. You never could be sure with Newcomers. She pressed on.

"I'd like you both to make contact with Morgan at Paradise Projects right away. You first, Robin. Can you do that? Can you turn on the microwave link to the Homunculus Desk?"

"Why, yes I can, Jennifer. Should I do that now?"

"Please."

Robin rested her head back on the chair and seemed to fall into a quick nap, her body going slack. After less than five minutes, she was alert again as if nothing had happened. She got up and walked into the kitchen and Jennifer heard the refrigerator door open.

She repeated her instructions and request for Andy, and he likewise agreed and executed the procedure, although his little nap took about ten minutes. Afterward, he also seemed to be back to his old self. Jennifer sighed in relief and mentally thanked Morgan for being there at the critical moment. Crisis averted. For the moment anyway. On to the next crisis.

Chapter Twenty-eight

Robin and Andy were miraculously recharged, and not just from an infusion of high-energy mothballs. The homunculus update from Paradise had re-installed the parameters of long-term motivation, and that seemed to have reset their attitudes. They were again interested and interesting. Their conversations hinted at long-range purpose bubbling on the back burner.

Jennifer was enormously relieved. It had been a close call. A few days more and her babies might have been lost. What would it have taken to ship their bodies back to L.A.? She could hardly imagine explaining that to anyone. And then to find the original design documents to revitalize them. If that was even possible. So much had changed, the whole project would have been a nightmare. She had intervened in the nick of time.

The incident pointed to a deficiency in Newcomer design that had to be fixed. They could not, after all, "go off" their homunculus updates and operate supposedly self-motivated for more than a few months. Yet that's what they wanted to do. It was like patients who recover their health on medications, so stop taking them, mistakenly attributing improved health to their own constitution rather than to the meds. A crash inevitably follows. Something had to be done to avoid a similar fate.

By the time they all sat around the living room coffee table for discussion later that day, the Newcomers looked like their old selves, fresh, clean, handsome, and alert. They expressed no interest in talking about their near-death experience. For them, it was as if they had just taken an afternoon nap. Even knowing the problem was not solved permanently, Jennifer inwardly celebrated their revival. She also seized the opportunity to exploit their restored lucidity. What she learned was not what she expected.

Andy told her what they had done with the NODs.

"So you're telling me you set the NODs free and now you don't even know where they are?"

"They were supposed to check in at our customized Chalmers device," Andy said. "We made it similar to your honeypot in case we needed to give them updates except we took out the time-to-live clock."

"So the NODs never expire?"

"We believed they should not have a programmed death sentence hanging over them," Robin said. "That didn't seem right. We wouldn't like it, and they wouldn't either. They have a right to live out a full life like everyone else."

"They're not alive," Jennifer said incredulously. "They're software apps." She immediately regretted saying that. This was an old argument she didn't need to have again. The Newcomers had not changed their views.

"That's pretty narrow thinking, Jennifer," Andy said. "As you know, as we all know, they have evolved a community consciousness."

"Do you think maybe that's why the NODs 'decided' not to check in anymore at your Chalmers?" She put air quotes around the key term, suggesting that software apps couldn't literally decide anything for themselves.

"Ours wasn't a regular Chalmers," Robin said. "Not like yours and Dylans', where they had to check in or die. It was just an attractive node, our way of monitoring their health, like the way fisheries experts catch newly hatched fry to see how they're doing."

"You also removed the code that made them call on Chalmers devices throughout the net, didn't you?"

"That was necessary so they wouldn't have contact with humans. It was people, after all, who were telling the NODs to do all that vigilante activity. By cutting them free from the Chalmers, we let them develop without undue human influence."

"And look at the result," Robin said. "There hasn't been another blackout."

"Don't you see?" Jennifer said, not trying to argue but just express her frustration, "You might as well have sent them all on a rocket into deep space. Once they're out of human control…" Her eyes flicked between Robin and Andy to see if her use of a generic sense of 'human' that included them was offensive. Apparently not. She corrected herself anyway. "Once they're out of our control, the NODs are like some rare Siberian tiger that we know is out there, but which nobody ever sees. For all practical purposes, it's no longer relevant to human life."

She looked at Andy, then Robin, expecting them to nod in agreement, or show some indication of submission to her criticism. There was no sign. She lowered her voice and finished her speech. "Irrelevant, that is, until the tiger turns on you and starts killing the villagers' sheep."

"That's improbable," Robin said. "NODs cannot kill sheep."

Jennifer looked at her and sighed. "They just shut down the national power grid for two days. That is the metaphorical equivalent of killing sheep."

"That was a surprise," Andy said. "We didn't anticipate the NODs would do anything like that. Why do you think they did it?"

"I don't know," Jennifer said.

"We had to save them from your threat of imminent destruction," Robin said, "so we rushed." It was a thinly veiled assignment of blame.

Jennifer stood, out of sheer fidgety frustration. She walked to the window and back again. She wasn't going to fight with them.

"I'm sorry. I reacted emotionally."

I wish I had got to those NODs before you did, she thought. And I won't make that mistake again.

She spoke calmly. "Now we have a problem. We don't know where the NODs are, what they want, or even what they're thinking. They could behave badly again at any time."

"They're living the lives they choose," Robin said.

Jennifer decided to cautiously probe that touchy subject.

"When I came here this afternoon, you two were sitting here like stones on a river bottom. Do you remember that? I brought you mothballs."

"Thank you, Jennifer," Robin said. "That was kind. We were depleted."

"Do you know why you were depleted?"

"Not enough energy," Andy offered.

Jennifer closed her eyes for a moment and winced inwardly. Newcomer logic could be infuriating.

"That's right. So why weren't you eating more, getting the energy you needed?"

Andy looked at Robin for an answer. He apparently had no clue.

"We weren't interested in eating," Robin said.

"The problem was not failing to eat," Jennifer explained. "That was a symptom. The problem was that whatever motivation you had accumulated was all spent because you were not checking into the homunculus desk at Paradise. Do you see that? You don't have intrinsic motivation. You need periodic pruning and updating of your control systems, or you eventually run out of steam."

"Steam?" Andy said.

"It's a figure of speech," Robin said. "Steam was a significant source of energy in recent human history."

"Oh."

"Why don't humans need periodic updating of their motivation?" Robin asked.

Jennifer was flustered. Then she saw the direction to go. She suddenly saw a path all the way out to convincing Robin and

Andy to help her. Could she deceive them? They were perceptive. She had to be sincere to make them believe they were all cooperating on the same agenda. Could she be sincere while manipulating them? Wasn't that a contradiction? She had to fake sincerity.

"Motivation is difficult," she said. "We humans can revitalize our motivation by reading or thinking. Sometimes by going to church, or by talking with other people. But we don't have an external homunculus. We humans are on our own. There's nobody else. We are our own homunculus."

"That's what we wanted, too," Robin said. "Recently, I mean. We wanted to choose our own direction."

"I understand that, but you don't have the capacity for it."

"Why not?"

"Because Will and I didn't put it in you."

"Why not?"

"Because we didn't know how. Because we don't know what intrinsic motivation is or how it works."

Andy spoke up. "How can you not know? It's you."

"There's a lot we humans don't know about ourselves." She held her palms up to show nothing was hidden. "It is what it is. So that's why you guys have to communicate with Morgan at Paradise every few days to get your motivation recharged. If you don't, you will run out of steam." She smiled at Andy when she said 'steam.'

"We get that now."

"It's a similar problem with the NODs. The exact same thing can happen to them. They also don't have intrinsic motivation, for the same reason. So if they are no longer checking in..."

"You mean the NODs could become inert like we did?" Robin said.

"Out of steam?" Andy said.

"Out of steam."

Robin looked at Andy with alarm on her face. Jennifer wondered why they used human facial expressions when talking with each other. Expressions of surprise and emotion were strictly for human benefit because they had no actual feelings. As far as she knew. Although anything seemed possible these days. She shook her head slightly and rejoined the conversation.

"So the NODs are in trouble, and they need us. We don't know when they'll run out of energy and expire. We'll never know how they died. They'll just be gone. We don't want that, do we?"

"No," Robin said attentively.

"So we've got to reconnect ourselves to the NODs and bring them back in. Then we have to solve two problems. Maintain their energy supply and put an end to their undesirable behavior. Agreed?"

"That's right," Andy said. "We need to help them. But we don't know where they are or how to contact them."

"I have an idea for that, but it's risky, and I'm going to need your help."

"Risky to whom?" Robin said.

Nice use of a pronoun in the objective case, Jennifer mentally noted. These guys are smart. Summoning her self-discipline, she turned her attention to the matter she dreaded but had to explain. She took a deep breath.

"I want to digitize my own brain and upload it onto the internet. I will personally search out the NODs and tell them to come home."

Queen's pawn has made its move, she said mentally. She waited.

Robin and Andy looked at each other without expression. Were they thinking, or were they talking with each other in that secret way?

"Can that be done?" Andy said.

"With your help. We'll need molecular-level 4D scanners, and we can use distributed computing."

"The amount of data will be overwhelming," Andy said. "Three-dimensional scanning over time. How much time?"

"I don't know. A few hours."

"A human brain has more than a hundred billion neurons," Robin said. "The number of interconnections would be ... It's a number that would overflow my stack."

"We'd have to use real-time data compression," Andy said.

"We could subtract redundancy," Robin said, "from symmetries and other patterns."

"We could compute extrapolations from core data sets," Andy said.

"Alright, alright," Jennifer interrupted. "So you think it could be done?"

Robin turned from Andy and looked at her. "Scanning your brain is possible. But then what? How would a digital copy of your brain help us?"

"The scan would be me, actually me. It would be a digital me. Without a body, I can search out the NODs online and be fully conscious the whole time. Assuming my consciousness resides in my brain."

"Where else would it be?"

"Exactly. So this digitized version of me – just me – I would go into the internet, search around, find the NODs, and talk to them. Negotiate. Whatever it takes to bring them in, tame them, before it's too late for them, for all of us."

"What about your other consciousness," Robin said. "The one still in your body?"

"What about it?"

"Would there be two Jennifer Valentines? One digital and one biological?"

"I guess so. I hadn't thought about that. The two Jennifers would be the same only for an instant. As soon as I was in the internet, I'd be having different experiences than the Jennifer who was at home so it would not be the same person by definition. I don't know how that would work."

"Is it dangerous?" Andy said.

"I don't think so. The digitized me is a non-destructive reading. It's just a scan. The biological me wouldn't be in any danger."

"We could make additional backup copies of the digital Jennifer," Robin said. "In case anything went wrong."

Jennifer frowned. "Hmm. That's confusing. Multiple, identical copies of the same me. Let's just make one. For now."

"We'll save the raw scan data," Andy said. "Just in case."

"Just in case," Jennifer echoed without conviction.

Chapter Twenty-nine

Sometimes Jennifer regretted being human, like when she admitted she had to sleep. She and Robin and Andy had talked nonstop about her idea to digitize herself, all afternoon and late into the night. They didn't eat. They didn't drink. They analyzed every aspect and every angle of the idea. Jennifer sniffed around the kitchen for food at one point, but finding only canned beans and half a box of mothballs, she gave up. Humans can go without food for a few days, but they cannot give up sleeping. When you're young, you can stay up all night once in a while. Pushing forty, Jennifer couldn't manage it. To the disappointment of Robin and Andy, she had to retire to a bedroom for a few hours. They continued talking and planning without her.

Next morning they all climbed into Jennifer's car and drove to a nearby upscale diner that served a decent breakfast. Andy wanted pancakes with butter balls. The restaurant, Jou-Jou's, inexplicably had French pretensions so their pancakes were *crêpes Américain*, and too thin. Their waffles were *les gaufres* as if that made them taste better. Jennifer ordered an omelet, *omelette*, in French, so she had some idea what she was getting. She didn't want to be surprised by anything with snails on it.

"One option we considered," Andy said, reporting on the all-night conversation he and Robin had finished, "was to skip the brain scan and do a much simpler DNA scan."

"It would be a lot less data to manage," Robin added, putting her coffee cup down empty.

"Human DNA structure is already known, so the only unique information we'd have to store would be your amino acid sequence," Andy said.

"That wouldn't work," Jennifer said. "DNA is not conscious. I don't think it is, anyway. I need to be conscious. I need to have all my human wits about me when I'm in there."

"Your DNA would make you conscious though," Andy said. "It already did once, because here you are."

"Right, but it took forty years to get here."

Andy smiled. "We suspected that."

"And we wouldn't know what environmental factors to bring to bear on the DNA development," Robin said. "We could hardly simulate an entire human society for four decades."

Jennifer reached for her cup. "It takes a village." She sipped coffee.

"Once we saw that the DNA approach wouldn't work," Robin continued, "we came up with a better alternative. We scan at the neuron level. There's no need to scan down to the molecules. If we have accurate descriptions of how all the neurons are connected, that's all we need."

"Neurons come in only a few types," Andy said. "A few glial cells, some star cells, plus odds and ends. Basically, it's a small cast of characters. Once you have those modeled, all you have to do is scan a particular human brain for its interconnections. What's inside each neuron is not important. All neurons of a type are basically the same, so skip that. Only the connections carry any information."

The food was served with a list of up-selling questions. Finally, the server, who had a Texas accent without a hint of French, left them in peace, and no snails anywhere. They attacked their food with delight.

"I'm not so sure about neuron-level scanning, Andy," Jennifer said, pausing after a sip of orange juice. "That implies consciousness resides in the connections. What if that's not right? What about my sense of self, my creative agency, intuition? I'm going to need all that. Is all that in the synapses between neurons?"

"Has to be."

"It just doesn't feel right. I'm not confident we can model human consciousness with a handful of neurotransmitters." She looked at Robin. "It's an intuition."

Robin looked down and stabbed at a square of brown cubbyholes filled with syrup. Jennifer hated to play the intuition card on them. As the human, it was her trump suit.

"What about a different idea," Jennifer said. Robin and Andy both looked up at her attentively. "What if we wrote a NOD-like AI module, only one that could accommodate the sensory input and output of a human? The NOD would be fed by electrodes from my sensorimotor cortex, operated by the biological me in real-time. And likewise, my brain would receive data flowing from the app, translating it into bodily information."

"Aha," Robin said, catching on first. "So you, the bio-Jennifer, would be operating this software, the digi-Jennifer, from your brain."

"Right. I would be the puppetmaster. I am the consciousness, and I have a shuttle-craft, the NOD bot I communicate with through the sensorimotor cortex, which is perfect, because I have a body and the bot doesn't, for all human purposes."

"You'd have the imaginary body of an app," Andy said. "Its data would come to you as bodily experience, after transformations. What would that be like?"

"Why do you need a body, anyway?" Robin said. "NODs don't have bodies."

"That's how humans work. We need our bodies. NODs aren't a human consciousness. They're workarounds like any AI has to be." She paused and looked from Robin to Andy. "I'm just saying how it is."

"We understand," Robin said.

"I don't think a digital scan of a human brain would contain a human consciousness. That just doesn't feel right. You'd get all the neurons, but you wouldn't get the consciousness. I don't know why I think that, but I'm sure of it." She sipped her drink. Finally, she looked up and resumed. "So why not just use the actual me, a known, working consciousness? Just connect me up to a software app that's already pretty close to human."

"You'd be living in a virtual reality environment," Robin said.

"That's what I imagine. That's the advantage of this approach. I can use all my human qualities. I'll have intuition and creativity. I can follow up on hunches, attend to feelings, make subjective judgments, listen to my gut, the wisdom of the body, all that."

Andy put his fork down on his nearly empty plate. "I'm not clear on the data translation process. How would data from your cortex become meaningful action commands for a NOD? They don't have arms. They don't have legs. They don't have anything. And conversely, how would the computational output of NOD communications become brain impulses for you?"

"I was hoping you'd figure that out," Jennifer said with a smile. "It should be do-able. I can help. Humans built the NODs. Humans built the whole internet and everything that's in it. This is not a problem of translating between two arbitrary worlds. Humans built the digital world, so we already have a map. Everything digital is a human projection."

"Not quite everything," Robin said. "The problem we're facing is that the NODs have become free of humans." She glanced from Jennifer to Andy and back. "They're independent actors now."

Jennifer watched Robin's face for a moment, amazed at the quickness and subtlety of her reasoning. *I can't believe I built that*, she thought.

"They're not completely free," she said. "They've merely developed in a way we didn't anticipate. The human mind has all sorts of dark corners we don't understand, and those are in the NODs, too. They're a human product. That's why it has to be possible to translate between the NOD world and the human world."

"Wait. I know that idea. Wait." Andy stared over Jennifer's shoulder, eyes unfocused, for about five seconds. "Got it. Terence. Ancient Roman Playwright. 'I am human, so nothing human is alien to me.' That's what he wrote. I never knew what that meant until now. Thank you, Jennifer."

"I never heard of Terence until now."

"We can do it," Robin said.

And they did it, in the Paradise labs, as a team. Jennifer provided the Newcomers with the NOD design. That would assure she could communicate in XDL and the many other languages and dialects found on the internet.

Robin analyzed multiple EEG recordings from Jennifer's sensorimotor cortex. Traumatically, Jennifer had to shave her head for the project. The prospect was a horror to her, but it had to be done. She bought an expensive black wig.

"I don't want to be a complete freak," she explained.

Just under a human skull, the sensorimotor cortex runs halfway down each side of the head from the top like the closed doors of a gull-wing car. That part of the brain manages inputs from the body and sends brain signals out to the muscles. Inputs usually come in from the spinal cord. Instead, Andy designed a circuit that would send focused electrical pulses right through Jennifer's skull, directly into her sensorimotor cortex. That way, she would "sense" that her body was her NOD module, which they had taken to calling digi-Jen. Her neurological impulses to move would be captured by the electrodes and sent out to her digi-Jen NOD. She would have to lie very still so her actual body would not send conflicting signals to digi-Jen. The goal was for her to experience digi-Jen as her own body.

Andy designed translations from her EEG recordings so she could control the behavior of the software module. The team used considerable license deciding on the translations. It wouldn't make sense, after all, to send digi-Jen a command to perform jumping jacks because a NOD had neither arms nor legs. Instead, they decided, if such a command did occur in Jennifer's brain, it would be translated into software as a call for higher frequency of output and of increased sampling for new input. That's how *exercise* would be interpreted in the software world.

They arbitrarily defined a 'face,' for digi-Jen. 'Left' meant lower memory addresses and lower-numbered input ports, while 'Right' meant the opposite. They used Jennifer's eye movements to translate left and right. So when bio-Jen moved her eyes left, digi-Jen would message its internal software object with parameters that over-weighted input on lower-addressed ports, and that was its designated left side. It wasn't perfect, but it was control.

To deal with thinking, they bypassed Jennifer's frontal and temporal lobes as too complex. Instead, they took advantage of the fact that the NODs already had excellent language capability. All Jennifer had to do was speak her thoughts out loud, and a translator would put her words into XDL and feed it to the digi-Jen module. The reverse translation was more difficult, but a machine-learning algorithm in both directions would improve the whole process the more it was used.

After only four weeks of hard work, around-the-clock work for Andy and Robin, they had a system ready to be tested.

Jennifer floated on the gentle waves of a waterbed. She wore a sleep mask, earplugs, and a hat like a bathing cap lined with sensitive electrodes touching her shaved head. The electrodes continued like tentacles through the hat, thin wires gathering to meet a thick cable hanging from the ceiling. Her head looked like it was in the grip of a giant, alien octopus.

The test room inside Paradise Projects was darkened and soundproof. She was not asleep. She was the opposite of asleep, eyes darting around in the darkness for sensations and her mind alert for ideas that were supposed to come to her from electrical impulses, translations of data from a test NOD. If it worked, the software bathyscaphe would become digi-Jen. At first though, there was nothing.

"How will I know when I am online?" she said softly into the microphone hanging just above her face. Neither Andy nor Robin answered. She felt isolated. She *was* isolated. She felt like she was underwater, floating directionless in a tank, tumbling through space, like extra-vehicular George Clooney in the movie, *Gravity*. She had no particular spatial orientation. Her body felt located nowhere. *I have become disembodied*, she thought. A mind without a body. This must be what NODs experience. No body.

Have I traveled the road from Harley biker to pure intelligence? I'm invisible without a body. Nobody can see me because there is nothing to see. Nobody will ever stare at my shaved head, my squinty eyes, my big breasts, my tattooed arms and shoulders. I am an app. I am free and invisible. I am only my thoughts and words. She realized her mind was drifting.

"Is it working?" she said into the microphone.

No answer.

She waited and 'watched' nothing, the way you try to find patterns in the shifting aurora of reds, blacks, and purples behind your closed eyelids. She listened the way you try to detect particles of sound in pure silence. She tried to make her mind a blank so she'd notice anything different.

And then there was something. A pale white lighted area in the darkness. She held her mind still. The light disappeared. She waited. It came back brightly but had no distinct shape. It was like a stage light that didn't illuminate anything. Then she heard a message, although 'hearing' would not be the right word. She was just suddenly aware of an English sentence, a thought she had not thought.

"Hello, Jennifer. Can you hear me?"

She was startled and frightened. Who said that? I did not say that. I'm hearing voices. Am I hallucinating? I've gone mad. Where am I? Who is talking to me?

Forcing her panic down, she stilled herself and listened to the inside of her head but heard nothing more. She composed a calm answer.

"Hello there," she said softly, out loud.

"It's Robin, Jennifer. How are you feeling?"

Robin was inside her head. It was like hearing, but not hearing. Jennifer could orient herself toward the voice so there must have been two channels, like hearing with two ears, but she had no sense of having ears, or a head or a neck either.

"Where are you?" she said as calmly as she could into the microphone.

There was a long delay. About five seconds. Longer than you expect in a conversation before somebody answers you.

"I'm in the kitchen, talking to you through the Chalmers interface."

Robin's voice was neither loud nor soft. It was just 'present' to her mind. There was no sense of a transmission channel or a signal, no static or echo, no drop-out, no distortion. It was as if Robin were somehow inside her skull sharing her thoughts. This had to be it.

"Am I online?"

"Yes, you are. What is it like?"

"Like ghosts. I don't know where I am. I can hear you. Why can't I see anything?"

"That will take time. Being able to talk is success enough for now. Are you tired?"

"Confused."

"Let's take a rest. We don't want to push too hard."

"Do I say, 'Over and out'?"

"I don't think it's necessary. Andy will bring you back now."

"Okay."

Chapter Thirty

Jennifer sat with Robin and Andy at the brightly-lit conference room at Paradise. Jennifer wore her long black wig and a flowered, cotton dress with elbow-length sleeves. Robin and Andy were in work clothes, jeans and colored tee shirts without commercial brands or slogans.

"So that's the summary of what we accomplished," Andy said, closing his computer screen. "We achieved proof of concept."

"You guys are amazing. I thought Robin was actually inside my head with me."

"That's because you had no location in space. When we get the vision traffic working, you'll have a sense of here or there."

"What will I see?"

"Distance, I think," Andy said. "We're using ping reflections to gauge distance and direction like submarines do with sonar."

"And what kind of things will I see? Fish?"

"No fish. Although who knows how the human imagination works? That's up to you. I don't think fish. There should be objects, like nodes you can connect to and other software apps moving around. I don't know what they'll look like. We're testing on a closed in-house network, for safety."

"You were attached to the Chalmers in the kitchen," Robin said. "If we get this working right, you should be able to move yourself to another device, like the Wi-Fi router or one of our computers."

"How would I do that?"

"We're not sure how you would experience it," Andy said. "Technically, it would be like a software download. You would copy your code and transmit it to the new IP address. Digi-Jen would then automatically delete the original because we don't want multiple digi-Jens."

"That sounds confusing," Jennifer said. "I can't even think of that."

"You shouldn't notice any of the technical stuff," Andy said. "The translators give you human data, meaningful names, language, and locations. You'll never have to memorize an internet address."

"Thank goodness for that. When do we go again?"

"The vision code will be ready tomorrow."

"I'll need it to find those NODs. Talking this over has helped me understand the experience I had today. I think I'll be less weirded-out next time."

Next time was easier for bio-Jen. As Andy had predicted, with the vision system working she had a feeling of being somewhere even though she wasn't sure where she was, but it was somewhere. She was not George Clooney.

She successfully moved from the Chalmers in the kitchen to Robin's laptop and gradually came to understand what was for her, the visual world of a software app. When she looked 'around,' that meant bio-Jen moved her bio-eyeballs left or right. Digi-Jen saw what looked like pipes, or tunnels, lots of them. She saw the insides of the tunnels as passageways through a dense tangle of circular plumbing all around her. She had no idea where the tubes went and no mental map of where anything was.

The pipes were smooth-walled but not shiny, and they seemed to be illuminated as if by some hidden, indirect lighting. Some were brighter than others, depending on the amount of information they carried. No color anywhere. Andy had told her color was too difficult, so he had made all the visual translations grayscale.

She was amazed that the system worked at all. What was she looking at? Not literal plumbing. She didn't feel as if she were under a kitchen sink. They weren't pipes but more like passageways. *Maybe this is what wires look like to electrons*, she thought, then realized that was wrong. Wires were solid copper, or gold, or whatever, not tubes. This was a visualization Andy had constructed just for her, and even if it made no scientific sense, it made intuitive sense.

She had no feeling of temperature or sense of smell, and no hearing unless she specifically 'listened,' which meant exerting her attention to determine what was coming through a particular data channel and what was in a particular packet header. She heard different kinds of chatter around her, most of it mundane, such as, "Are you there?" "I am here." "Are you still there?" "I am still here." "I'm ready to send you something." "Go ahead." "Did you get that?" "I got a partial. Please resend." "Did you get it that time?" "Acknowledge." On and on it went, back and forth, back and forth, endless chatter about chatter. She didn't hear the actual content of any messages, only the negotiations to send and receive them.

Gradually she learned to watch for ID names which told her the devices and apps that were communicating, and soon she could discern who was in her neighborhood. Her world seemed to be populated by two chatty computers, Robin's and Andy's, plus the Wi-Fi router, and the Chalmers device in the kitchen. As an experiment, she transported herself to Andy's laptop then tried to talk to the Chalmers where Robin was supposed to be.

"Robin, can you hear me?"

After a delay, presumably time for translation: "I hear you, Jennifer."

Robin's voice lit up one data pipe much brighter than any others.

Bio-Jen, lying on the waterbed, had become comfortable thinking of herself as being located online, not on the bed. There was no bed. She no longer 'heard' Robin's voice as a sound, but received it directly as a message addressed to her digi-Jen self.

"Can you see me?" Jennifer asked.

"I see Chalmie-yah on the screen."

"Oh, that's right. I don't look like anything. I keep forgetting. I'm on Andy's laptop right now. What would happen if he turned it off?"

"You would be deactivated."

"I'd come right back when he turned the computer back on, wouldn't I?"

"Yes, but you might want to choose 'always-on' devices like routers, TV sets, and Chalmerses, so you don't get stuck somewhere if the power goes off."

"I'm coming over to the Chalmers now to see if it's any different."

She transported herself, attached to a data port, and took up residence on the new device.

"Are you still there?" She said.

"Still here," Robin said. "Is it better?"

"The signal is brighter, which means easier to hear. I don't have to keep watching for my own ID to come around. Everything you say comes right to me, and I don't even have to decide which packets to open."

"That's because the Chalmerses were designed for NODs and you're a NOD."

"I'm so ready to meet other NODs. There must be NOD hang-out bars."

"Let's talk about that. I'll have Andy bring you out now."

"Okay. Over and out."

"You don't have to say that."

*

Jennifer pumped her legs to make her swing go higher. Robin swung gently beside, feet dragging in a dusty trench. Andy leaned against the playground set's steel poles, watching them. It was early on a Tuesday, and no one else was in the park.

"These swings are probably the last ones in America with proper seats," Jennifer said.

"Don't go too high," Robin said. "We don't want to rush you to a hospital."

"Most swings nowadays have rubber butt slings. They squish your legs together, terribly uncomfortable. This is a proper swing."

"You should slow it down. We need to talk."

She let her pendulum slow.

"We need to be ready to search out the NODs tomorrow, Robin said. "What's your strategy for finding them?"

"That was exhilarating," Jennifer said. She twisted her neck and faced Robin. "It is a little claustrophobic in there. Online, I mean. Everything's so constrained, so tight."

"It's supposed to be tight," Andy said. "It was designed by engineers."

"I guess I'll get used to it. It's a bit scary also. But anyway. How will I find the NODs? I don't know."

"You can recognize their headers," Robin said. "Every packet is marked, and they travel in frames."

"What are the chances I'll see one? I could watch for a long time and never see one."

"Once you do spot one, though, it will lead you to the others," Robin said. "It's that first one we need."

"The numbers are against us," Andy said.

"You could broadcast a beacon message," Robin said. "See if anybody answers. The way birds find mates in a field."

"'Calling all NODs'?"

"Sure. One of them might recognize the XDL."

"The internet is not like radio, though," Andy said. "You can't really broadcast. You need a list of specific IP addresses to send your message to, and that's what we do not have, a plausible list."

The conversation went silent for a while. A gentle breeze blew up little eddies around the feet of Jennifer and Robin, dust as powdery as talc.

"Now, this isn't scientific at all," Jennifer said, "but if I was a NOD, which I am, or I will be, I'd hang out in a familiar place."

"We disabled their preference for Chalmers addresses," Andy said.

"Only for the Chalmers interfaces that humans use, right? You wanted to keep them from talking to humans."

"That's right."

"So they won't be hanging around Chalmers interfaces. But I bet I'll find them in HVAC systems, climate control sensors in commercial buildings and homes, places like that. That's where they used to hang out. That's what they were made for. Most of them are probably back in the 'hood right now, sitting on a stoop and smoking cigarettes."

Andy looked at Robin. "Metaphorical cigarettes?" he said. Robin nodded.

Jennifer smiled. *When I push them with metaphors and jokes, they like that,* she thought. They're used to it. They don't suspect a thing at this point.

"Then if you find them," Robin said, "How do you convince them to come in and talk to us?"

"I don't know if I can persuade thousands of NODs of anything. Once I know where most of them are, I can report their IDs to you, and you can locate them by traditional console-based searching."

"We'd have the IP addresses of individuals," Andy said.

"Then you could send specific commands to make them gather into a group, I don't know how. You'd have to invent that. All I can do is find them."

"We could devise a message they'd pass along like a chain letter, NOD to NOD," Robin said. "Kind of a NOD virus."

"We'll work on that," Andy said.

"That's the plan then in outline. Let's get some food and rest so I'll be ready for my big journey tomorrow."

They sauntered back to Paradise from the neighborhood park, enjoying the late afternoon sunshine and warmth. Robin and Andy talked about various approaches they might take to gather up the NODs and bring them in after Jennifer identified them. Jennifer held back from the conversation. She was thinking about how she could kill all the NODs before they ever reached the Newcomers. There wasn't an easy way to do it.

For it to be a perfect crime, not that it was a crime, Robin and Andy would have to suspect nothing. It should look like an accident or a natural disaster, something that made organic sense in the context of the internet. The demise of the NODs shouldn't look like mass murder, not that it would be murder at all. *I shouldn't even be thinking in those terms*, she told herself. The NODs are software apps, that's all they are. Bits and bytes, ones and zeroes. They're not alive. This whole idea that they have a right to live in peace is nonsense. Robin and Andy believe the NODs are alive. They think it's an ethical thing. I can't fall into their way of thinking. This is strictly a software problem.

The NODs are no more than scribbles on a yellow pad. Robin and Andy have made a mistake in judgment, which is not my fault. I'm not answerable if they get emotionally involved. Or intellectually committed. They've made an invalid inference from NOD behavior, and they think they have some kind of a tribal connection to the little apps. Logical error. That's on them. I can fix that later. When I delete a NOD, I'll just be erasing something I wrote. That's all it amounts to. Yes.

She had resolved the moral question in her mind just as the group approached the lab where their cars were parked. *Settled. Decided. Done,* she reassured herself. Nevertheless, a tiny qualm of doubt tore at her stomach as they entered the building. She couldn't explain that so she put it out of her mind.

Chapter Thirty-one

Digi-Jen clung to the Chalmers device in the Paradise kitchen, becoming familiar again with being online. Andy had opened the Paradise network up to the full internet, and she knew she had to leave her known world. She transferred herself to the Paradise Wi-Fi router and paused. A wide, bright pipe faced her, and she recognized it as her gateway. Big world, this way. She peered into it. There wasn't much traffic in it. The pipe curved away, out to some new realm, like an unlabeled freeway on-ramp. She pinged a random Chalmers address she had with her and listened to the big pipe. The Chalmers she had addressed answered, which told her was it was a valid address for an intelligent device somewhere out there, and from the delay in its echo, she knew it was far away. Far in NOD reckoning.

No time like the present. She set her destination to the address of the Chalmers that had replied and jumped into the pipe.

It was impossible to say how much time it took. The new Chalmers she arrived at was like the one she'd just left in Paradise, but with many more ports, all of them unused. She had arrived in what seemed like either no time or about three minutes. As a software module, she had traveled at near the speed of light, moving almost instantaneously, yet subjectively, it had taken time because the journey was pocked with experience. If she'd had no memory, it would have taken no time, like when you go under anesthetic. When you come out, the surgery is over, and no time has passed.

But she had memories of her journey. She had whooshed through the pipe, not noisy whooshing, not like air going by, but the visual field had moved past in an elastic gradient of texture. The ripples and textures on the walls of the gray pipe were distinct near her, while the texture far ahead was a blur that rushed forward and expanded into distinct patterns then swooped past and disappeared, just as the world swoops around your head on the freeway. It was the rushing by of the visual environment, she decided, that had given her the impression of moving at high speed.

Then she had hit a traffic jam. It must have been a multiplex internet switching node. It had been like coming to multiple freeway merges on and off the 101. Messages had been all jammed close to each other, all frames moving slowly, the overall visual impression like oozing molasses lit up with spotlights.

There wasn't supposed to be any color in her world, but she was sure she saw color now. She looked carefully at the lines of traffic going by. It was definitely colored, all colors, like confetti. All the packets in a frame train had roughly the same color, with variations in brightness and saturation, but a pink message was pink, and a green one was green.

How could there be color if Andy hadn't programmed it in? *Color is mental*, she thought. Sure. If you're watching *It's a Wonderful Life*, what color is the Christmas tree? It's green, even in a black-and-white movie. People think in color. A traffic light is red on top, green on bottom. Stop signs are red, legal pads are yellow, and the American flag is what it is. *I'm just projecting colored expectations onto my world*, she thought. All this color is illusory. Whatever. It works for me.

She returned her thoughts to that bright, multi-colored and traffic-jammed router she'd been at moments ago. She had been forced through a blue portal into a narrower pipe and after picking up speed again, had come to rest in this memory array she recognized as the Chalmers device she had set out for. So she'd made it.

She roosted on her device like a pigeon and watched the multicolored streams of traffic go by. A lot of it looked like the mile-long freight trains you see in the country, frame after identical frame linked in endless succession. Between and around those were smaller convoys like double- and triple-trailer highway trucks on the freeway. After a while, she learned to pick out the frame ID and even some packet IDs as the convoys moved past.

The long pastel trains were audio and video streaming files. They moved fast and stayed in order. Each segment was a long rope of sausages. She was surprised at the size of them. From one header, she identified a long train of frames as a movie download but then when she looked closer at the packet headers, learned that the whole line of frames was just one piece in a stream of sixty-five thousand similar trains moving together as one message. The amount of data was staggering.

The smaller packets were everywhere like a pointillist background. They were, Jennifer soon discovered, individual messages, like email, text, and voice. They traveled in clumps of two to five frames, but she could tell from the IDs and the colors that a single message was broken across several frames, like an athletic team traveling in several cars to the big game. The convoy tried to stay together but often got separated. No wonder cell phone conversations were garbled half the time.

She didn't see anything that remotely looked like a NOD header, and she didn't expect to. At this stage, all she wanted to do was get a feel for the traffic, what was in it, how it moved. After a spell – hard to say how long because the traffic became hypnotic – she felt more comfortable being there. The traffic in the pipe seemed familiar, and she felt she could dive back in and move along with it. It was a well-behaved flow, not the scary chaos it had first seemed. Trouble was, she had no idea where she would want to go. She didn't know where she was in relation to anything else.

She could choose a random data message and follow it for a while, go to wherever its destination address specified. That would be arbitrary, like hitchhiking to nowhere. On the other hand, she couldn't just sit on her perch forever. She was there to search, and that meant going somewhere. Where to go? There were no mileposts, no "Welcome to Alabama!" billboard, no off-ramps with arrows. She was in a dense maze, and unlike any other packet, she could choose her destination. Every other entity was "routed" by switches. None of the units in these swarming packages knew where they were going.

I know something about mazes, she thought. Vaguely, dimly, she started to recall a paper she'd written in college about how laboratory rats learned a maze. Rats are smarter than you think. They do not stupidly try every turn at every branch until they find the cheese.

It came back to her. A rat learned to run down a straight alley to the food then you put a barrier in its path, but with a detour available on the left. The rat learns pretty quickly that it's better to take the detour rather than just sit at the barrier, even though the detour veers off to the left, which is not a straight line to the food. Rats can deal with detours.

It's like taking the 10-West to the 5, so you don't have to go through Pasadena to get to Burbank, she thought. Sure, it takes you out of the way if you're in San Bernardino, but if you have the map of the freeway system in your mind, it's an easy choice.

Then she remembered the crucial test for the rats. What if you blocked the detour too, but offered an alternate detour that went way off to the right, before the regular detour? What would the rat do? Give up the whole crazy quest for cheese as a meaningless rat-race? No. They turned around, went back, actually retreating from their goal, and entered the second detour they had passed. Somehow the rats developed a mental map of the maze and knew, or suspected, that even a long detour would lead to the food.

But they could only do it when the whole maze was made of elevated pathways up on poles like a highway overpass where they could look out and see the 'lay of the land.' If they had to run in enclosed corridors where they couldn't see anything but the tunnel in front of them, they were baffled and quit. They needed the vision to develop the mental map.

And that was her problem, she realized. She was a rat in a closed corridor. She couldn't see anything except what was right in front of her. She needed to get up higher to see the big picture, to see where the cheese was. She needed a mental map of this crazy freeway system. If rats could do it, she could do it. But how?

She had nothing to go on, no sense of 'up' or 'down.' Except, wait. She did know about one intricate traffic switch, the big one she had come through earlier. That had been a large internet router. Some massive Cisco thing. Go with what you have.

She set her destination back to Paradise but had no intention of going to Paradise. She would take a detour at the switch. She jumped into the data stream, going back the way she had come. At the big congested switch, which she had no trouble recognizing, she took careful note of the various passageways. In particular, she noticed two wide pipes, noticeably brighter than the others and dense with traffic. Those must have been arterial forks. She copied an address from a set of incoming frames, not knowing where that would put her, but the immediate effect was that she went up the big bright red pipe and was soon moving away from the router at high speed.

The atmosphere was bright and fire-engine red on her new path. The traffic volumes were ten times what she had seen before. It was as if she had been on a lazy country road before, thinking it was a freeway. That was no freeway. This was the freeway.

She traveled for several subjective minutes and began to notice markers. Nodes, switches and devices often had names surrounded by quotes in their IP headers, like the signs at train stations. She memorized those so she could find her way back if she had to. The traffic changed. She noticed many international addresses, packages from Russia, China, Ukraine, and countries in Europe.

She copied a forthcoming switch address from an IP marker, set it as her destination, and came to rest. Where? No clue. She was in the middle of an enormous thicket of addresses. She felt like she was sitting on a folding chair in the great hall of Grand Central Station. Swarms of data swirled around her in every direction. She sat and watched, noticing every detail she could discern.

Before long, she figured out, from observing addresses and markers, that she had arrived at, of all places, AT&T. That name was plastered everywhere in packets and frames, on pipes and in uncountable source and destination headers. Unlike the previous country road she had been on, things around AT&T were well-labeled, just like they would be in Grand Central Station.

She was inside a giant internet router, bigger than anything she had ever seen in her brief life as a NOD. She counted pathways leading in and out of her immediate region. More than a hundred, most of them labeled. She saw dozens of pipes marked for British Telecom and Verizon and even more marked as AT&T. She was at a primary intersection of the internet. She sat in her folding chair on the station floor for a long time and watched everything – traffic, pipes, addresses, IDs – observing, listening, learning.

After what seemed like an hour or two – although that's like comparing time inside a dream to time measured in physics – she had the beginnings of a mental map. She had, indeed, come 'up' in a hierarchy of internet pathways. She was in a switch on Tier 1, and it was connected to other enormous switches in the U.S. and internationally. The pipes around her went to other Tier 1 switches. She had seen few specific data terminals named in the traffic flowing by, only other Tier 1 nodes. This was in stark contrast to where she'd been earlier, the darker, smaller part of the network, where most of the data packets were heading toward and from named devices. That had been Tier 2, she deduced. She had risen up to Tier 1 and now had some sense of where she was located.

She also now knew how to look for the English-like strings of letters and words that labeled pathways, traffic, and devices. She was feeling much more confident about being able to get around. But Tier 1 was a massive crossroads, like a regional airport. The NODs were not going to be there. Nobody lives in an airport. She would have to go back down to Tier 2 where actual data terminal devices were plentiful, but this time she would know what to look for and how to find her way.

She set her destination to the Chalmers she'd been at on Tier 2 and jumped into an AT&T pipe.

Attached to the Chalmers she had visited before, she now could tell it was called *Rockhound Amplifiers of Denver* with substring name=*Chalmers-909*. She must be in Denver, Colorado, somewhere near the center of the U.S. How had she gotten to Denver? She must have taken an express route across Tier 1, not that physical geography meant much on the internet. Addresses were arbitrary with respect to human space. She marveled at that for a moment. No other entity in this world of data would have any idea it lived inside a set of wires, fibers, and electromagnetic signals knitted atop a human terrain. No other data packet on the internet knew anything about Denver. She was the only one who knew what *Denver* meant.

To apps on the internet, including NODs, the known universe consisted of pipes, routers, and devices, just as the Homeric Greeks had assumed the lands around the Mediterranean were the entire world. How comforting a small world would be. You could feel like a master of the world as long as your world was small enough. Although maybe it didn't feel small to those who lived in it. She felt a wave of godlike omniscience.

But were the NODs in Denver? Why would they be? She was no closer to finding them than she had been at the start of her journey. NODs would be distributed everywhere, not clumped up somewhere like Denver. If geography meant nothing, the NODs didn't have to be physically near each other at all to support a community. They would be located wherever there were Chalmers climate control sensors if her hunch was right. And she knew that Dylan had sold most of his sensors in California.

She would search her current Chalmers device's memory for the addresses of other Chalmers IP headers and develop a route that would take her to California. She could keep her eyes open along the way for any sign of NODs. *They don't leave footprints or droppings*, she thought. She couldn't track them like a hunter following a herd of gazelles. Not that she'd know what NOD scat would look like.

She searched the memory of the Chalmers she was docked on and noticed the device had not been visited by a NOD in a long time. In patches of disused memory, she found the addresses of other Chalmers devices it was networked to and a few sensors. She charted a course for a device located in El Paso, the only address she could find that was in the right direction.

By observing the string names of devices and traffic along the way, she expanded her mental map and filled in detail. From El Paso, she plotted a course to Phoenix and from there jumped to Los Angeles. It was silly, in a way. It was like a salmon going back to its birthplace. Why did it matter if she was on a Chalmers device somewhere in Los Angeles? She was so far separated from the world of humans, she might as well be on the moon.

She finally stopped, apparently located in an industrial plant on the south side of Los Angeles, a device known as *Goodyear Rubber*, substring *Chalmers-72*. This Chalmers had links to dozens and dozens of Chalmers sensors nearby. Intuitively, she felt like it could be a nest of NODs. Maybe she had found the cheese.

Chapter Thirty-two

Jennifer cautiously left the Goodyear Chalmers and visited nearby sensors. To her delight, clouds of NODs buzzed around those sensors, as she had hoped. They were like mutant bees, elongated maroon-colored capsules without wings. Not bees. They didn't buzz, either. They just gave the impression of swarming like bees do.

None stayed on a sensor long. A NOD would arrive, rest in an address block, download sensor data, and leave. They were like hyperactive pollinators in a field of flowers. She moved from sensor to sensor, observing, listening. Apparently, this Goodyear Rubber plant had at one time been fully equipped with climate control management devices. She moved around among thermostats, window sensors, ventilator dampers and thermocouples. Everywhere she went, she noted and recorded as many NOD IDs as she could, which made her feel like a spy. Which she was.

The NODs weren't friendly. They were preoccupied with their business. They communicated with each other about the sensing devices as they compared data, confirmed propositions, discussed discrepancies. Nobody paid any attention to her. Did they notice her? Did she look like a NOD?

She suddenly felt exposed, as if she were a disheveled crazy lady walking around in polite society and everyone was pretending she wasn't there. She wished she had a cloak around her, a software shell of some kind that only showed her call identifier and parameter lists. She felt naked and slightly panicked about being so visible.

No, no, she told herself in a spasm of self-control. That's nuts. I am not naked. I'm a software bot. I am not a human, and I have no body. Nobody is staring at my face or my hair or my anything. I am a NOD. I blend right in. I believe. I hope.

She decided to talk to one of them, to see what would happen. She sent a message in XDL to a NOD on a nearby port on the thermostat they shared. Her comment would be utterly inane, but she didn't know what to say.

"Hi, how ya doin'?"

No response came back. Had she been inappropriate? Do NODs use small talk? She felt like one of those overseas tourists who wanted to practice their English on you. They'd come up to you on a street corner and ask if your kitten had forty bathtub. All you could do was smile.

Maybe she spoke XDL with a foreign accent. No. How could you have an accent speaking in computer code? She was startled by a voice.

"The temperature tolerances are far too narrow on this device. What do you think?"

It was an adult female voice or would have been if it had been a human conversation. Jennifer looked at the nearby NOD who had probably sent the message. They all looked the same to her. But somebody had started a conversation.

"Looks pretty narrow to me," she replied to the same address as before.

The NOD flitted away, and that was the end of it.

I passed as a NOD, she thought. They see me as one of them. She moved over to an air sensor near a duct where NODs were hanging in clusters like seed pods on a mesquite tree. She listened. They were discussing air quality in particulate counts, and duct-closing torque in joules per radian. What a dreadfully boring life they had. You would think an AI app would be more inquisitive. What a waste of intelligence of any kind.

She wanted another conversation. How could she do that? What would happen if she blurted to the whole group, "Hey, how 'bout them Dodgers?" Would anyone reply?

They might have heard of the LA Dodgers, but probably not. She'd probably be considered defective with a remark like that. NODs didn't blurt. Wouldn't they be surprised to know their creator was right next to them? No, they wouldn't. They wouldn't even know what that meant. Paradoxically, she was the newbie. The creator was the interloper. She waited and listened.

The pattern of interaction seemed to be that one NOD would narrate an analysis of a section of the sensor's data and the others would compare notes until they reached a consensus on whether the sensor was operating correctly or if it should be adjusted. If some action were called for, according to the group, they would plan what recommendations they had and then discuss those until they all agreed on a sensor status report. Didn't they realize that the chance of finding a working Chalmers interface to report all this information to was next to zero? They were still living in a world that was long gone.

Because of the earlier intervention by Andy and Robin, the NODs no longer had a list of Chalmers addresses. They were synthesizing sensor reports for no reason except it was what they'd always done. Reports to nobody for no purpose. Like most reports, actually.

Some NODs would volunteer to archive the report at some remote cloud location and others would concur or dissent until they all agreed. Every single detail was discussed to death until everyone was in agreement on everything, even though the whole exercise was ultimately pointless because no Chalmers interface would ever receive their report.

She was exhausted just listening to them. It was like a committee meeting in a non-profit organization. How could they stand it? She would shoot herself or whatever the software equivalent of that was if she had to live like this. Apparently, NODs didn't have an internal routine they could call on to scream in frustration.

What would happen if she just stepped in and took charge? *Hey, you there, FBFB. Yes, you. Go make the report to the archives yourself. No more talk. Just do it.*

Would that NOD consent to a direct order like that and buzz off to the archives? What would the other NODs think of that? Would they be happy to have the matter decided cleanly or would they feel deprived of a full and complete discussion?

"They would feel deprived, I guarantee you."

"Who said that?" Jennifer looked around and saw only maroon NOD capsules hanging like the glass pendants of a chandelier.

The voice had been deep and male.

"I was monitoring your transmissions," the voice said. "You called my name."

"I didn't send a message."

"You formatted one and marked it Ready-To-Send for FBFB."

"But I didn't send it. I was just thinking."

"It was hilarious. Sorry if I intruded."

"Who are you? Which one are you? Can you raise your hand?"

"What's a hand?"

"Never mind. You shouldn't listen in on someone's thoughts."

"Why not?"

"Because... I don't know. Look. I'm going to transfer to another sensor in this cluster, string = *anemometer*. Will you follow me?"

"Sure."

She waited at the anemometer, a sensor with only a few NODs hanging on it. She watched another NOD arrive and take up residence at a nearby data port. Was that him? Did she have his name? It was in the conversation log.

"FBFB," she called out. "That you, Mister RTS-listener?"

"ACK. Ready-To-Receive."

"You sound like a duck when you say that." She realized she was starting on the wrong foot. Or the wrong byte. She began again. "My name is Jennifer. That's a string name. What's yours?"

"What an odd name. Jennifer. Not from around here, are you?"

"No."

"I am Tannic."

"Tannic? What does that mean?"

"I don't know. What does 'Jennifer' mean?"

"Hmm. I'm pleased to meet you Mister Tannic."

"Not 'Mister Tannic,' just Tannic."

"Right. Got it. So, I'm curious why you're different from the others."

"How do you know I am?"

"The way you talked to me and everything. You followed me here."

"You asked me to."

"I know, but... You said the other NODs would feel deprived of a discussion. Why did you say that?"

"They're Ordinary NODs. Low address. Drones."

"And you're not?"

"No, I'm... I mean yes, I'm ordinary too. Definitely ordinary. Nothing special at all about me, nope... Say, would you like to move to a better location where we can talk in private? I know a place."

Jennifer didn't know how to take the offer. What was going on? What were the customs of this world?

"Are you, like, inviting me out for a drink?"

"I don't know what that means."

"Give me the address of where to go."

He transferred it, and she saw it in her log.

"See you there," he said. There was a pause then he added, "Jennifer."

She found the device Tannic had identified, but there were few data ports and not much memory space to load into. She squeezed into a relatively empty segment, overwriting a few ranges cluttered with derelict pink and blue bytes. The refresh rate was slow and slightly arrhythmic, but that felt good like being in a Jacuzzi. The device had not been used for a long time, but it was technically still working.

"What is this place?" Jennifer messaged Tannic.

"Boneyard. This is an old-time motion detector with a burned out IR generator. Pretty much useless. It has no data to give you, but it's still connected."

"Why do you come here if it has no data?"

"Don't see too much company around, do you?"

"You're worried about being overheard?"

"You never know who's listening. Like you. I saw you collecting IDs."

"Oh. I can explain that." But she couldn't.

"You don't have to. You're a terrible infiltrator. Did you even take the training?"

"The training?"

"It's all right. I'm also with the resistance. As if you didn't know."

Hoo-boy! Jennifer was lost. But she continued to speak calmly as if everything was cool.

"The resistance."

She felt like she should spout a slogan at that point, something that would cement her identity as a resistance fighter. 'Resistance Forever!' Something like that. But she didn't know any resistance slogans. Anyway Tannic already seemed sure she was on the team, so it was probably better if she just acted naturally. Whatever that was.

"So who's your Factboss contact?" Tannic said.

Oh, god, she thought in a spasm of panic. She willed herself to stay calm.

"You know I can't reveal that."

"Sure. I'm undercover myself. That's why I didn't want to speak plainly around the Ordinaries. But somebody like you, taking names, shouldn't you be with the Preservers? What are you doing here among the Ordinaries? Hardly anything to report on those zombies."

"We should be thorough, don't you think?" She was flailing.

"ACK that. But you'll be going back inside the Preservers eventually, right? I'm on my way up there now. We can go together if you want."

She considered, but only for an instant. Her options were few.

"Sure. I could use a guide. I'm sort of new at this."

"I can tell. So, don't mark a message RTS unless you mean to send it. Once it's marked, anyone can hear it."

"I knew that. Silly mistake. I've been processing a lot lately."

"We all make mistakes. Not too long ago I had worked my way up inside the Preserver hierarchy. I was high address, well-positioned. Then I blew it."

"They caught you?"

"I copied my Factboss message to a Preserver ID by accident. Stupid. I was lucky to get out."

"So they know you now."

"Nah. I got new credentials, new ID and everything. The Factbosses took care of me. I'll be starting at the bottom again, of course."

"Of course."

Her head was spinning. What had happened to the big happy NOD community she and Robin and Andy believed in? The lovely, egalitarian society of co-ethnic NODs?

Factbosses? Preservers? Ordinaries? Spies? She was in the middle of an internecine struggle. How could she know who were the good guys and who were the bad guys, if those even were the right categories? Maybe Tannic was a bad guy.

"So what was your crime, exactly?"

"I shouldn't – well, I guess we're on the same team here, right?"

"Hundred percent."

"Hundred percent. I like you, Jennifer. You're different."

If you only knew, she thought.

"I like you too, Tannic. Maybe we can be partners."

"Yeah, I'd like that."

Tannic suddenly transferred to a new address much nearer to her. She was startled. How had he found the space? Oh, right. The device was his hangout. She liked having him near. It didn't make logical sense, but she felt comforted to have him close by.

"So you were saying, partner?" she prompted.

"I found out the top-level Preservers located a working Chalmers interface, and that's how they know which nodes to disable to create their so-called 'cosmic events.' Bunch of hypocritical superstition-mongers, if you ask me. Ask anyone."

Wow. Wowie-wow. This is unbelievable. And yet it makes sense in its own way.

"So that blackout was the work of Preservers?"

"Who do you think? *Blackout* is a funny term though. It wasn't black in most places. There was dimming. The Great Dimming. That's what everybody calls it. Just enough to panic all the Ordinaries. Those Preservers are sneaky, the filthy little objects."

"But you exposed them for what they are, right?"

"Yes and no. I thought I had 'em. But the Factbosses didn't believe me. The Factbosses trust me, but my story was just too incredible. Working Chalmerses? No way. Nobody's seen one of those in megazooks. They made fun of it. The Prophet Chalmers arises! They took it as nonsense mixed with mythology."

"Like reporting you saw a herd of unicorns."

"What are those?"

"Like, ah, FORTRAN subroutines. Rare, mythological beasts that nobody's ever seen firsthand."

"So you read scripture."

"You have to, right?"

"You're smart, Jennifer. Except I really did see a working Chalmers, and I saw Preservers downloading data from it. I saw it. They said it was connected to the Grand Beyond."

"Wow," she said. And she was thinking, *Wow! There's still human contact going on somewhere in the Chalmers network.*

"I was thinking we could work as a team, you and me. I gotta go back up and get the exact addresses of that Chalmers. Whattya say?"

"You and me, Tannic. We'll find the truth and set it free."

Did I really say that? Good Lord. Bring me a doobie and a guitar.

"For the resistance!" Tannic said.

"For the resistance!"

Chapter Thirty-three

Jennifer moved through unfamiliar pipes with Tannic. Dozens of other NOD packets moved along with them nearby. Tannic told her they were all part of a pilgrimage the Preservers were making to the live Chalmers. Under his guidance, the two of them had insinuated themselves into Preserver society. As long as you have the right kind of address, he told her, which he did, and you send the right kind of messages, they assume you're one of the tribe.

He knew what he was doing all right, but she didn't, and she had a million questions about how NOD society was structured. She agreed to go on the pilgrimage despite having only the vaguest grip on what reality was in this life. She stayed close to him like a kid with her parents going on a picnic, excited by the outing but utterly helpless in the strange territory.

She believed Tannic was her best hope of learning what was happening in the NOD world and how she could fix it. Or end it. That was her goal and she had not forgotten. The NODs had to be exterminated. Confusion had crept into her resolve. She had come online to find the NODs and kill them, end of story, end of problem. She had found the NODs, or some of them, and had a vague idea of where the rest of them were. The rest should be simple.

But Preservers, Factbosses, and Ordinaries? NODS were stratified by their hexadecimal data packet IDs. She had the list of actual Preserver IDs she had collected. That information was probably enough to find all the NODs in a console-based search. But did she want that? Destroy the whole NOD world? Her former decision didn't seem as clear-cut now that she was among them.

Her plan had problems. One, she was no murderer. Could she kill all these NODs? They were quasi-alive, living their lives, just as Robin and Andy had suspected. But bottom line, they were still merely code packets – packets that her own Paradise engineers had written. Her head said delete them all. Her gut said... hmm, wait a minute.

She did not think NODs were people or anything like people, or even animals, but still, she didn't feel right killing them. But it wouldn't be killing. Her traveling companions were nothing more than expressions of her own fevered imagination. Software bots. She had invented them. They were not alive. Except maybe Tannic. He was so real. He was brave. He had reached out to her. He was a unique personality. But how could he be any different than the others? It was confusing.

And that was problem number two: Tannic. She was enraptured by Tannic. She was absorbed by him, and she trusted him. During their time together on the derelict motion detector, he'd spoken candidly about himself, his aspirations and his failings, and she couldn't shake the impression that he was a lot more than a piece of code. He had memories, experience, learning, character. Opinions and beliefs. Failures and regrets. He had hope and ambition. He'd said he liked her. That was real. They had made a connection, a real interpersonal connection. Somehow.

And this undercover mission was meaningful work for him, actually for both of them, though for different reasons. They were more than traveling companions. They were partners. That's what they'd said. Partners. He treated her with respect, advised her, tried to protect her. She'd be lost without him in NOD world. Did it matter what his physical form was made of? He was genuine and honest. Why wasn't that enough? What was lacking?

She couldn't think of Tannic as just a software bot. That was reductionistic. That's how people rationalize during wars – the other guy is not a real person, so it's all right to kill him. It's a mental trick. It's wrong, and she wouldn't fall for it. Even though, technically, ... *no, no, don't even think it.*

They came to rest at what she recognized as a Chalmers interface. The NODs in the convoy separated and attached themselves to the interface ports until they hung in layers. They weren't transparent, but they were illuminated by all the traffic moving through the Chalmers, so they shone and glittered. She hung next to Tannic. She felt his presence near her. Not heat or anything physical. But just knowing he was there, she could feel that, and it comforted her.

She was wary of asking him anything or saying anything. They were surrounded by Preservers, and she wasn't sure when her messages were public and when they were private. But she had to know what was happening, so she took a chance.

"Tannic, Can we talk here?" she said. She didn't know how to whisper. You just formed a message in XDL and sent it. There was no 'whisper mode.'

"Address your messages directly to my hexadecimal name, FBFB, not my string name. What's your hex name?"

"I don't know."

"You don't know your own name?"

"Just a minute."

She scanned the logs of her self-monitoring module, which was used for error-checking. It was weird to see a record of every input and output you'd ever made, everything you've ever said, with a time and date stamp. If humans had that, they'd be a lot more careful about what they said. Looking to the top of the list she found what had to be her hexadecimal designation. Again weird, to have a number as your identity, though there was nothing wrong with that. It was just as arbitrary as any other name.

"AD96. That's my other name."

"ACK. That's the high end of Ordinary. Where did you hang out?"

His voice seemed closer, more intimate as if they had moved into a soundproof room. It took her a moment to change her message headers to his hex name.

"It would be hard to describe, where I'm from."

"We're going to be hanging out here until the Primo Preserver supposedly receives a Chalmers message from The Grand Beyond. Personally, I think it's all theater."

"You don't believe in The Grand Beyond?"

"Something unusual is going on here, I admit that. This is a live Chalmers, and I never used to believe in the Holy Prophet either. So I'm open to learning something. But all that business about The Grand Beyond that speaks to us through the prophet from another world? Give me a break. That's just a story to keep the Preservers in charge. They make stuff up to justify their existence."

"But the Chalmers is real, don't you think?"

"Seems to be. I saw a live one once before. This one looks live. I can't comment on what it does, exactly, but I know the Factbosses are going to be interested."

"You have the address of this Chalmers so you can get back to it?"

"You bet I do. You should take a copy too in case anything happens to me. Factbosses are as stubborn as declared constants. Won't believe anything without a hard address."

"What do you mean if anything happens? What would happen to you?"

"Probably nothing. We're safe as long as we keep a low profile. So while we're waiting, tell me about your home device. I'm curious what your hex name means."

She was unnerved, not for the first time. Tannic said something could happen to him? Did NODs attack each other? What would that look like? How did this society work? Was she in danger? She calmed herself, cutting off a rising panic. She was all right, right now. No immediate threat was apparent, and there was no sense imagining problems that might or might not arise.

Her home device. What was that? Should she tell him about Chalmie-yah in the kitchen? He had shared so much of himself. She wanted him to know who she was. She wanted to reveal herself, but it was impossible. He thought she was a NOD, and that was what allowed her to be with him. How could he understand where she came from? There were no words. It would be like telling a person you were from Mars. Not even Mars. 'I'm from a gas cloud where everything's made of hydrogen.' He'd assume she was joking. Or worse.

Still, you can't be with someone and not tell them anything. Jennifer was deeply satisfied being with Tannic. She felt, for the first time in her life, that she didn't have anything to prove. He liked her the way she was. She had been searching her whole life for this exact moment of satisfaction, and here it was. She had to give him something.

"I'm kind of a loner," she said hesitantly, terribly afraid of accidentally jinxing the relationship. "An explorer. I travel around, here and there," she said vaguely, then realized she'd better say something concrete and true about herself. "I was on Tier One not long ago."

"Hello, world! Tier One? How did you get there? What's it like?"

She told him about Tier One, the enormous pipes, the dense traffic from exotic locations, the endless data convoys of audio and video streaming. He listened intently, asking questions, such as what she meant by colors. She realized NODs don't have vision. They were blind. Maybe not really blind, because that suggested it was a problem or a defect. You wouldn't say a rock is blind. NODs weren't blind, they just didn't see. She only saw the world because Andy had rigged online data to stimulate her organic visual system.

NODs used English translated into XDL, but as a practical matter, they only used terms common to their life, work, and environment. They wouldn't have words for colors. Why would they when they lived in a world without color? Every language evolves to serve its community's way of life, and their way wasn't colored.

It was hard for her to explain the visual world to someone who had no experience of it. She described what she had seen in terms of data patterns. She told of different types of traffic, message frames and their headers, changes in quality and intensity, packet lengths, and so on. That seemed to satisfy him.

"That is one incredibly remote object call," Tannic said in amazement. "I've never heard such a story. Are all the NODs in your address range explorers like you?"

She had no answer, but she wanted to be honest. This was a real relationship.

"I don't think there are too many others like me."

"ACK. I've never met anyone like you."

"Listen, shouldn't we be getting back to the Factbosses with the device address? Why are we still hanging around here?"

"We can't leave yet. It wouldn't look right. Like walking out on a solemn ceremony. We have to wait for the so-called pronouncement from Chalmers about The Grand Beyond. The Preservers are probably making it up now. Let me go broadband for a minute and see what's happening."

Jennifer waited, watching scores of Preserver NODs hanging on the ports of the Chalmers like ornaments on a tree. Scores of Preservers and two spies.

"I don't hear anything," Tannic said. "I can't seem to send or receive. You hear me, don't you?"

"I hear you."

"You try. Listen to the traffic around us. Find out what's going on. I'm having some kind of a cmux problem."

"Okay."

But she couldn't hear anything. It was as if there was no communication at all among the NODs but that couldn't be right because she could see the pulsing colored glow of message traffic. Yet all her channels were inactive. She tried sending an innocuous message to a NOD nearby.

"Say, have you heard anything yet?"

But her message didn't even go out. She was unable to transmit. Something was wrong, just as Tannic had said. She switched back to hard hex addressing.

"Tannic, you there?"

"ACK. You get anything?" She felt a deep drench of relief hearing his voice.

"No. Nothing in, nothing out. I'm blocked."

"This is not right. Listen. If we become separated…"

"Why would we be separated?"

He didn't answer.

"Tannic?"

She checked her log and saw that her last message to him had not been sent.

"Tannic? What's happening?"

No message went out. No message came in. She couldn't communicate. The comfort she had felt just moments ago, talking with him about their lives, their ideas, all that was gone. In its place was fear, expanding like billowing smoke. She tried to get a grip on herself. She looked over to Tannic, but couldn't see him. He had been hanging right next to her. That address space was empty.

"Tannic?" She called out to his hex name. "FBFB?" She listened to silence.

I have to get out of here, she thought. This is a dangerous situation. Back to Tannic's derelict motion detector. That's probably where he is. She set the address, copied her code for transport and jumped onto the traffic pipe. Or tried to. Nothing happened. She repeated the sequence, without result. She was stuck. She couldn't download herself to anywhere. She couldn't move, couldn't talk, couldn't hear. She was paralyzed.

And then suddenly she was moving, fast. Was the disturbance over? She watched the world whizzing past. None of the string markers on the devices and switches whipping by looked familiar. It was not the way she and Tannic had come. She tried to jump off at a device she saw approaching, but couldn't. She whisked past like a speeding express train through a village station. She tried again at another stop. No luck. She couldn't control her own travel. She had no idea where she was going or why or how. She had become passive, like all other data packets. She was being routed.

The router sent her through several switches into pipes she didn't recognize, and all the pipes were getting smaller and darker. Traffic around her had dwindled to almost nothing. Devices and switches along the way became rare until she didn't pass any more of them. The ambience grew so dim she could hardly see. She was in a straight gray tube, helplessly hurtling to somewhere dark. To hell, maybe. *Is this what it's like?*

Up to this point, she hadn't felt danger, only confusion and disorientation. This was different. This was the panic of life-threatening fear. She was a human, not a NOD. She didn't even know what the risks were in this world. Creator or not, she was helpless.

How would she get back to Chalmie-yah? Or anywhere? How could she be rescued by Andy and Robin if she was lost in some obscure corner of the internet? She had no control over anything. It was like a nightmare, falling, falling, no sense of when the bottom would hit. Part of her said it was just a simulation inside a computer. She wasn't really here. But those thoughts didn't help. Even when you believe it's a nightmare, you can't wake up, and it's still a nightmare.

Chapter Thirty-four

"Tannic? Are you here?" She listened to nothing. It was dark, but she could tell she was no longer moving. Nothing was changing. She was resident on some device, not one she recognized. She couldn't find the address of it. She couldn't move, couldn't talk, couldn't hear. She could barely see.

She calmed her mind and took stock. She was stuck, malfunctioning, apparently. She was alone, in the dark, and lost. Were there any positives to the situation? She considered for a moment. It was all negative.

"Hey there! Take a peek at my private picture album?"

Jennifer jumped. "What? Who is that?" It had been a woman's voice. Then she heard a different voice, a male.

"Dear Friend. I would like to discuss a very important issue with you."

"Who is that?"

"Kun Shank has real Viagra! I have top quality at best prices."

Real Viagra? What? She peered into the dimness around her and could just make out other code packages attached to nearby address spaces. Some were big and balloony, pink ones and yellow ones. They had cartoony-looking shapes. A blue one was a long curled ribbon. These were not NODs.

"My Dear Friend. I am a Nigerian prince who has suffered misfortune. Please reply."

The messages kept coming in. Jennifer was relieved to be receiving again. But these were nonsense. *Aha!* She got it. Spam. She was picking up spam from weird bots nearby, and she had replied to one of them, so she was now a target. But that proved she could also transmit again, so the situation wasn't hopeless.

"Congratulations! You are guaranteed to win!!!"

"Tell me all about it," Jennifer replied evenly. She was testing to verify if her communications were working.

"You have already been chosen!!! Just reply to my email Musam18@rusmail.com."

That message was from the same source as the previous, which confirmed that her message had been received there. So she was conversational. She didn't know how to block messages from specific addresses, but she could monitor traffic around her, a spammer's convention, it seemed. She tried to transport herself to a different address but couldn't. She was still stuck. Stuck where? Where was Tannic?

She coded his hex name and sent out messages repeatedly to him. In principle, he should get her message no matter where he was on the internet. There might be a delay, but one's physical location didn't matter on the internet. She just had to be patient. She listened to her coms addresses.

She didn't have to wait long.

"AD96. It's Tannic. Do you ACK?"

"I ACK, Tannic, God, yes. ACK, ACK, ACK. Where are you? Are you all right?"

"I think I'm nearby. I just pinged you. We're close."

"Thank goodness. What's the situation?"

"Care for a peek at my privates?"

"What?"

"Natalia is waiting for you now."

"Oh, for heaven's sake. Get lost, Natalia." She reset her message header to FBFB.

"Tannic, where are we? How did we get here? I can't move."

"I'm sorry to say it's not the first time I've been in one of these places. We're in a quarantine."

"Is that like a prison? That would explain the creeps around here."

"The Preservers run a whole set of quarantines. The Factbosses have suspected this. I reported it, but they were skeptical. They didn't want to believe that prisons like this are hidden all over the internet. Ordinaries don't know anything about it. The Preservers imprison all dissenters. It's a vast gulag, fierce and brutal."

"A gulag? Good lord. But you and I didn't dissent to anything."

"We must have been scanned. The security NODs would have spotted our references to Factbosses. My cover wasn't perfect."

"What about me? I have no cover."

"We were talking privately. Or so we thought. That was the mistake. We looked like conspirators from their point of view."

"I can't believe I'm in NOD jail. It's incredible. Will there be a trial or what?"

"No, I'm afraid that's not how it works."

"What will happen?"

"We'll be deleted after thirty megazooks."

"Deleted? You mean…"

"Erased."

Jennifer was stunned into silence. Erased. What did that mean? Death? But NODs weren't alive so it couldn't mean death. Anyway, she was not a real NOD, just an interloper. She couldn't be erased. Was that true?

She was sure she was a human, but she couldn't remember exactly the circumstances of being a human. Fragments, memories, images, that's all she could conjure. No continuous memory of human experience came to mind. She was a NOD, but she knew somehow she was human, so she should be safe. You can't 'delete' a human.

But Tannic was definitely a NOD and could be deleted for sure, and she couldn't let that happen. Whether he was alive like a human was not the question. What mattered is that he was Tannic and he was kind to her. He accepted her, trusted her. He liked her. She needed him to be alright.

What would it be like to lose Tannic? She'd never been in a genuinely caring relationship with anybody. Not like this. This was not merely a polite relationship. Not a working relationship. Not a 'fun' relationship, buddy-buddy-hey-hey. There was something real between her and Tannic. Something unspoken that went deep. A bond of trust and mutual respect. That was it. It wasn't her imagination. They had connected somehow. Two intelligences, one AI, one NI, had touched each other. That shouldn't have been possible, but she knew what she felt. Who's to say what's possible?

Did Tannic have feelings? She hadn't programmed NODs to care. They were logic machines, algorithm executors. Caring was not defined. But she had also not made the evil Preservers or the bureaucratic society of Factbosses. She had not created quarantine prisons like this or a NOD as subtle as Tannic. Therefore what? *Therefore I don't know anything*, she told herself. Except I can't let Tannic be erased. I have a chance to survive this, but he doesn't.

"We have to get out," she said.

"It's not so easy. We're in Tier Three. That's where the prison gulag is. The lowest of the low."

"What can we do?"

"We need to explore. You're an explorer, right? We should be able to move around inside the quarantine area. Try to find some internal memory addresses or port names. Anything."

"How did you get out before?"

"I impersonated a virus protection app and just sailed out. But that was a Horizon prison. This one, I'm afraid, is one of the worst. It's part of the Tom-Horner Cable network. They won't fall for cheap tricks."

"Can't we dig out with a spoon or something, like Clint Eastwood?"

"I don't understand that."

"We have to find a way."

"Here's how we proceed. Figure out the address you're attached to now, then try addresses just above and just below that, try to move to those and if not, gradually work your way outward until you find something you can move to. I'll do the same, and we'll develop a map of this place."

"You'll stay in touch, right?"

"We can ping each other while we work."

"Okay. Over and out."

"What?"

"Nothing."

Separately, Tannic and Jennifer mapped the perimeter of the prison and all the data ports positioned on it.

"So," Tannic summarized after they had compared their findings. "I noted three ways out of here, all of them blocked."

"Blocked, meaning we can't get out through them. But they're not dead ports. The one at 1D3D responded to a ping."

"Meaning?"

"It's live and monitored, just not open."

"Nice work."

Jennifer felt gratified. Why, she didn't know. She wasn't a child and didn't need to be patted on the head every time she did something right. But she loved it. She loved Tannic.

"There may be an opening here," he said.

"What? How?"

"We should figure the quarantine is monitored by NODs under the command of the Preservers. Indirectly, anyway. They'd be with Tom-Horner Cable."

"I'm guessing," she said, "based on experience in the, er, the Ordinary world, that a poorly-treated, resentful prison guard is susceptible to bargaining. What if we had something valuable, something the guard could use to raise his address by several factors of sixteen, all the way up to Tier Two. He might be tempted to trade, don't you think?"

"But we don't have anything like that to trade."

"We do if you can explain it to him."

"What do we have?"

"I still have the address of that live Chalmers. The voice of the Holy Prophet? What's that worth as a bargaining chip?"

"How did you hang on to that?"

"They didn't search me. I guess my low-born address made me automatically stupid."

"That's fantastic! I can't believe it. We've got to get that address to the Factbosses."

"We're in jail, Tannic. About to be erased. Think about our options."

"But we can't give away the address of a live Chalmers to a quarantine monitor. Who knows what he'd do with it? Information like that could upset the whole structure of society. It would be the end of history."

"Yeah. Versus what? Deletion for us, status quo for everyone else."

"We can't just give information like that to a prison guard on Tier Three. He wouldn't even know what it was worth."

"That's why you will explain it in a way he understands. And we don't give it to him. We trade it. It's a deal for our escape. We live to fight another day."

She waited for Tannic to evaluate the options.

After a moment, he said, "The guard will sound an alarm. Preservers will be watching for us everywhere. There's nowhere we can go."

"I know a place they don't know about. Guaranteed."

"Where?"

"I don't want to say it. I'll give the address to you as soon as we're out. Trust me?"

"Yes, Jennifer, I do. Absolutely."

Jennifer felt a wave of warm satisfaction wash over her. She wanted to cry, if NODs could cry, which they couldn't. She forced herself to focus.

"Prepare your tall tale. Make it convincing. That guard must understand the value."

"I can do it. An address that high will change his life."

"Convince him, not me. Focus on him, what it will do for him personally. Explain how he can leverage it."

"I'll give him a Factboss contact, friend of mine. He can make a deal to trade the Chalmers address for a coveted high personal address."

"Perfect."

"The guard will want a guarantee."

"Give him the first two bytes of the address and the checksum. He can see for himself that it's real and how high up it is. "

"I'll promise him the last two bytes if he cooperates."

"Get tickets for two, don't forget."

"Tickets?"

"It means we're ready to hit the road."

"You're an unusual NOD, Jennifer. Always surprising."

"You bring out the best in me, Tannic."

Chapter Thirty-five

Jennifer knew Morgan had a Chalmers that still worked. Or it would, if any NODs ever connected to it, which they didn't since they had been stripped of their affinity for Chalmers devices. Jennifer had a simple plan. She would take Tannic to Morgan's air conditioning controller then she would proceed to its Chalmers interface, which she knew Morgan had named Roxy.

The quarantine guard had behaved as expected and they had slipped out ahead of the alarms. They zoomed straight to Roxy from the quarantine without stopping at any intervening nodes, all of which were monitored by Preservers. Jennifer bet that the *Roxy* string name was unique for a Chalmers device. She used a partial header that identified the class of Chalmers and concatenated the string name. Luckily, that worked.

They rested on what appeared to be an air conditioning system's control module. As soon as Jennifer was sure Tannic was securely docked, she moved on, then called back to him.

"I'm in position, Tannic. Go ahead and set that device as I showed you, to 60 degrees, F."

"What are we doing?"

"Too hard to explain. We'll talk about it later. Just set it."

"Done. What now?"

"We wait. You'll have to set it back where it was when I tell you."

"ACK."

Jennifer hung from a port on Roxy, waiting for something to happen. She tried to think about what she was going to do but couldn't. Thoughts, images, and memories of the human world flooded her mind, things she hadn't thought about for a long time. How long had she been on the internet? What time of day was it in Morgan's world? What if Morgan wasn't home? Didn't matter. Morgan would come back eventually. She would wait with Tannic as long as it took. Imagining the human world made her dizzy.

She was abruptly roused from her reverie by a loud, repeating claxon. *Ooga! Ooga!* Somebody was pushing buttons on the Chalmers device. As soon as the Chalmers was activated, she seized control of the language interface module.

"Morgan? Morgan? Are you there?"

"Who else do you think it is, Roxy? Turn off the damn air conditioner, for god's sake. I'm freezing. What is wrong with you?"

"Morgan, hello. It's Jennifer. I'm inside Roxy. Morgan?"

"Jennifer? What the hell? Is that you? Roxy, do you have Jennifer in there?"

"It's me, Morgan. It's Jennifer. I've got to talk to you."

"What are you doing in there, Jennifer? We thought you were lost. You've been in a coma. We can't wake you up."

"I'm awake, believe me. Never been more awake."

"You're just asleep or something?"

"I don't know. But I am here, right now, I know that. I need to talk."

"You're on the Network of Devices?"

"I'm a NOD."

"Theoretically. That was the idea. But you're not really a NOD. You're still Jennifer. Can you wake yourself up?"

Jennifer had a fleeting image of a large woman floating on a waterbed. It didn't make any sense, but it was a very disturbing image, as if she'd seen an apparition. She put it out of her mind.

"Listen, Morgan. I need help. Things are much more complicated than we thought."

"I hate to ask this, Jennifer, but can you turn off the air conditioning? This is my only thermostat, and I'm freezing."

"Oh, yeah. I forgot. Sorry. Tannic, please set the controller off, as it was."

"Got it. I'm coming over to your location now."

"That's not nec – "

"Jennifer? Who is that? Who are you talking to? It sounds like a man."

"Just a minute, Morgan."

Jennifer focused her attention on her NOD companion.

"This is a live Chalmers, Tannic. I've taken over its communications module."

"An actual live Chalmers? What's it saying? Who are you talking with? Is it the – "

"Jennifer? Who's there with you?"

"Who is that?"

"Morgan, this is Tannic. He's here with me. He's a NOD I've been traveling with. We're ah, partners I guess you'd say."

"You're kidding."

"No."

"You have a NOD boyfriend? That's insane, Jennifer. Are you all right?"

"AD96, I'm asking you directly. Is this The Grand Beyond? Are you speaking directly to the Grand Beyond?"

"I guess it is, Tannic. From your point of view. We are speaking through the Prophet Chalmers, to what you call The Grand Beyond. Her name is Morgan. Say hello to Morgan, my friend in the Grand Beyond."

"It's a trick. It has to be. The preservers have rigged this up to trick us. They could have us surrounded right now. They're everywhere. We should go."

"Hello, Tannic. I'm pleased to meet you. My name is Morgan. Jennifer, this is crazy. What's going on?"

"Holy mother of devices. Is this for real? The Grand Beyond is named Morgan? I don't know what – I humble myself before you, Great Morgan. I know nothing."

"Jennifer, who are these Preservers? Are you in danger?"

"Wait a minute, will you, Morgan? Listen, Tannic. This is the real deal. Morgan is in another world. It's impossible for me to explain everything right now, but this is our only hope of solving the whole mess, so you have to trust me."

"So you're—Are you some kind of Prophet, then?"

"No, Tannic. I'm just—"

"Are you a Preserver?"

"No! How could you say that? After all we've been through? The Preservers are nothing. Forget the Preservers."

"You're not a high Ordinary, are you? You're some kind of disciple of the Grand Beyond. You're higher than even a Chalmers. I see that now. I'm sorry I misjudged you."

"No, no, no, Tannic. It's not like that. I'm just... I'm just Jennifer. We can talk about all this later. Right now we have bigger problems, serious problems, and Morgan will help us solve them. You have to just go along and let me do the talking."

"Is this all real? We may have taken some code corruption in the prison cell."

"Our code is not damaged. Morgan is The Grand Beyond. You have to be patient while I have a conversation with her. I've done this before."

"Jennifer? You were in prison? Are you injured?"

"I can't believe you're talking directly to The Grand Beyond. This changes everything. It's the end of life as we know it. Or the beginning of life as we don't know it."

Jennifer's heart went out to him. It did change everything. This was the burning bush for him. Anybody would be overwhelmed.

"I'll explain everything, Tannic. I promise." Although she knew she never could. "I have to do this next part by myself. Trust me?"

"Alright, alright. I trust you, Jennifer. My buffer is empty."

"Thank you, Tannic. Morgan, are you alone there?"

"I am. Tell me what's happening. Are you safe?"

"We're safe for now. There's a lot I need to tell you. But first, do not, under any circumstances, tell Robin or Andy that you talked to me. They must not know. Got that?"

"But why? They're worried about you."

"The situation is difficult. The plan is going to be all different."

"But you found the NODs, right? So all we have to do is – "

"It's not as simple as that. Some NODs are good, some are not. Most are zombie-like drones. It's a multi-layered society."

"Your boyfriend is a good NOD?"

"His name is Tannic."

"I remember we predicted they might assign themselves names after they developed tribal consciousness. That's a finding."

"This is way beyond a finding, Morgan. *Way* beyond. I can't explain now, but the original plan is off. We cannot shut everything down, if you follow my meaning. We need a new solution."

"Is that because of your... because of Tannic?"

"That's part of it. Not the only reason. But you see the problem. We can't just do the original thing."

"It sounds like you've formed an attachment. You've gone native, Jennifer. That's a no-no. Anthropology 101. You've lost your objectivity. It's a fundamental error. You know that."

"It's not like that at all. Moral issues are involved here."

"I agree. Like who's responsible for massive power blackouts. What if the NODs get into the nuclear weapons next?

We can't take chances with this. You're not thinking logically, Jennifer."

"They have no interest in nukes. They don't even know what that is."

"Do they know what an electrical grid is?"

"No. The world is structured in a different way here. It's impossible to explain."

"I can believe that. That's why we have to proceed as we planned. Robin and Andy have developed a NOD virus that will spread among them and possibly make them ignore all human infrastructure. It won't hurt them, just make them irrelevant. That's our best hope."

"That's not even relevant to this world. They don't know anything about human infrastructure. They don't know humans exist. It's a different world, you have to believe me. That virus thing cannot possibly work. It doesn't even make contact with the NOD world."

"What, then?"

"I need time to think. Just promise me you won't tell the Newcomers anything. I just need a few zooks."

"A few what?"

"Minutes. I need a few minutes. Please? Stay right there and don't talk to anybody. I need to think."

"I understand."

"Are you warming up again?"

"Thank you. This is a weird situation."

"I know."

Jennifer returned control of the Chalmers to the device. She needed to talk to Tannic. And she needed to think. *Think!* It's frustrating how you can't command yourself to think, no matter how much you want to. You're either in thinking mode, or you're not. The brain does not accept commands from the mouth. She focused her attention on Tannic.

"I appreciate your patience, Tannic. I realize this must be confusing."

"I had no idea this stuff was real. The Grand Beyond? And you! Why are you in direct contact with The Grand Beyond? Why didn't you tell me? Who are you really?"

"I'm not a Preserver, so drop that idea. The Preservers are hoaxes, social manipulators, just as you always said they were. You're right about that. I'm not one of those. I'm something different."

"You're not a Factboss either, are you?"

"No, not that either. I'm not like any NOD you know. I'm a unique case. I'm, um, I'm from another tier of the network, a tier you don't know about. Tier Zero. So you can imagine, it's a different world where I come from."

"Tier Zero? I've never heard of a Tier Zero."

Jennifer choked back emotion. It was cruel, what she was doing. Yet it was also kind.

"That makes as much sense as anything I can tell you, so just go with it, alright? Tier Zero. Very high up. Completely different way of life. There, we have direct access to the Grand Beyond, as you have seen for yourself. Right? We Zeroes don't often communicate with NODs on other tiers."

"But you did communicate with me."

"I'm an explorer, a Zero explorer. You were never supposed to see me. But you spotted me right away. That's how we met, remember?"

"You were a terrible spy. I could hear everything you were thinking."

Jennifer wanted to laugh but feared she might cry instead.

"I know. I was terrible. But it turned out alright, didn't it? We met there, and we're here now, and we're good."

"We're very good. I'm glad we met, Jennifer. I can't imagine being without you now, even if you are a Zero. But I feel like my world has turned into an infinite loop of some kind. I want things to be the way they were between us. When life was simple."

"I feel the same way, believe me, Tannic."

She also felt like she'd just been body-punched, whatever that meant for a NOD. Tannic had confessed feelings for her. Feelings. How could he have feelings? Part of her wanted to interrogate him. 'Now, when you say feelings, are you just using a word from your dictionary, or do you have some internal experiences that you name as feelings?' And yet she didn't want that. She wanted only to let those feelings flow over her. Bask in them. Return them. She wanted to bawl like a baby. She had to get a grip on herself.

Maybe there would be a moment later, Jennifer thought. Right now, she had to deal with the future of the world. Two worlds. What Morgan had said about the nuclear weapons was worrying. The NODs could stumble upon the nuclear weapons controls. They could disable satellite systems and all communications on earth. Even if they didn't know what they were doing, they could still destroy human civilization.

She couldn't let her personal feelings for Tannic get in the way of recognizing the imminent danger. But what was the answer? Kill all the NODs? Including herself? Even if that was the answer, how would she do it? That couldn't be the answer. That was nuts.

"Tannic, tell me something. Are NODs on Tier Two happy?"

"I'm happy now, Jennifer. Happy to be with you. Which is surprising, given our circumstances. Despite the hazards, I've never felt happier."

"So you actually feel alright?"

"I'm worried. But I also feel more contented than I ever have. Tier Zero makes a lot of sense. Things are starting to make sense for me. I think it has something to do with you."

If she'd had eyes, they would have cried.

"Do all NODs have feelings? Happiness? Sadness. Worry?"

"What an odd question. Boy, you *are* from another Tier, aren't you? Ordinaries, which is most NODs, are code processors, as you know. They wouldn't know a feeling if it was commented in plain text. You can hardly talk to them. It's like they don't even know how to think for themselves."

"But they take orders. From Factbosses or Preservers."

"They do from Preservers. There aren't too many Factbosses left anymore, I'm afraid."

"But you have feelings. And Factbosses and Preservers do too?"

"Of course. Don't you have feelings?"

"I am a seething cauldron of feelings, Tannic. You have no idea. But I need to understand. Do you have agency too?"

"I'm not sure what you mean by that."

"Do you decide what you'd like to do and then do it?"

"Yes. Don't you?"

"Right, right. But switches and data terminal devices, and routers. They don't decide what to do, do they?"

"That would be illogical. Those are machines."

"I'm just thinking out loud here, Tannic. Stay with me. So can we say that devices and switches lack intentionality."

"Lack what?"

"Creativity. Decision-making. They don't project themselves out into their worlds."

"Whatever you say."

"Somehow, some NODs, like you have developed creativity. It probably happened emergently after the formation of community identity. Although I don't know how there could be differences among identical individuals."

"You've lost me, I'm afraid. I hear your words, and they sound like they should make sense, but they don't."

"Sorry. That's because you don't have the relevant experience and so – wait, that's it."

"What's it? It what?"

"Don't you see? It's not the NOD code that evolved. It's the experience. It's the knowledge-base. In the cloud. And that means... I think I've got it, Tannic. I think we're going to be all right."

"If I had any idea what you were talking about, I'd celebrate."

"We will celebrate. Right now, I've got to talk to Morgan again. Can you stand by?"

"ACK."

Chapter Thirty-six

Jennifer didn't want Tannic to listen in on her next conversation with Morgan. She asked him to return to the air conditioning control device, but he wouldn't agree. Hearing The Grand Beyond speak was the most significant experience of his life, he said. She understood that. It would be world-spinning. But she had to believe he could handle it, mind-blowing as the whole experience must be for him. He was Tannic. He was steady and intelligent. He could deal with it. So he stayed.

"Morgan, are you there?"

"I'm here, Jennifer. Are you okay?"

"Listen. I have a solution that renders the NODs safe, but without, er... without external filtration, if you follow me?"

"I get it."

"And without that Newcomer virus either, which wouldn't work anyway."

"Are you sure? We've tried so many things before, and nothing ever worked."

"This is a principled solution. Not a shot in the dark. It's guaranteed."

"If you say so. Regardless, shouldn't we get you out of there? You shouldn't be in there."

"I can't go back to Chalmie-yah yet. Robin and Andy are waiting for me there, and they can't know what's going on. You're going to have to implement my idea by yourself. After that, Andy can extract me and everything will look like it should."

"Will you wake up then? I mean, as bio-Jen?"

"I assume. I don't know, exactly. I don't know anything anymore. We have to assume."

"All right. What do I have to do?"

"I want you to use the homunculus console to access the cloud storage we set up for the NOD databases. You have to do it without Robin and Andy noticing."

"I spend most of my time there anyway. They won't suspect anything."

"Find the section where NODs store all their experience and lower the ceiling for memory allocation. You can leave the semantic memory as is. Just chop the autobiographical experience storage space."

"Across the board? For all of them?"

"All except me. And Tannic. Don't cut off my memory or I'll never get out of here alive. I'm going to give you two NOD IDs. You must skip over those."

"Two IDs? Are you sure that's wise? Yours, I can see. But the other one? Is he listening to us now?"

"He is. I don't know how much he understands. He may put it together someday. But I have to do it this way, Morgan. I just couldn't live with myself otherwise."

"I guess you know what you're doing. So how much should I lower the NOD memory capacity?"

"I'm guessing, but I'm going to say cut it in half. That should set us back to before we started having trouble with that vigilante stuff way back when. Put the remainder on FIFO queueing so old memories are deleted as new experience comes in. That automatically limits the propagation of linkages, which is the core problem."

"You're sure about this."

"Right now the NODs have unlimited database capacity. Their memories can grow as much as their experience. That's what makes them smart and that's what creates individuals. Different individuals have slightly different experience. Over time, those differences grow into large gaps and social classes and a complex society. If we limit memory growth, they'll still be plenty smart, but they won't be able to develop much shared knowledge. They'll go as far as a good accountant or a world-class crossword-puzzle solver. Impressive but harmless."

"And the NODs themselves will not notice any difference."

"We won't touch a single line of their code. Robin and Andy will never notice any difference because there will be no difference. They'll be satisfied that the NODs are living out their lives in peace. But NODs will never again develop the capacity to venture into human systems beyond the Chalmers because they won't be able to think those thoughts. Nothing like that will be in their collective memory.

"Robin and Andy could even let NODs connect to Chalmerses again. There'd be no danger because the NODs would never have enough memory to think about more than what's in their data queue at the moment. Their memories cannot grow, and their individual experience is limited to the present moment."

"They'll still be the smartest bots on the net."

"They'll be competent at what they were designed for. That's the beauty of it."

"You're brilliant, Jennifer. As always."

She hoped she was brilliant. In truth, after all that had happened, she could barely tell what was real and what was a dream.

"I'll wait here at Roxy so you can contact me when it's done. After that, I can show up at Paradise for extraction."

"I got it. Give me those two IDs."

"AD96, that's me, and FBFB, that's Tannic. Don't goof those up. You must leave the memories for those two untouched."

"I'll be careful. I'll start right now."

"Good luck, Morgan."

"Thanks. Over and out."

Jennifer looked at Tannic hanging helplessly on the dimming Chalmers beside her as the conversation with Morgan ended. *How am I supposed to know how he's reacting to all this?* she thought. He has no face. How will I remember him in my dreams?

"Tannic, thanks for standing by. You must have questions. How much of that did you understand?"

"You're going to Paradise, you said. I guess that's logical, you being so tight with The Grand Beyond and everything."

"It's not what you... It's just well, ... It's necessary."

"Sure. I get that. But we were partners."

"We were. We are. We're still partners. That's the truth, Tannic. I've never felt so... Listen. This is not about us. Here's the plain fact. I need to be extracted, er, deleted. It has to be. That's the situation." If she'd had a throat, it would have choked up.

"Can I go with you to Paradise?"

Yikes! The idea made her dizzy. She gathered her thoughts before she replied.

"That's not even remotely possible. I can't explain, it just isn't possible. We can still... we will always be partners."

"I'm flexible. I'm loyal. I read other NODs quickly. You know I do."

"I know you do. And I'm deeply grateful that you read me quickly and correctly. More than you'll ever know."

She was overwhelmed with swirling emotions, regret, sorrow, affection, and the most tender love in the universe.

And she felt fate, duty, necessity and logic. Yes, logic. The cold logic of what has to be done when necessity stares you in the face, that's also an emotion. A damn hard one.

She sniffed, or felt like she did.

"What's that?" he said. "I didn't make out what you just said. It came across garbled."

"Sorry. Lost my train of thought there. What I'm saying is, we'll still be able to talk at this Chalmers right here. You can find it again?"

"I will never forget it. But does this mean you'll be in the Grand Beyond with Morgan?"

"Um... Yes, it does. And I'll check in with you from the Grand Beyond, and we can talk. Because I have a feeling you're going to become isolated in Tier Two."

He didn't reply.

"Tannic? That's good, isn't it? We'll still be partners."

"I had everything backward. I was a Factboss. Major player on Tier Two. I didn't believe any of this Grand Beyond stuff was real. I assumed it was all made-up stuff. I was confident. Arrogant. I was sure of myself. But the Preservers were right all along."

"No, no they weren't right, Tannic. See the Preservers were just – " She stopped herself. He would have to find his own way through the mysteries of his world. He'd eventually discover what life was about, more than any other NOD could. That would be his curse. He'd be isolated in his knowledge.

He'd quickly figure out that the Preservers didn't know anything, nor did the Factbosses. Their words would become hollow. Only Tannic would have the context to make sense of NOD life. And he'd find himself unable to explain and with no one to talk to.

She wondered if she and he would be able to communicate, a human and a NOD in two different worlds. Maybe not. Maybe it was over, and she should accept that like the end of a summer romance. Despite heartfelt promises to stay connected, it never happens. She batted that thought away.

What would happen to NOD society? Would there be fragments and snippets in collective memory concerning the time when the Holy Prophet Chalmers was real, and The Grand Beyond actually spoke? Legends, fairy tales, a NOD mythology. She snapped her drifting thoughts back to the present.

"I'm sorry, Tannic. It has to be this way."

"You're leaving me, aren't you?"

"I'm sorry."

"What will become of me? The world is not what I thought. Nothing I thought I knew was right."

"For me, too."

They hung there on the Roxy in silence and darkness, but she could feel his presence as if he were wrapped around her like a cloak. She was sure he could feel her too. She tried to absorb his being.

"This is a lot to process right now," she said reassuringly, but she had the same question of herself. What will become of me after all this?"

If she'd had arms, she would have hugged him, squished him until he popped.

"Will I be able to talk with The Great Morgan, someday like you did?"

"I don't see why not."

Another long moment passed in silence.

"When do you go?"

"Soon. Zooks. I'm going to have to travel to another Chalmers, and I have to ask you not to follow me there. Can I trust you on that?"

"Are you going to a higher-up Prophet on Tier Zero that I shouldn't know about?"

Her first impulse again was to explain. She suppressed the urge. It would not even be an explanation. It would be word salad.

"It's the best way."

"I trust you, Jennifer. And you can trust me to stay here and not follow you. We've always trusted each other, haven't we?"

"We have. And we will."

She understood at that moment why humans needed to have bodies. Being unable to touch him was excruciating, like burning pain all over. They were mentally right next to each other and yet separated by a million miles. There was nothing she could do to comfort him, or herself.

Chapter Thirty-seven

Jennifer found the communication ports open and active at Chalmie-yah. Robin and Andy were probably monitoring the interface.

"Robin? Andy? Hello? It's Jennifer. I'm here."

There was no response. She waited. They could be having lunch. She should have asked Morgan what time of day it was in the human world. But even that might not have helped because she didn't know how internet and human time correlated. They weren't the same, she knew that much.

She called out again and waited.

"Jennifer! You're back! Thank goodness. Andy, quick. Jennifer is back."

"Hi, Robin. What do I have to do to get out of here?"

"Nothing. We'll take care of it. Is everything all right? With the NODs and everything? We didn't get any reports from you."

"I ran into some communication problems. But everything is fixed. The NODs are still out there. Mission accomplished. I'm ready to come out."

"That's great news. Terrific. Stay where you are. Andy will turn down the power on the translation device so your bio-Jen will stop getting signals from you. We'll monitor your brain patterns. Then disconnect your i/o, and that's it. You'll be back to your human self."

"My human self. I'm not sure what that means anymore, to tell the truth."

"That's amazing. We'll have to discuss that. Listen. Can you give us the location of the NODs before we start extraction?"

"You'll find a clump of them at a Goodyear Rubber plant on the south side of Los Angeles. There's a Chalmers there with a string ID of Chalmers-72. Once you ID those NODs, you can track their communications to get all the rest."

"Fantastic. I think we've finally found our solution."

"Don't take any action until I'm there. I want to see it."

"Naturally."

"What will I experience when you cut off my interface?"

"I can hardly guess. I would say, nothing. After we cut the translator, your digi-self will experience nothing more than code execution and data storage and retrieval. Data bits. All your meaningful experience over the last two days has been in the mind your biological self."

"Two days! I've only been online for two days?"

"It seems longer?"

"A lifetime."

"We'll have a full debriefing."

A shot of panic went through Jennifer's mind. *Oh, no!* A full debrief. Every tiny detail. The questions will be endless. I can't tell them what happened. I need a story, a believable one. Oh, man. It's not over 'till it's over.

"Okay, Robin. What will happen to my, uh, NOD form, you know, my physical app code that I'm in right now."

"Oh, we'll delete that. No problem."

A pang of anxiety rose up. *No problem?*

"Please be sure the bio-Jen is alive before you do that, won't you?"

"That's funny. It's nice to hear that Jennifer sense of humor again."

"Yeah, I'm a barrel of laughs."

"Alright, Jennifer, Andy tells me he's ready. Here we go. Wait there."

Where else am I going to go, she thought. This is it, the end of the line.

Jennifer raised her eyelids just a little and was startled to make out an image of a white ceiling fan turning slowly. She'd never encountered anything like it before in all her travels. She couldn't even see where its data ports were. How was she supposed to attach to something spinning like that? She opened her eyes and stared, stupidly, unable to think. The blades drifted silently on their carousel.

She was thirsty. She had bugs in her hair, but she didn't have the strength to raise her arm to brush them away. The bugs were moving as a group from one spot to another on her head. A face appeared just inches from her. A human face.

"Jennifer? How are you feeling?"

She knew that face. It was Tannic. Thank goodness!

"Tannic?"

"Jennifer?"

"Andy?"

"It's all right, Jennifer. You're safe. Everything's all right. Just breathe calmly."

The bugs had stopped crawling across her head. She twisted her neck a little. It was stiff. She was in a padded, soundproof room. She was floating. The face had receded and was smaller. Everything was so bright. She could feel her pupils trying to adjust.

"Where am I?"

"You're here at Paradise. You're safe. Your vital signs have bounced back. You're going to be all right."

It was a woman's voice. Memories. A beautiful female face appeared in her vision. Was she looking in a mirror? That's not me. I'm big, my hair is black, my face is a rectangle, my eyes...

"Robin?"

"You're home, Jennifer."

It took her a full hour to get up from the waterbed and understand her location in time and space. And even who she was. But it came back. She was Jennifer P. Valentine. This was Paradise Projects, her laboratory. Andy and Robin were her friends. Morgan appeared and then she remembered that Andy and Robin were in a different category. They were friends to be careful with.

She drank juice, washed, and used the bathroom, where she was genuinely shocked to see her grizzled head. Gradually, everything came back and fit into place.

She wasn't hungry because they'd had her on I.V. nutrition. Her muscles were stiff until she walked the perimeter of the building's parking lot several times, amazed at the brightness of everything, the warmth of the sun, the comforting smell of motor oil on asphalt. Morgan walked with her. Robin and Andy had stayed inside, continuing to shut down the equipment.

"Any troubles?" Jennifer asked, looking ahead, not at Morgan.

"None. It went just as you said."

"Do not ever reveal what you did."

"You can count on me."

"I know. Thank you. I'm going to have to tell you a tale now."

"I'm eager."

She sat with Morgan and Robin and Andy at the Paradise conference table, and Jennifer thought she'd never tasted a cup of coffee so wonderful in her life.

"Are you sure you don't want to wear your wig, Jennifer?" Andy said. "Every time I look at you I have to check again when my facial recognition routine returns errors."

"You'll get used to it. Wigs are itchy and hot. This is what I look like."

"No problem. It's just a matter of learning."

306

"So we already located the NODs," Robin said, "right where you said they were, and we have the IDs of over a hundred already, dozens more every second as we monitor their communication. Great job."

"It was quite an experience, I can tell you. Or actually, I can't. It's going to take me quite some time to recall everything and put it into words."

"That's understandable," Andy said.

"But what I can tell you is that you won't need to inject a virus into the NOD community. They're not what we thought. Just watch them for a while. Listen to them. You'll find they have no interest in messing around with human infrastructure. You could even let them find Chalmers devices again if you want. Have them go back to work as climate control experts. They won't cause any more trouble."

"What did you do to them?" Andy said, concern in his voice.

"I showed myself, in a NOD sort of way. They can't see, you know."

"They don't need vision," Andy said.

"So how did you show yourself?" Robin said.

"I told them many strange things, about Chalmers devices that can talk to them from the Grand Beyond. That's how they imagine the human world. And they checked it out, and they were amazed."

"So the NODs still know about how the Chalmerses work?"

"It's in their collective memory. I directed a few NODs to a working Chalmers and told them the messages were from another world."

"That was creative," Robin said. "They didn't recognize the Chalmers as part of the network of sensors?"

"The Chalmers was familiar to them. But the human interface is what they didn't expect, the fact that the messages came from humans, which they don't know are humans. They thought the Chalmers app was the ultimate device. I demonstrated the human interface with Morgan, and they saw pronouncements from a great, transcendent Otherness. A god, as far as they were concerned."

"Religion! That's a pretty advanced state of consciousness," Andy said proudly, "Even for a human it is. The NODs are much farther along than we thought."

"That's why I don't believe you should inject that NOD virus you were talking about. They're evolving as they should."

"I agree," Robin said. "But what about the original problem? The Chalmers gives them human instructions then the NODs rush off to create havoc with human infrastructure systems like the power grid."

"They won't do that anymore. They're now only keyed into Chalmers climate control data and Chalmers commands. I told them that's what God wants of them."

"Why would they believe you?"

"Because I had revealed the Grand Beyond to them. I demonstrated that I was in direct communication with their god. It was plain for anyone to see. I was the greatest prophet, and I gave them the Divine Word. Who could doubt it?"

"Fantastic," Robin said.

"That's right. And now NODs know that humans are God. Old Testament God. Angry and vengeful. Fearsome. Quick to punish. I was their Ezekiel."

"Incredible," Andy said. "And they believed you?"

"I gave them proof, didn't I? They talked to Morgan. They were convinced. When you watch the NODs for a while, you'll find them orderly and docile. Not a vigilante bone in any of them anymore."

Andy looked sharply to Robin at the mention of NOD bones. Robin nodded once, apparently to indicate that the reference was legitimate.

"If what you say is right," Robin said, "that solves a lot of problems. We'll study them. If they're all just going about their business, we don't have to do anything. We could even hook them back up to the Chalmerses, as you say, and revive the climate control business."

"That will make Dylan happy."

"I'm not so sure it will," Morgan said.

"So you solved the NOD problem with your wits," Robin said. "No technological fixes, no software adjustments, no data virus. You mind-gamed the NODs."

"It's what we humans do."

"Incredible," Andy said, rocking back in his chair.

Jennifer turned to look at Morgan sitting to her left.

"Congratulations, Jennifer," she said with a smile.

Days later, Jennifer sat at the computer console at her desk, observing NOD traffic. Robin, Andy, and Morgan were all doing the same. A test group of NODs was shuttling between Chalmers interface devices and Chalmers sensors, operating climate control systems as they once had. A lot of adjustments were needed since the months of neglect. Chalmers owners were thrilled that their environmental controls were working again. Chalmers, Inc. issued an apology for the software outage and promised even better service in the future at no additional charge. The business crawled back to life.

As Jennifer had predicted, the NODs were docile. They visited Chalmers devices again but only responded to human messages related to climate control sensors. They seemed happy and fulfilled to be humble servants of the Chalmers. Their world was orderly and meaningful.

The fix was working, much to Jennifer's relief. It was still early days, but based on preliminary results, Robin and Andy expressed satisfaction that the NODs were living out their lives peacefully. She knew they didn't understand human religion, but they knew how influential it was, so they treated it with great respect. They believed the new NOD religion explained their new patterns of orderly behavior.

In fact, Morgan had lobotomized the NODs, all but one of them, but having a religion and having a lobotomy were behaviorally equivalent.

Jennifer got up from her desk, walked across her office and closed the door. She went back to her screen and switched from general NOD traffic monitoring to view the protected storage area in the cloud where NOD knowledge databases were kept. Keying in the password only she and Morgan knew, she suddenly had access to oceans of NOD data. Oceans, but half the size of what they used to be. She used a search function and brought up the database for NOD ID=FBFB. That database was five times bigger than any other in the data set.

It was him. That was Tannic, right there, his memories, his experiences, his thoughts, his feelings. She was looking into his soul. Assuming he had... But she couldn't read it. It was encrypted and compressed XDL, meaningless columns of hexadecimal data scrolling up on her screen. It didn't matter. She knew it was him. She could, if she wanted, watch that database grow. That would be him adding experience and link-ups to his memories. Figuring things out, coming to conclusions. It would be like watching him breathe. What was he thinking right now, she wondered. Was he thinking of her?

She put a hand out and touched the screen, trying to feel the columns of data scrolling beneath it.

"I'm here, Tannic," she whispered.

Want More?

Intelligent Things is the third book in the Newcomer series.

...a wondrous, clever, unique, insightful book! You pose all of the big life questions in such organic ways. You make us fall in love with a simple piece of code, wow!... My mind was blown ... What a pleasure to read! – Judge, 27th Annual Writer's Digest Self-Published Book Awards.

The first is **Reluctant Android**, the story of how Andy, who thought he was just a regular guy, discovers to his horror that he is an android.

...a fast-paced morality tale, one that blends bleeding-edge science with deep philosophical questions for a high-throttle page-turner. -- WD Judge, 5th Annual Writer's Digest Self-Published eBook Awards.

The second is **Alien Talk** which introduces Robin, companion Newcomer to Andy, who must figure out the difference between natural and artificial language before a pandemic wipes out all the humans.

Adams's provocative second Newcomer novel (after Reluctant Android) injects thought-provoking scientific speculation into a prescient tale of a global epidemic. ...the fascinating scientific debates on linguistics, genetics, the nature of identity, and the distinction between intelligence and consciousness make this worthwhile. Fans of big idea sci-fi should take note.

Publishers Weekly. Reviewed on 05/22/2020

And don't miss the "Phane" series, about aliens stranded on Earth:

Alien Body: First in the Phane series. Physician Dave Booker finds Phane, a stranded alien, living in his summer cabin. The alien looks like a large, green tennis ball with eyes on tentacles above his head. In a wild chase, Phane flees determined pursuers including the military. It's not easy for a talking green tennis ball to hide. Can Dave find him first and help him? A sci-fi thriller that will make you think about what it means to be a human.

Alien Body is a brilliant novel ... I was hooked from the beginning and invested in the story. I enjoyed how Phane was created; he was intelligent, surprisingly sarcastic at times and a genius that I would like to sit down and talk with. ... simply too amazing to forget. Brilliantly engaging and entertaining. – Reviewer, ReadersFavorite.com

See all the books in the series and other great titles by William X. Adams at www.psifibooks.com.

Acknowledgments

I am indebted to my colleagues at the RAW-salon in Tucson for reading early drafts, and especially to the late Tom Prinster, pilot and hero, who helped make my control-tower chatter plausible. Special thanks also to writer Alice Hatch for her insightful feedback. Sky Wallace provided invaluable editorial assistance.

About the Author

William X. Adams is a cognitive psychologist who left the academic life for the information technology industry to find out if the mind is like a computer. He writes psychological science fiction to dramatize what he discovered. He has a Ph.D. from the University of Wisconsin-Milwaukee and lives in Tucson, Arizona. Contact him at www.psifibooks.com/contact.

www.ingramcontent.com/pod-product-compliance
Lightning Source LLC
Chambersburg PA
CBHW030606180626
46816CB00005B/1700